PRAISE FOR THE AWAKENED SERIES

Obliteration

"My kind of book—tense and frightening and twisted and FUN. I guarantee you—everything from EEKS to SHRIEKS!"

—R.L. Stine, #1 bestselling author of the Goosebumps and Fear Street series

"*Obliteration* is a bloody war zone of throat-clutching suspense and horror, showcasing humanity at its best and worst. The action is unrelenting, a true roller coaster of savage twists, turns, and rolls. So strap in and get ready for the ride of your life!"

—James Rollins, #1 *New York Times* bestselling author of *Crucible*

"What a finale to the trilogy. *Obliteration* is exactly what it says: loads of action, explosive fights, and of course . . . even more creatures. Join the fight and see how it ends. So much fun!"

—Brad Meltzer, #1 *New York Times* bestselling author of *The Escape Artist*

"The book is all action, with a thrilling showdown between the Queen, Van Ness and Cafferty, that keeps the reader on the edge of their seat."

—Red Carpet Crash

"This pulpy and fast-paced narrative follows not only Cafferty and Van Ness as they arm themselves with some of the Foundation's deadliest creations, but also the few desperate survivors of the creatures' carnage. . . . With a tone and energy similar to Brian Keene and other 2000s-era pulpy horror writers, this grim vision of humanity's possible extinction should satisfy those looking for a gruesome, diverting read." —*Booklist*

The Brink

"*Awakened* goes international, and the terror skyrockets. *The Brink* is proof that sometimes the most horrible creatures lurk closer than you think. Powerful and horrifying. Curse you, Murray and Wearmouth, for keeping me awake so late."

—Brad Meltzer, #1 *New York Times* bestselling author of *The Escape Artist*

"It's monsters. It's horror. It's danger and shocks and scream-out-loud surprises! And mainly, it's *fun*. A tense and haunting thriller. Don't miss out."

—R.L. Stine, #1 bestselling author of the Goosebumps and Fear Street series

"Murray and Wearmouth's latest, *The Brink*, is a white-knuckled roller coaster. This novel is chock-full of everything I love: strange creatures, a world teetering on the edge, and heroes who I'd want at my side during any firefight. This isn't just a story hopped on steroids but one injected with nitrous and blazing on all cylinders. Give me more!"

—James Rollins, #1 *New York Times* bestselling author of *Crucible*

Awakened

"This book is no joke. Get ready to not sleep tonight. *Awakened* does exactly what it advertises. Scary-amazing fun."

—Brad Meltzer, #1 *New York Times* bestselling author of *The Escape Artist*

"Murray and coauthor Wearmouth . . . sculpt a briskly moving narrative that includes a plethora of short-burst action sequences and pacing fit for a Brad Meltzer novel. Along the way, they plant the seeds for sequels and craft a tight, pulse-pounding story that practically cries out for a film adaptation."

—*Booklist*

"*Awakened* is a tautly written, brilliantly unexpected thriller from authorial duo James S. Murray and Darren Wearmouth. . . . *Awakened* hits the high notes of Douglas Preston and Lincoln Child's *Relic* and Scott Snyder's *The Wake* . . . but its scope actually extends much further."

—*Kirkus Reviews*

"*Awakened* is a good old-fashioned monster story with devious new twists. Creepy and disturbing in all the right ways!"

—Jonathan Maberry, *New York Times* bestselling author of *Glimpse* and *V-Wars*

"A great book with both science fiction and horror elements, along with some mystery. I highly recommend this."

—Naomi Downing, Sci-Fi Movie Page

OBLITERATION

By James S. Murray
and Darren Wearmouth

AWAKENED
THE BRINK
OBLITERATION

JAMES S. MURRAY AND DARREN WEARMOUTH

OBLITERATION

AN AWAKENED NOVEL

HARPER Voyager

An Imprint of HarperCollinsPublishers

First Harper Voyager premium printing: April 2021
First Harper Voyager hardcover printing: June 2020

Print Edition ISBN: 978-0-06-286900-5
Digital Edition ISBN: 978-0-06-286901-2

Cover design by Richard L. Aquan
Cover illustration © Larry Rostant

Harper Voyager and the Harper Voyager logo are trademarks of HarperCollins Publishers in the United States of America and other countries.

HarperCollins is a registered trademark of HarperCollins Publishers in the United States of America and other countries.

21 22 23 24 25 BVGM 10 9 8 7 6 5 4 3 2 1

OBLITERATION

T he fierce Hurricane Melyssa moved ominously across the Atlantic Ocean with formidable power. Reports claimed it would batter the East Coast of the United States like nothing before. It had the potential to dramatically change lives. Whole swaths of the Carolinas were being evacuated. Traffic jams clogged I-95. And the front end of the weather system hadn't even neared land yet.

For now, it was closing in on a lone steel-and-concrete rig precariously anchored in the roaring sea. Rain lashed down on the listing platform. A howling wind whipped against it.

Light punched out of ten portholes into the darkness. In the far one, the shadow of a man hunched in his chair.

A lone man at ease with himself.

A man unperturbed by the constant sea spray lashing his window. Untroubled by the lightning splitting the sky, followed by the crash of thunder. Undisturbed by the creaking of steel and the swaying floor.

A man who knew his true destiny.

The wheelchair-bound Albert Van Ness lazily waved his finger around to the crackling strains of Schubert's String Quintet in C Major. A dose of proper culture massaged his mind. It enriched him. Gave him a welcome break from the brainless interrogations and the terrible food.

He closed his eyes and relaxed.

The composition he was listening to went right to his heart. A true classic by a man of quality. It reminded him of the library in his French chateau, where he directed Foundation proceedings for the sake of humanity.

Now the entire planet was at risk, thanks to his shortsighted captors. So naturally, why should he care about anything but music at a time like this?

A record player was all he was afforded in this mid-Atlantic prison, a claustrophobic cell that afforded no creature comforts. He smiled at the phrase, knowing what little comfort creatures truly provided. The world thought itself safe now that he was locked away in this place.

The same fools who marooned him here would eventually come begging for his help.

At this moment, though, it didn't matter. His concerns were for the here and now. He was listening to a master. Someone like him.

Van Ness wasn't scared by the weather, the relentless rocking of the waves, or his uninviting prison cell. The starched lapels of his orange coverall remained vomit-free. He was clean-shaven. Sharp. After a year of this demented incarceration, he remained in control—of everything. His faculties, sure. But also beyond.

Not that they knew it yet. He let out a deep, satisfying breath.

His thoughts drifted from his father, Otto, cutting down a creature in Barcelona during the early sixties, to the look on American president John Reynolds' face when he plummeted to his deserved death. Everything had a purpose, for better or for worse. Even being here, in the path of a hurricane.

Van Ness let out a purr of satisfaction.

He could sleep easy, and that's what he intended to do.

Another wave crashed against the rig, spraying his porthole window with salty water. The needle of the player scratched across the record, pulling him out of his reverie. Van Ness winced at the butchery of the music. The same kind of vandalism that had stopped him from saving the world and re-creating it in his image.

Memories of Paris flooded his mind.

His eyes slammed open in disgust, all pretense of tranquility shot when that god-awful man's face haunted him once more.

Thomas Cafferty, the failed mayor of New York City and second-rate impostor, deluded in thinking he had won the day.

The fool.

And yet—and this was where the bitterness lay, tearing at even Van Ness' sizable ego—he, too, was a fool. It was Van Ness' trusted right-hand man,

Edwards, who had betrayed him, slicing off his hand moments before he could ignite the nuclear bombs planted underneath cities around the world. It was Edwards who had stopped Van Ness. Not Cafferty and his ragtag group of incompetents.

Van Ness' remaining hand clenched tightly, and he thought he could feel the phantom fist of the other. He stared down at his healed stump. Anger and pain washed through him.

Another image flashed in Van Ness' mind: Mayor Cafferty's fist striking him in the face. The disrespect. The audacity. The sign of a man who had no control.

If the world now relied on Thomas Cafferty to save it from the impending apocalypse, it was sorely mistaken.

The prison rig listed in the swell of a force nine gale. More spray battered the window of his cell with such strength as to threaten its very integrity. But these structures were built to withstand seeming devastation. Just like him.

Van Ness didn't blink an eye as the record steadily resumed and Schubert continued to play.

Remain calm, Albert.

He looked across to the calendar on the wall and counted the days.

It's been one year. Any time now, he thought.

They are coming for me, and I will answer the call.

I will save humanity, and my price hasn't changed. But now there is one more demand they must meet.

Thomas Cafferty is a dead man.

CHAPTER TWO

The early-morning sun had just risen over the already scorching Nevada desert, bathing the vast plains and peaks in a deep orange glow. A soldier on the top of an MRAP tactical vehicle silently aimed toward the mouth of an old gold mine. To his rear, former New York City mayor Tom Cafferty stood behind the open back door, focused determination on his face.

Cafferty peered at a screen displaying footage from a drone sweeping the immediate area for any signs of a ground-level breach. During the last year, the creatures had ventured higher and higher toward the surface of the earth, ever more tolerant to oxygen and light. Cafferty suspected a land-based war was inevitable.

But we still have time.

Because now they knew what they were up against, and resources were finally being deployed on a global scale. The drone was a testament to that, its transmitted image showing the jagged peaks of the Toquima Range, before dipping down to the

Mineral City ghost town. The skeletal remains of buildings and rusting machinery were partly shrouded in the shadow of the mountains, though clearly visible in their terminal decline. People had flocked here during the mid-nineteenth century when the excitement of the California gold rush spilled over to this seemingly empty desert. Like most other settlements during this period, it had a short and intense life.

Cafferty was preparing for a short and intense battle. Another step in the fight against these gruesome underground creatures that had attacked New York City three years earlier, to ensure other global cities didn't suffer the same fate as the ghost towns here. The thought of the huge underground networks beneath his feet—created first by humans and now used by creatures and their enormous nests—made him wince. Tunnels stretched for miles. They went deep. A massive home inadvertently created for a deadly enemy. It was as if humanity had invited its own destruction all those years ago.

But that same enemy now had an unrelenting opponent.

He wiped a thin sheen of sweat from his brow and ran his hand through his salt-and-pepper hair. Even at this time in the morning, the temperature had already risen to uncomfortable levels. It was shaping up to be one of the hottest days of late spring, and he was eager to get this operation started.

The drone camera closed on Cafferty's location. Twenty MRAP vehicles circled the old gold mine. Ten black SUVs sat behind on a rutted dirt track.

Two Apache helicopters hovered in the air, their downdrafts throwing up thin dust clouds. Farther back, three trucks transmitted data and images back to the White House Situation Room, where President Amanda Brogan and her team watched.

"Move in," Cafferty commanded over his mic.

With that order, two mechanized robots powered into the tunnel, brightening its walls with their powerful lights. Every hundred yards, they would fire rocket-propelled strobe grenades into the far distance, designed to keep any creatures at bay.

Forty Special Forces soldiers, dressed in all black, immediately followed in an overwatch formation with their laser guns raised. A cable ran from every weapon's grip to a newly designed battery on each soldier's back. It ensured a superlong charge, which should be more than enough for this particular mission.

The first four soldiers carried drills to bore holes in the tunnel wall at regular intervals. The next four would twist screw eyes into the created gaps. It gave everyone an anchor point if the creatures tried to use their unstoppable telekinetic force on the soldiers' bodies. They'd hook their belts in place. During tests in their previous missions, this had proven a solid safety mechanism.

Cafferty swatted a fly away with his second-generation laser pistol, using the same ease to kill an insect as a creature would when butchering a person. He marveled at the slick movements of the soldiers. A highly trained, heavily armed group. Powerful, with the right tools for the job. Experienced from previous encounters with the creatures.

And he was in charge.

After all he'd been through, all he'd seen, and all the begging and groveling he'd seemingly had to do to get to this moment, here he was: at the head of a government-backed mission that filled him with pride.

Just as important, this was out in the daylight. This wasn't a shadowy operation, run by a despot like Albert Van Ness and his deranged Foundation. Cafferty was proud of how much he had done to keep this aboveboard, to try to involve everyone in fighting the creatures. He wasn't holding the world at ransom . . .

At that thought, Cafferty's hand tightened around the laser. That maniac Van Ness had caused the Z Train disaster in New York, which had almost killed him, not to mention his wife, and *had* killed hundreds of people. Only through quick thinking and the sacrifice of some incredibly brave people were he and his team able to somehow pull through a nearly impossible situation below the Hudson River. That same day he'd learned about the now dismantled Foundation for Human Advancement, and his mission was set.

But at that point, he and his team were basically all alone, with no support from anyone. They had to take down Van Ness by themselves.

He had to watch as the wheelchair-bound lunatic nuked cities in a twisted attempt to stop these creatures. Rapid City, South Dakota—gone. Lincoln, Nebraska—gone. Van Ness had killed an untold number of civilians. Irradiated land that would be uninhabitable for decades, if not more. Kidnapped, then killed former president John Reynolds. Killed British prime minister Simpson. Blackmailed numerous world governments for decades, amassing a fortune on the blood and sweat and fear Van Ness considered beneath him. Did all of this with impunity until a small team had finally taken him down in his underground Paris headquarters. Cafferty's team. That feat alone had saved millions of lives. Van Ness now rotted in a remote prison.

And now I run the show.

This time, the hunters were about to become the hunted without any loss of human life. Only one species was dying en masse in the desert today.

To him, the way to win this fight remained simple: identify the creatures' locations around the world, hit them hard with the tech the Foundation had developed, and destroy the nests. Then move on until every subterranean infestation around the world was completely annihilated. He understood it lacked the nuances of Sun Tzu's *The Art of War,* but that also made sense: he was taking down something far more deadly—and decidedly less human—than ancient armies.

That strategy had brought him to this scorched landscape. This abandoned Nevada gold mine was a confirmed nest site.

People had gone missing here.

A film crew from a popular ghost-hunting show had already gotten more than what they bargained for in the gold mine. They followed a voice that they mistook for a friendly spirit. The recovered footage showed them getting unceremoniously slaughtered, carved to pieces in seconds. The only other things recovered were the host's broken glasses, their measurement equipment, and traces of DNA.

Earlier this morning, Cafferty's tech expert, Diego Munoz, had remotely navigated a bomb disposal robot into the depths of the mine. The robot's camera captured images of advancing creatures before a tail lashed down, ending the transmission. It wasn't a lot, but it was enough—Cafferty had all the proof he needed to launch his strike.

President Brogan had sensibly taken the threat to humanity seriously, meaning the required resources were at Cafferty's disposal. This was only America, however. The global situation remained problematic. Governments still wouldn't pay his reasonable costs or naively thought they could deal with the creature threat themselves. Why they thought this, when for so long they were willing to pay Van Ness his blood money, made no sense. Still, they held out.

But not for long . . .

This was the site where he and his team would prove their strategy, then break free of the bureaucratic chains that had bound them since ending Van Ness' global reign of terror. Actions spoke louder than words. Once they'd recorded the whole end-to-end operation, no government in the world could deny the way forward. A path to victory, forged by Cafferty's organization, the David M. North Foundation.

Boots crunched on the parched ground toward him. Diego Munoz moved to Cafferty's side, followed by former NYPD SWAT team member Sarah Bowcut. She glared at the mine's flashing tunnel through steely eyes. The tech expert took a deep breath in anticipation of what was about to happen.

Cafferty could feel their excitement. He felt it, too.

Three other capable members of his close team remained to Cafferty's rear, ready to follow him in once the soldiers had secured the area.

"Move your vehicle into position," Cafferty commanded into his mic.

A recovery truck's engine roared to life. Dust puffed around its tires as it reversed to the side of the group. The hydraulic brakes let out a sharp hiss.

"Connect yourselves up," Bowcut said.

All six took turns to secure cables from their waists to winches on the back of the truck. The superstrong, mile-long carbon fiber tethers gave them extra protection if they had to enter the breach. If the telekinetic force became too strong when planting their bomb, they would radio the topside team and get immediately dragged out one after another, in order to avoid tangling.

"*No new seismic readings,*" Cafferty's wife, Ellen, said through his earpiece. "*Still got live images from every helmet cam.*"

"Thanks, baby," Cafferty replied. "You get the slightest movement on that dial—"

"*Yeah, yeah, Tom. Just don't take any stupid risks.*"

"Would I?"

"*Yes.*"

Cafferty glanced back at the SUVs and winked at his wife. Ellen was sitting behind the tinted window of the front one, overseeing the operation from his team's perspective. She'd insisted on coming along, even though he'd wanted her to stay out of harm's way for the sake of their son, David. Especially since it seemed she was here to specifically watch over *him*.

Cafferty's thoughts drifted back to his speech a year ago at the UN General Assembly. Ellen had implied that just like his obsession with the Z Train, Tom was now equally obsessed with his global mission to destroy these creatures. She feared he was becoming like Albert Van Ness. A bolt of irritation shot through him.

This trivialization can wait for now.

Not everyone sees the threat with the same clarity as me.

Yes, the same clarity as Van Ness, but without his murderous intent. With the actual good of humanity in mind.

Cafferty returned his attention to the entrance.

Only the sounds of drilling and a faint whine from the robots' engines came from the tunnel. No screeches. No shouts over the radio. No reported laser shots. They would come soon enough. He knew it. Knew that creatures never remained idle in the presence of their enemy.

"You're looking tired, Tom," Bowcut said.

"No time to rest," he replied. "We'll have plenty of time for sleep later."

"Then let's get in there."

Munoz grunted as he readjusted his shoulder straps. His pack contained the C-4 bomb. Tech experts from DARPA had helped design the shaped charge to rocket toward a nest, then detonate on remote command. The creatures wouldn't have a chance to destroy the graphene-concealed working parts.

"You ready, Diego?" Cafferty asked.

"Oh, don't you worry, Tom," he replied. "We'll blow these motherfuckers to kingdom come."

A thin smile stretched across Cafferty's face. "Same old Diego. Straight to the point. As subtle as a sledgehammer."

Munoz peered at his tablet showing the robot video feeds inside the mine. He flashed the screen at Cafferty, confused.

"I don't see any sign of the creatures," Munoz said. "Maybe they've hightailed it back to their nest."

"They'll come for us. It's just a matter of when."

"Up here or down there?" Diego asked rhetorically.

Cafferty shrugged. It didn't matter. The fight was going to play out one way or another, preferably belowground while they still had time.

During the last year, Cafferty's team had become the best he could ever imagine. Bowcut had trained Munoz to become the meanest, most badass nerd on the planet. Munoz, in turn, had showed her how to use all of their new toys they'd gathered. Together, the three of them had been to hell and back. Escaping the carnage underneath the Hudson River. Battling monstrosities in London and Paris. Stopping Van Ness in his lair. These events—and their collective adversary—had created an unbreakable bond and a determination to see this through. He trusted them with his life.

"*All clear. We're over the breach,*" came through Cafferty's earpiece.

"We're coming down," he replied. "Any contact?"

"*None.*"

Cafferty extended his laser toward the mine and strode forward.

Everyone followed in single file.

So far, everything was running like clockwork.

The team had perfected this plan while destroying nests in Virginia and Kentucky. Nobody required hand-holding. Everyone knew their job. They cleared a path to the nest. Planted the bomb. Retreated. Then boom. Three down, maybe another thousand to go.

He stooped inside the mine entrance. His footsteps echoed off the low ceiling and pit-scarred walls. As he descended, soldiers lined the route, kneeling with their laser weapons raised.

Cafferty slowed his stride as he neared the breach in the tunnel—the point where the creatures burst through to the surface. He tensed, waiting for the first earsplitting shriek that would announce an attack.

The two robots had stopped in front of a pile of rubble. One blasted light along the distant shaft. The other angled its beam into the depths below.

His heart hammered against his chest. He gulped in a breath of the cloying air.

Everything going according to plan didn't stop the butterflies in his gut.

Cafferty glanced over his shoulder. "Never gets any easier," he said.

Munoz nodded. "They're smart all right. But they can't outsmart a blast of C-4."

"For now."

All the information retrieved from Van Ness' organization told him that much. The creatures had a chilling knack of outthinking any tactics deployed against them, usually within weeks, in different locations, like they could communicate with each other on a global scale.

The robot's light brightened the breach below, revealing a stadium-sized cavern right below the mineshaft. The creatures' nest was massive. Hundreds of caves lined the walls in all directions, like ants might carve out of their tunnels. Debris from the creatures' victims littered the ground on perches below: backpacks, bloodstained clothing, glimmering jewelry, a mangled TV camera, a shredded blue blanket.

But . . . no creatures.

A deathly silence filled the air.

Silence in a cavern usually meant the creatures were focusing their telekinetic powers in the shadows and were trying to drag people toward a terrible end, courtesy of razor-sharp teeth, claws, and tails. But none of Cafferty's team members seemed affected in any way. Everything remained calm and still.

A minute passed. Nothing.

The cavern was empty of life.

This isn't right.

"Where the hell are they?" Cafferty said to himself.

Munoz and Bowcut appeared by his side.

The tech expert peered downward. "What the hell, Tom?" he asked, confused. "They were here hours ago."

"You took the words right out of my mouth," Bowcut added.

All three exchanged nervous glances.

The ground-penetrating radar had confirmed that this tunnel led directly to an enclosed nest. Cafferty reached into the side pocket of his cargo pants. He pulled out his methane-measuring device, which confirmed what he expected: the creatures could survive at this level of higher oxygen. They'd seen it before in Kentucky and Virginia. But those lairs had been full of the creatures, while the entire cavern before them remained empty, not a single shriek or lash of a tail.

Munoz gently elbowed him. "Tom, seriously, what the hell?"

"It doesn't make sense. They can't disappear into thin air."

"Maybe it does," Bowcut called from his side. She had advanced farther into the tunnel and angled her light toward a gap in the wall. "You better see this."

Cafferty walked over. Her beam stabbed into an upward tunnel, not previously identified on any of their geophysical surveys. It stretched as far as the beam reached, extending to the southwest.

Right toward Las Vegas.

Right toward civilization.

CHAPTER THREE

Shafts of radiant sunshine broke through the cloudy sky over San Francisco, brightening Lombard Street's steep, snaking route. Karen Green gripped the handles of the stroller containing her four-year-old son, Joey, as she approached the block-long section of eight hairpin turns. Her husband, Daniel, walked by her side. He marveled at the vibrant array of flowers and bushes that hugged the crookedest street in the world's packed sidewalk.

T-shirts and shorts for the family was the right idea today, she thought. The gentle breeze coming off the Pacific Ocean provided only light relief from the oppressive humidity. The buildings lining the road gave welcome sporadic shade, though tourists ascending in the opposite direction sucked in deep breaths and mopped their brows.

Better them than me.

A continuous stream of cars steadily wound down toward Pioneer Park. Heat haze rose from their hoods. In the far distance, ferries plowed across the glistening deep blue bay. Somewhere close, the noise of a trolley's bell tinkled.

San Francisco always seemed so alive. A breathing metropolis that drew Karen in from San Bruno every time she had a day off from the stress of her job as a paramedic.

"Just another day in paradise," Daniel said, winking at his wife. "Hungry?"

"Of course." She glanced across to him. "I'm guessing the usual?"

"Wild horses couldn't stop me," he replied. "Lead the way, love."

She smiled. "You got it."

The relaxed grin on her husband's sweat-sheened face said it all. Contentment and anticipation. Daniel shared her love for a sourdough bread bowl full of clam chowder at Fisherman's Wharf. It was how they had met seven years ago, catching each other's eye from opposite tables while devouring their favorite meal. Back then, they were both twenty-four years old with the world ahead of them. On their first date they had watched the 49ers crush the Giants. Second date: Alcatraz. Third date was a weekend movie sequel marathon: *Aliens*, *Terminator 2*, *Superman II*, *The Godfather Part II*. The best sequels in the history of motion pictures. They had fallen in love fast. Married a year and a half later. Then came their son, Joey, their pride and joy.

Joey loved the sights and sounds of the city, too, craning his neck around the seat at regular intervals to watch the bigger cars rumble past. Only a truck got him more excited. To his young eyes and ears, the city provided a sensory overload compared with the tranquility of suburbia.

Karen twisted the stroller around a group of tourists to head down the steep switchbacks and toward Taylor Street. A left turn there took them all the way to the Boudin Bakery Café and the holy grail of food, New England style.

Daniel abruptly grabbed Karen's arm and stopped. She turned to look at him, confused by his sudden movement.

"Do you hear that?" he said curiously.

"No. Hear what?"

"Listen."

"Danny, stop fooling around," she replied jokingly.

"I'm not. Listen."

His tone and the stern look on his face told her something wasn't right. Daniel reserved this expression only for serious moments, or for when he tackled the final boss in his video games.

At first, she detected only the usual sounds of the city.

Then, vaguely in the distance . . . something else. Growing louder.

It sounded like . . .

Faint cries.

Was it . . . ?

Cries of desperation. Panic. And above this, an odd shriek, like a scream queen crying out in the dead of night.

Suddenly, a gunshot echoed between the buildings. Karen's body jumped at the distinct sound.

Most tourists on the street froze. Pedestrians exchanged anxious glances.

Then a hundred yards ahead, a manhole cover flipped high into the air. As she observed its arcing trajectory against the cloudy sky, the world seemed to revolve in slow motion.

The manhole cover spun down and crashed into an SUV's windshield, shattering the glass and embedding into its center.

"What the hell?" Daniel uttered. He stepped closer to her and Joey. They edged toward the entrance of an apartment building, moving to shelter.

Tires skidded.

Metal crashed against metal as two cars collided ahead at the intersection.

Multiple gunshots rang out and they instinctively ducked.

Then an odd silence.

She could feel the energy in the air, but for a brief moment, everything turned still. No pedestrians moved; cars came to a standstill.

Karen didn't know what to make of it all. She attempted to process her surroundings. A gas explosion perhaps, or maybe a portent of an earthquake.

But why the gunshots then?

She had no answer. In fact, she had more questions as a lone man turned the corner, running in the middle of the street silently, panic on his face. His white linen shirt was torn to shreds and had red stains running down it.

Karen gasped. Her paramedic instincts kicked in and she took a step toward the man to help. Before she could get there, though, he suddenly stopped midstride on the street, as if his body were tied to an invisible rope that had reached its full length. The abruptness of his stop made Karen pause. The frightened man turned to look at her with desperation in his eyes. She was about to call out to him—

His legs jerked backward and he fell facefirst onto the asphalt. He desperately reached for anything he could, even dug his fingernails into the concrete.

It was no use. An invisible force yanked him backward with tremendous power, like a bungee cord snapping him back around the corner he had come from. His fingernails ripped off and his horrifying scream broke the silence. The man's body disappeared and then the scream abruptly cut off.

Karen gulped in a shuddering breath. Joey's safety rocketed to the front of her mind, whatever was happening. She turned back to her son.

Distant, painful screams filled the air again, growing louder and louder, closing in on their location, rapidly.

"Mommy, what's happening?" Joey asked in a panicked voice.

She faked a smile at him and placed a reassuring hand on his shoulder. "I don't know, baby. But we have to get out of here."

"What the . . ." Daniel trembled.

Karen followed his eyeline down the street.

A dozen frantic people charged back up the hill with horror etched across their faces.

Daniel grabbed Karen's arm.

She raised her eyes toward the road.

Near the manhole entrance, an enormous black creature, at least seven feet tall, stood on top of a car's hood. Its serrated tail wafted from side to side. Karen blinked several times to check she wasn't hallucinating. She remembered seeing an image of one on TV. It was nothing as horrific as the real thing. The thing bared three rows of razor-sharp teeth. It hunched before letting out an earsplitting screech.

The creature rammed its tail directly through the windshield, penetrating it with the ease of a pin through plastic wrap. Blood spattered against the internal windows. A bloody hand momentarily slammed against the driver's-side window, then slowly slid down.

Another creature exploded out of the manhole. Then another. Then another. At least forty in the time it took her to stumble back with the stroller and bang against the apartment building's glass entrance.

Before she could even utter a word, the creatures spread to the sidewalks at unbelievable speeds, springing forward on their muscular legs. They charged up Lombard Street, cutting down everything and everyone in their path. Tails lashed through pedestrians, slicing through their torsos and limbs. Blood sprayed across the white concrete in every direction.

More creatures burst out of the manhole. They systematically attacked the logjam of cars, ripping off the doors and turning the occupants into pink mist.

Joey screamed and covered his eyes.

Adrenaline coursed through Karen's body. She had witnessed many gruesome scenes in her job. This was off the scale.

She ripped Joey out of the stroller and clutched him tight. The sight was unbelievable. She had to do something. Anything to escape the carnage.

Daniel grabbed the chrome handle of the building's entrance. He heaved but the door was locked. He frantically pressed buzzers. Nobody responded.

The creatures closed in on them, continuing their butchery. They carved through the group of tourists only steps ahead. Cameras went flying. A map fluttered to the ground. Several bodies dropped shortly after. Intestines spilled across the sidewalk from an old man who had been sliced through at waist-level. The smell hit Karen, and she almost retched. A tail whipped across the old man's wife's neck. Her scythed head rolled along the street and came to rest against the curb.

Karen watched the onslaught in openmouthed terror.

Hundreds of the monstrosities infested Lombard Street. They leaped along the sides of buildings, smashed their tails against cars, and wiped out every living thing within a hundred yards of the manhole within seconds. They were only a stone's throw from Karen and her family's location. And they were closing fast.

Something clicked in her brain, knocking her out of her paralyzed state.

She had to find a safe place. She had to *move*.

Karen turned and frantically banged on the glass door.

A young woman, dressed in light blue yoga pants and a matching shirt, appeared in the corridor. She sprinted up to the door, peered beyond the family at the scene unfolding on the street. Her eyes bulged and she took a step back.

The creatures had closed to within seconds.

Karen never expected her life to end like this, or the life of her son and husband. She opened her mouth to scream, but her husband cut her off.

"Open the goddamn door!" Daniel yelled at the young woman inside.

Thankfully, the woman twisted the latch. He shoved his way in.

Karen immediately followed into the air-conditioned lobby, clasping Joey while shielding his eyes. The door slammed shut behind them, followed by a slight wave of relief. She turned to thank this young woman, their savior. Tears streamed down the woman's face. But there was no time for thanks.

The shadow of a creature loomed on the sidewalk and approached the door.

Slowly, a scaly black hand with sharp talons screeched along the glass, gouging out three deep lines.

It's toying with us . . .

The family backed away from the door.

"Watch out!" Karen shouted.

"What the—"

Suddenly, a sharp black tail whipped outside, punctured the glass entrance, and speared through the Good Samaritan's mouth. She let out a gurgle.

Her eyes rolled up to the top of her head. Blood dribbled from the glistening, sharp end.

The tail suspended the woman's limp body in the air for a few chilling seconds before it withdrew, sending her lifeless carcass to the carpeted floor. The tail then smashed against the entrance again. The crunching blow shattered more glass. Small shards battered the family. Humid air flooded in from the street.

"Run!" Karen bellowed.

Daniel pressed the elevator button. The overhead digital display read that it was on floor twelve. They didn't have time.

Karen headed straight for the staircase and powered up as fast as humanly possible. Joey held his mom tightly and cried out, drowning out the shrieks from the street.

"It'll be all right," she lied, trying to comfort him.

But comfort was the last thing on her mind.

This wasn't a bad dream. Her lungs burned as she ascended. Her thighs ached from the strain of rushing her son away from the slaughter, and she wasn't sure how much farther she could go. But fear propelled her forward. She looked over her shoulder every few seconds.

Daniel, though out of shape, matched her stride up the stairs. They might actually make it to safety.

But a creature had followed.

It tore after them at twice their speed, bounding up a few steps at a time.

Karen looked up. They couldn't risk stopping to knock on a door, not that she thought anyone who had seen the events outside would open one. Four more levels to go until they reached the roof. She didn't know where else to go. She had no idea if it was a futile move. Her only thought was getting Joey as far away as possible from the ground and where these monsters came from.

A bloodcurdling screech echoed up the staircase. The creature had closed to within a single flight. Daniel stopped and turned.

"Run," Karen cried out to her husband.

"You go, love. I'll stall it."

"Danny, no!"

"Save Joey. Now run. Right now!"

He stared up at her for a moment. Tears welled in her eyes. Tears welled in his. She knew exactly what this meant.

"For God's sake, Karen," he shouted. *"Run!"*

Heavy footsteps pounded on the floor toward them. Daniel turned away from his wife. He protectively raised his arms in a desperate attempt to stop the massive creature's ascent.

A tail lashed out, slicing clean through Daniel's forearm.

Blood sprayed the wall. He dropped to his knees and roared in agony.

"Daddy!" little Joey cried out.

The tail lashed down again. It sliced through Daniel's shoulder and stopped in the middle of his chest. He wavered on his knees. One didn't need to be a trained paramedic to recognize it was a killer blow, though he still attempted to throw a groggy punch with his dying breath.

"No!" Karen screamed.

Her mind snapped back to reality. It would all mean nothing if she didn't keep running. She spun and desperately sprinted up the stairs, clutching her son. Her world shattered. Her husband gone. She glanced back down once she had ascended two more flights. The creature had picked up Daniel's corpse and repeatedly smashed it against the bannister, brutally and sadistically. She had no frame of reference for what was unfolding.

Four deep breaths took her to the entrance of the roof. She thrust open the door and burst out into the bright sunshine. She spun and slammed a dead bolt shut on the roof door, expecting the creature to plow through it at any moment.

Adrenaline and fear flooded her veins, and she slowly backed away from the door. There was nowhere left to run.

Thrashing sounds and screams came from apartments below her feet, but the door to the roof remained quiet.

No creatures. At least, not yet.

A minute passed. Then another.

Karen's legs gave way and she collapsed to her knees on the shingled ground. Joey cried into her shoulder.

Shrieks filled the air, seemingly from all parts of the city.

Broken, she peered over the railing on the roof. Through her tears, she had a panoramic perspective of San Francisco.

Smoke billowed out of several high-rise buildings. Sirens blared, though the cops in the two police cars she could see had clearly been slaughtered.

Creatures bounded along every street within view, in all directions, like scattering cockroaches. They crawled over ferries in the bay, swamped Fisherman's Wharf, and tore apart tourist-filled trolleys, now soaked in blood.

All she could think was how long she had left to live. How long Joey did. Sooner or later, the same heavy footsteps that announced the death of her husband would come her way.

But until then, she'd be forced to witness the death of San Francisco.

CHAPTER FOUR

Frantic staffers rushed in and out of the White House Situation Room, panic across their faces. The usually orderly command center had devolved into utter chaos.

President Amanda Brogan sat rigid in her chair at the head of the conference table, her eyes fixated on the dizzying on-screen reports of the carnage happening countrywide and worldwide. She squeezed the chair's arms in a white-knuckled grip.

She had only been passively watching Cafferty's mission when the world had suddenly turned on its head. They had planned to monitor Hurricane Melyssa and deal with the damage. Now, the barely believable had become a barbaric reality. Damage beyond anyone's imagination. She'd funded Cafferty for his fight against the creatures, but nobody expected a mass attack this soon or of this magnitude. None of the dozen staff members around the table uttered a single word.

Vice President Webster shook his head. He had the pallor of a corpse, a blank expression, and his usually immaculate gray hair sagged from him constantly running his hands through it. For the first time in his life, the motormouthed New York politician appeared lost for words.

Only a few hours earlier, Brogan had been watching Tom Cafferty's mission in the Nevada desert with feigned interest. Now, she was shaken, terrified, watching America fall, city by city. Devastating creature attacks in San Francisco, Chicago, Miami, Houston, Detroit, and Atlanta. Reports of new cities under siege poured in every few minutes. Countless creatures had risen in unison, sweeping through streets and cities at a lightning pace.

One by one, news broadcasts from each city went dark, but not before the president had witnessed footage of thousands, maybe millions, of people dying at the hands of these monsters. Bitten. Slashed. Gouged. Methodically murdered. Bullets were essentially useless, though Cafferty had already warned her of that. The oxygen level and light that had protected humanity in the past were clearly no longer deterrents. The creatures had evolved faster than ever imagined to tolerate life aboveground. The rising had begun.

The president activated the national Emergency Broadcast System and quickly declared martial law, militarizing all local police and fire and mobilizing all armed forces.

Not that it would matter.

From what she'd seen, cities were falling at ferocious speeds. Any attempt to fight back was met with a swift end, and more frighteningly, it appeared that the creatures knew exactly what they were doing,

what targets to hit and in what order. They were relentless and coordinated, first attacking power grids
and infrastructure, then slaughtering the masses.
Dozens of cities within the span of a half hour.

"Madam President—" the secretary of defense
said.

"Wait," she snapped back.

The country, the world, was entering unchar-
tered territory. She needed time to think, and fast,
as people were dying at a rapid rate.

Television reports streamed in from around the
world of the same occurrence. Sydney, Auckland,
Toronto, Manchester, Delhi, Cape Town. She
slammed her fist on the table. It was almost as if
Albert Van Ness had this day planned all along. But
he didn't plan this. He couldn't have. The twisted
old man was safely locked away on a prison rig in
the middle of the Atlantic, unlike the population
currently being annihilated.

A young aide, visibly trembling in his charcoal
suit, put down a phone and turned to her. "Jack-
sonville, Indianapolis, and Columbus, too, Madam
President. God knows where else."

"Call Tom Cafferty," Brogan bellowed. "Right
now."

The former mayor had the weapons to fight back.
She had funded him to the tune of a billion dollars.
The government needed those weapons now. And
it was becoming clear that she'd need Cafferty for
another mission, one he would not want to hear.

The aide leaned down to punch in the number.
As he did, the overhead lights, screens, and phones
flickered off.

Darkness swamped the Situation Room.

Brogan sucked in a sharp breath. On her watch, the country was falling. Just like the White House, she was also powerless.

The ominous conclusion was that the creatures were rising in Washington, D.C., too, taking out electrical plants just now and then undoubtedly, methodically butchering the population.

A few seconds later the backup generators kicked in and the White House stuttered back to life.

"Get me Cafferty!" she commanded.

General Robert Emmer, a short balding man who had the nickname "911" because of his ability to deal with emergencies calmly, pushed through the door. "Madam President, creatures have reached Lafayette Square. We need to evacuate the White House now."

"We'll be safe in this bunker, General," she replied.

"No, ma'am, I don't believe we will."

Brogan was taken aback at the bluntness of his reply.

"You and Vice President Webster need to accompany me to Marine One. Air Force One is standing by, ready."

"General, I am not abandoning the—"

"Madam President, we've lost the ground war," the general interrupted. "The only safe place to be is in the air or on the sea. Evacuating the White House is not optional."

The gravity of his words sunk in.

A look of realization spread across President Brogan's face and she rose from her chair. "General Emmer, order the navy to launch every ship we have and the air force to scramble every single plane. Save as many of our armed forces as we can!"

The feed from the major D.C. TV networks went dark one by one, and one by one the White House phone lines stopped ringing.

"They've reached the Smithsonian!" a voice called out in the background. Panic began to spread in the Situation Room.

"Attention, everyone, we are evacuating the White House now!" President Brogan bellowed out. "General, get as many staffers in the choppers as possible."

Secret Service grabbed the president and vice president by the arms and the group bolted up the stairs and out of the entrance hall. Brogan was half in a daze at the unfolding events. Everything had happened so fast, so unexpectedly.

When they crossed a short section of lawn toward Marine One, whose propellers were already spinning, Brogan jolted to a stop.

A thick line of creatures approached down Pennsylvania Avenue, chopping down the fleeing citizens. Thousands of them. Heading straight for 1600 Pennsylvania Avenue. Like they knew their destination. No orders would save people right now.

Vice President Webster wheezed up the steps and entered the chopper.

Brogan had no choice. She grimaced at the distant screams, the sporadic gunshots that split the air that she knew wouldn't save anyone.

The creatures would be here in less than a minute. White House staffers raced across the lawn to reach other choppers. There was no way they'd make it in time.

With a silent prayer, President Brogan scrambled into the chopper, and Secret Service strapped her in tightly. The door slammed shut and Marine One immediately lifted into the air as creatures barreled through the White House gates.

Brogan let out a deep breath and peered out the window. Sickness swamped her stomach. Bile filled her mouth. She couldn't figure a way out of the onslaught.

Hundreds of creatures reached the White House and smashed through the windows—windows that were expected to stop machine-gun fire—crawled up the walls, and clambered over the roof. Guards, marines, and Secret Service briefly held firm outside the West Wing before the avalanche of creatures overwhelmed them.

As Marine One sped across the sky to rendezvous with Air Force One, Brogan and Webster stared out the windows, shocked.

The death toll below was incomprehensible. America's capital was lost. More though, America was lost. The world might be lost.

Humanity . . .

She knew this wasn't simply a one-off attack. America and the world faced an apocalypse. A fight for survival against an unyielding enemy. Humanity was facing its own extinction.

"Is Tom Cafferty in the air?" President Brogan finally said.

"He is, Madam President," General Emmer replied.

"I need to speak to him, General. Now!"

CHAPTER FIVE

The Black Hawk carrying Cafferty and his team thumped through the clear blue sky toward Las Vegas. It was now a race against time to reach the military jet on the Nellis Air Force Base runway. He peered through the window, down to the Calico Basin, where thousands of creatures—barely visible through a thick cloud of dust—bounded over rocks and through the sparse plains toward the western edge of the city, like an approaching dust storm, ready to wipe Las Vegas off the face of the earth.

Cafferty let out a long, resigned sigh of sadness. He then closed his eyes for a moment to compose himself. It was all too much to bear.

Everyone on the chopper had at least one family member or friend in the cities that had reportedly come under attack—how could they not, when pretty much every American city had been a site of slaughter? The black throng would reach Vegas in minutes, tearing into over half a million residents and tourists.

There was nothing Cafferty's team could do beyond a heroic yet suicidal charge.

And while they could at least take out some creatures with them, millions could not. Perhaps billions more were still in the firing line of tails, teeth, and talons.

So as they flew toward doom, Tom knew it was a mistake. They had to retreat to a safe place.

But is any place safe?

The fact was, probably not.

Another soul-destroying fact made him sick in the pit of his stomach. All the team's meticulous planning in the United States had been destroyed in less than an hour. They had barely begun their mission of destroying nests around the world, and now it was moot.

We dragged our feet. Van Ness kept his weapons from us. And now we're going to die because of him.

This wasn't an exaggeration. They didn't have the ability to take on this many creatures. Arms production had started in earnest only after the new prototypes had been tested and approved. Cafferty reckoned they had two thousand laser guns and ten thousand strobe grenades manufactured. Two thousand guns would barely create a dent in Las Vegas, let alone throughout the world. And the strobes were clearly useless now that the creatures had evolved to tolerate light and oxygen.

How did they evolve so fast?

Cafferty's mind drifted back to the creatures' cavern underneath the New York City subway system three years ago. Those pregnant women cocooned, being kept alive, being tested on by the

creatures. Then the newer, smaller creatures that
were more tolerant of oxygen and light. And now *this*.

*These monsters crossbred species in order to extermi-
nate humanity and managed it at a schedule that would
have boggled Darwin's mind.*

Pandora's box was open and would never ever be
closed again.

Bowcut rested a hand on his shoulder. "We'll
regroup and fight back, Tom. We'll find a way."

"No, Sarah," Cafferty replied. "No. We've lost.
I've lost."

Ellen squeezed her husband's hand tight. She
glanced back out the window at the carnage below.
"God help them."

Munoz looked up from his tablet. "Tom, it's
accelerating. Half of Europe has dropped off the
grid. It's carnage in Rio, Jakarta—"

"Enough!" Cafferty snapped back, rubbing his
temples.

"I'm just saying, Tom. This many simultaneous
attacks across the world? Attacking power grids
and infrastructure first, then genocide? This isn't
coincidence."

"What are you saying, Diego?" Ellen asked.

"This is strategy. This is command and control.
Tom, this is higher intelligence."

Cafferty's hands tightened into fists.

"Van Ness never said the creatures were *this*
smart," Diego continued.

Cafferty put his head down, beaten. "Oh yes,
he did. He knew this day would come, unless we
destroyed them first. He knew all along. That's
why . . ."

Cafferty's mind drifted back to Van Ness' plan to annihilate the nests with thermonuclear weapons, killing millions of people in the cities above along with them. The plan Cafferty and his team had stopped.

Would the madman's mass murder have prevented the even greater genocide now unfolding worldwide?

He fought back vomit threatening to spew forth. But he could feel it churning inside him. The failure. The guilt. The *anger*. He switched his gaze to the window and looked downward.

The Black Hawk passed over the first Vegas neighborhood. Creatures infested the streets, smashing through house windows and charging after anyone in sight. It took only seconds for the poor people to meet a swift end. Or maybe they were the lucky ones. Some vanished in a swarm of creatures, much like David North in the Jersey tunnel. The painful reminder sent a shudder through his body. In hindsight, that day was merely an appetizer to what was happening below.

It was a violent, gruesome tableau, made all the worse by the silence in which he experienced it from so far up.

The chopper banked and roared toward northern Vegas. As far as he could see, every place had been swamped by the first wave, which was probably more like a first tsunami.

They passed over Boulder Junction and neared the Strip. Even from here, as he attempted to view the length of the road, the fresh damage was obvious. At least half the windows on the Luxor hotel's tall black pyramid were smashed. Creatures crawled around the giant Sphinx outside, surrounded by blood-stained corpses. Farther ahead, smoke billowed out of the MGM Grand. Corpses floated in the fountain outside the Bellagio. Red clouds surrounded their bodies in the crystal-clear water.

The attack had reached Treasure Island. This gave Cafferty his first snapshot of the creatures hitting civilization en masse. The windows of the tall red hotel burst out in quick succession. Some had probably attempted to seek shelter in their rooms. It was clearly futile. Tom's imagination painted the picture of the creatures smashing through the doors, grabbing the occupants, and forcefully throwing them through the glass. Just like how they threw the passengers out of the Z Train car three years earlier.

Anyone attempting to escape on foot toward the old town met the same fate as the people on the outskirts of the city.

Blood raged along the Strip's gutters.

Creatures roamed supreme, darting around every corner, racing into other casinos' entrances, like the Pink Flamingo. The only place that remained untouched at this point was Circus Circus, but in a manner of minutes, it, too, would be overrun.

Those tourists have no idea what's about to hit them . . .

CHAPTER SIX

Mike Gianno walked along a corridor to his high-roller suite in Circus Circus. He grasped the hand of a lady he knew only as Cindy. She was wearing a tight red dress showing her voluptuous curves. Maybe thirty years old. He wasn't sure. She was most definitely out of his league, but his natural charm had clearly won her over.

This morning, he'd dressed to impress. Skinny jeans. A white linen shirt, unbuttoned to the center of his chest, ensuring he flashed his thick gold necklace. It was most likely real, too. He avoided tucking his shirt in to conceal his growing potbelly. A classic fat guy trick. The short sleeves flashed his inked biceps. He wasn't exactly ripped, but for a balding man approaching his midforties, he thought he looked pretty good. Distinguished, even.

To complement his appearance, a squirt of Stetson cologne had given him a woodsy, citrus aroma compared with his competition at the casino bars: morbidly overweight desperados with cigarettes constantly jammed between their lips. He didn't need to sink that low. The thought disgusted him. He'd upgraded to e-cigarettes long ago. And the ultimate ace in his pocket: he had a suite in the hotel. Women love suites, is what he had heard. He also had the decency to put his wedding ring in the safe, so all good there.

"You got booze?" Cindy asked.

Mike smiled. "Does a shark have a waterproof nose?"

"What?"

"Forget about it. There's a minibar."

It's expensive.

So what? I'll take the hit to impress her.

His excitement grew as they neared his room. He'd previously had no luck at the tables or the slots. Five hundred bucks, hosed in under two hours. Something he couldn't really afford with a wife and two kids back in Michigan. After his losing streak, he'd hung around the bar. Six rejections later, he'd met Cindy, a fitness instructor from Tyler, Texas. They'd immediately hit it off, talking about their love of action movies and barbecue.

Cindy and he had talked for half an hour. It felt like he'd known her for years. It was like she understood what he was all about. She had an insight into the male psyche that he'd never encountered before. She *knew* what men were about, clearly.

Here goes.

Mike placed his key card against the door. He opened it and waved Cindy inside with the flourish of a ringmaster. "After you, madam."

She frowned at him. "Are you sure you're not drunk?"

"Only had five Moscow mules," he replied proudly. "I could have easily had six."

She shook her head and entered the room.

Mike closed the door behind him and spun to face her. Sure, the high-roller suite at Circus Circus had cost him only one hundred bucks, but it was the best room in the hotel, with a living area, a separate bedroom, and a huge bathroom.

Cindy peered around. "Is this really the presidential suite?"

Mike nodded. "Uh-huh."

"Which president? Carter?" Cindy sassed back. She slipped off her purse and reached for the zip on the back of her dress.

Holy shit, this is happening . . .

"Oh, one last thing . . ." Cindy said while unzipping her dress.

"Anything for you, baby."

"You need to pay up front."

Mike's eyes widened. "Oh . . . uh . . . excuse me?"

"That's standard here in Vegas, baby. It's not that I don't trust you."

"Oh . . . you're . . . uh . . . working right now?"

Cindy rolled her eyes. "Does a shark have a waterproof nose?"

Mike hadn't realized. The revelation momentarily hurt his ego. He imagined the bums in the casino bar laughing after he'd left. He'd given most of them a triumphant grin on the way past, like he'd been the victor in their unspoken competition. He might have even given one the finger.

"Uh, yeah. So how much are we talking?" he asked.

"Depends on what you want."

Mike did fast math in his head. Five hundred lost on the casino floor, a hundred for the room, five Moscow mules, pay-per-view last night to watch that new hidden-camera comedy movie that just came out, UberX from the airport . . .

Damn, adds up fast.

"Um . . . two hundred?" he replied.

She shook her head and held up one hand. "That's what you get. I'm gonna use the bathroom first."

"Okay, um, it's right through there."

Cindy sauntered through to the bedroom and headed for the bathroom.

Excitement rose inside him, a feeling he hadn't experienced since his last "business" trip. He stripped naked and slipped on a terry cloth bathrobe, leaving it loosely fastened around his waist. Mike checked himself out in the mirror. He sucked in and puffed out his chest.

A clatter of noise came from the bathroom, followed by silence.

"Hey," he shouted. "You all right in there?"

"You need to pay up front," Cindy's voice said from behind the closed door.

This sent a wave of irritation through him. If she planned on talking turkey all the way through their experience, it promised to be a total turnoff.

"Okay, I get it," he replied, opening his wallet and counting out two hundred dollars. That left eighty dollars in his wallet. Plenty for the taxi back to the airport and maybe another pay-per-view tonight. He had already maxed out his credit card, so reception would have to take cash. He was dying to watch *Anaconda* again.

Then, her identical voice again, from behind the bathroom door. "You need to pay up front," she repeated.

"I said I get it," he said, annoyed.

Mike entered the bedroom, attempting to push her parroted comment to the back of his mind. The crisp ivory sheets had been spread to one side, and her dress lay across the top of them. He sat on the edge of the bed, waiting for her to finish whatever she was doing in the bathroom.

He reached across to the bedside cabinet and grabbed the half-drunk glass of wine he'd left there the previous night. It tasted warm and sour as it gushed down his throat. He squeezed one eye shut, wincing.

"You need to pay up front," she called again.

"What the frick?" Mike replied.

He strode over to the bathroom and flung the door open, ready to demand that she leave his suite immediately. Enough was enough.

The large bathroom had a mirrored shower to the side. No water was running. Cindy wasn't on the toilet or at the sink. The curtain was drawn across the bath at the far end and had stains across its white surface.

What the hell has she done?

Mike stormed over and swept the curtain to one side. Cindy lay slumped in the bathtub, eyes rolled back in her head. She had huge slash marks across her stomach, and a shallow pool of blood lapped against the lower parts of her body.

He clasped a hand over his mouth to stifle his scream.

How? Suicide?

What do I do now?

He glanced up for signs of any security cameras. None.

They'll think I did it . . .

What do I tell my wife?

Mike spun to face the bathroom door. He needed to think this through.

As he turned, a massive black creature exploded through the mirrored shower door. Blood dripped from its razor-sharp teeth. Its tail whipped from side to side as it advanced toward him, blocking off his escape.

Mike stumbled back in shock. His legs hit the bath and he collapsed. His backside crashed against Cindy's wounded stomach and he whacked his head on the edge of the tub. His eyes went hazy, possibly from a concussion. Cindy's warm blood saturated his white robe.

The creature approached, wide-eyed with excitement as it towered over its prey. It leaned down close to Mike's face. "You need to pay up front," the creature said, its vocal chords mimicking Cindy's voice precisely.

Equal parts terror and regret instantly spread across Mike's slumped-down face. Before he had a chance to look up, two powerful hands clamped around his head. Claws immediately sunk into his temples. The hands crushed hard against his skull.

The creature ripped him out of the bathtub and held him a few feet in the air. Cindy's blood dripped from his robe to the tiled floor.

Mike screamed, long and loud, hoping somebody would hear, hoping somebody would help.

The creature swung his body toward the towel hook on the door.

Then it thrust him downward with tremendous force.

The blunt hook crunched through his spine, just below his neck. His legs went numb, and he could no longer move his arms. The creature took a step back and watched as Mike swung gently from side to side on the door hook, the life draining from his body.

He wheezed out a gurgling, dying breath.

Not yet sated, the creature raised its thick black arm and rammed three razor-sharp claws into Mike's neck.

Everything instantly went black.

Just like that, Mike's business trip had come to an end.

CHAPTER SEVEN

A s the Black Hawk raced over Las Vegas, Cafferty silently shook his head at the thousands of dead bodies below, at the thousands of bounding creatures in full sunlight, having no problem breathing oxygen anymore.

The city was lost.

Massive questions flooded his mind.

Where does the world go from here?

Will anyone even live to see next week?

Am I to blame?

Ellen squeezed her husband's hand more firmly, sensing his despair. She rested her head on his shoulder for a moment.

Bowcut ripped a satphone from a front pouch on her black body armor. She planted it to her ear, listened intently, then passed the device to Tom. "It's President Brogan."

Cafferty put the satphone on speaker, trying to collect himself. "Madam President."

"Tom, has your chopper reached the air base yet?" Her tone was stern, for obvious reasons.

He replied, "Approaching west of Vegas now, fifteen minutes out. We're just ahead of the creatures. The pilots say we should beat them to the base in time."

"Get on that military plane and get airborne again the moment you land."

"Yes, Madam President."

"Tom, Washington has fallen," Brogan said.

Munoz's mouth dropped open. Bowcut shook her head in disbelief.

"My God," Ellen replied. "Madam President, our son David? My parents?"

"A helicopter got them before Fairfax was overrun," Brogan replied. *"They are safe at the moment, heading to one of our aircraft carriers that made it out of Norfolk in time."*

Cafferty welled up with tears, clutching Ellen close.

Thank God David is safe.

"Where are you now, Madam President?" Cafferty asked, collecting himself.

"I'm in Air Force One, along with Vice President Webster and the Joint Chiefs," President Brogan replied. *"We're staying airborne indefinitely. Midair refueling planes got off the ground before Andrews Air Force Base fell to the creatures. We should have enough fuel to stay in the sky for a few days while we come up with a plan."*

"Good, good," Cafferty replied.

"Tom, I need you to do something for me . . . and for your country," Brogan said softly. Her sudden change of tone made Cafferty listen more intently. *"Something only you can do . . ."*

She paused, and Cafferty sensed the hesitation in her voice. He also suspected what was about to come but didn't believe it quite yet. Not until the awful words had spewed out of her mouth.

"I need you to go see Albert Van Ness."

Cafferty put the phone down for a moment.

Munoz and Bowcut, who had leaned in close to listen, both stared in disbelief.

Cafferty raised the phone again. "Are. You. Kidding. Me?" he said.

The chopper closed in on the air base and began its descent. A fence surrounding the base remained intact. Soldiers hunched behind twenty vehicles on the airstrip. They aimed toward the city, waiting for the inevitable attack.

"He might have information on how we can stop this attack. But you see . . ."

Cafferty knew the president's next words before she said them.

". . . he'll only talk to you."

"You mean you've already reached out to him, Madam President?" Cafferty asked incredulously.

The president's silence on the other end said it all. Cafferty swelled with anger that threatened to burst him apart from the inside.

"You know this is his final twist of the knife, don't you, Madam President? You're playing right into his hand. He's *baiting* you to get to *me*. If Van Ness had any contingency plans for this, we would have already uncovered them when we raided the Foundation and its servers. He's lying."

Cafferty squeezed the satphone harder in his hand, looked up at his team, and shook his head.

"No, Madam President," Cafferty continued. "No. I will *not* visit that murderer. I won't give him the satisfaction of an audience while we could be planning and launching a counterattack instead. We need to regroup and—"

"*Now you listen to me, Tom,*" President Brogan shot back defiantly. "*The world is on its knees. If there's even the slightest chance that madman can help us stop these creatures, then so help me God,* you're going. *Is that understood?*"

The chopper began its final descent, closing in on the military jet that had its side door open and engines running, ready to depart.

"The world can't leave its fate in the hands of a lunatic, Madam President. Not again," Cafferty replied, sounding defeated.

Van Ness had made the same arrogant claim to him before, that the former mayor was destined to fail and *only he* had a way of winning the final battle.

"We're approaching the runway, Tom," Diego interjected. "And this is gonna be close."

Cafferty peered out the window as the chopper approached the landing strip. In the distance, hundreds of creatures raced across the lush fairways of the Sunrise Vista Golf Course, heading directly toward the base's perimeter fence. Muffled shots rang out as soldiers responded to their presence. Cafferty knew bullets wouldn't have any effect against the attack.

"*Get onto that plane as fast as possible, Tom!*" the president shouted through the satphone. "*Then get to Van Ness.*"

The Black Hawk's wheels hit the ground next to the military aircraft. Cafferty, Ellen, Bowcut, and Munoz jumped out and sprinted up the jet's small set of steps. A soldier immediately slammed the plane door shut, and the pilot fired the engines full force.

The aircraft picked up speed along the runway. The jet's engines whined, drowning out the external gunfire of soldiers quickly losing their lives.

Out of breath, Cafferty peered out the window of the plane. The jet's wheels lifted off the runway and they took to the sky. Below them, the creatures leaped over the perimeter and swarmed the remaining soldiers.

"They don't stand a chance," Munoz uttered.

"Heavily outnumbered with useless weapons," Bowcut added.

It didn't need to be said, but they needed to say something, to somehow come to terms with what they were witnessing.

It was all over in thirty seconds. Creatures overran the vehicles and rapidly set about slaughtering soldiers. They then headed for the main buildings to finish the job of destroying the air base in its entirety.

Cafferty slid down his window cover. He had seen enough.

Civilization was falling fast.

"We're airborne, Madam President," he finally said into the satphone, defeated.

"Thank God," she replied. *"And your mission?"*

He rested his head in his hands.

How has it come to this as my only option?

"Tom, maybe you should at least hear Van Ness out," Ellen said quietly to her husband.

Cafferty turned to his wife and gave her an angry look.

"Humanity is falling," she continued, not cowed by his anger. "If even a hint of truth exists in Van Ness' claim that he can stop this, we're going to need all the help we can get.

"Tom, our *son* is in danger. Wouldn't you do whatever it takes to keep him safe?"

Cafferty shot his wife an icy glare, incredulous and furious with her. *How dare she use David against me like this!* But again, she looked back with defiance. He looked at Munoz and Bowcut. They apparently both agreed with Ellen.

They all knew what Van Ness was. And yet they seemed to trust that maniac more than him. He felt surrounded by betrayal and hated that he had no choice but to acquiesce.

Cafferty lifted the satphone to his mouth.

"Fine. I'll go," he said, shaking his head in disbelief.

"But know this, Madam President," he continued, eyeing his three companions so that they knew the words were for them, too. "This is a *trap*. And more of us *will* die."

CHAPTER EIGHT

The sun had almost set in San Francisco, bathing the city in a warm orange glow. A shaken Karen Green sat cross-legged, away from the edge of the apartment building's roof. Little Joey knelt by her side, his arms locked around her waist.

The sounds of alarms and sirens filled the air, thousands of them blasting from cars and buildings.

But no more screams. Or cries of pain and suffering.

Only distant shrieks.

They made her skin crawl. Made the hairs on the back of her neck stand on end.

She figured anyone left alive remained hidden from facing a certain death. At least for now.

Nobody had answered her 911 call. She hadn't expected anyone to, but she had tried nevertheless— what else could she do? During the afternoon, her cell signal had died. She knew her fate and the fate of her son rested squarely in her hands. The only way to know if the creatures were coming back was to assess the situation on the ground. Once more, the thought crept through her mind:

I need to make Daniel's actions count, make sure he didn't die in vain.

Karen broke free of Joey's embrace. He tried to cling to her, but she eased him away. She placed her finger against her lips to encourage his silence. He replied by wiping tears away from his eyes. It didn't take him long to comply to this.

He'd seen too much.

Her hope was that he couldn't process the events. A slim hope, yes, but she couldn't stand the thought of those images seared into his mind for the rest of his life. Of his father being . . .

Of the images permanently seared in *her* mind.

This might be our last sunset.

"Baby," she whispered. "Be a good boy and stay quiet for Mommy. Please."

Thankfully, Joey nodded in acknowledgment, in part because he couldn't see her internal dread. As a paramedic, she needed a great poker face. Patients with serious injuries required reassurance on their way to the hospital, not a panic-stricken EMS worker telling them they'd die if they didn't beat the traffic in time. Joey needed his mother, not the victim of a vicious, living-nightmare attack.

Once confident he would follow her request, she dropped to her elbows and knees and crawled toward the edge of the roof. The asphalt scraped against her flesh. She grimaced as she advanced.

"Mommy, I'm hungry," Joey whispered a little too loudly for her comfort.

Karen's head snapped toward the bolted door. She listened for heavy footsteps, a snarl, an echoing shriek—any sound that would show that her son's voice had betrayed their location.

Something clattered below, like a steel pole plunging down a gap in the staircase, crashing against the old iron bannister as it descended.

She tensed, glanced back to Joey.

He gave her his doe-eyed look.

She pressed a finger to her lips once more and focused back on the door, expecting it to burst open at any second.

Roughly a minute passed.

Nothing came.

Then two.

Still no creatures. No sounds nearing the top flight of stairs.

Karen waited a little longer before she let out a deep breath through puffed cheeks.

They hadn't eaten since breakfast, so she understood her son's discomfort; he was used to regular meals. Lunch had been the next item on the agenda when the creatures attacked. The comfort of Fisherman's Wharf now seemed like a distant memory. A past life, away from this unfolding horror. And while they usually brought snacks, they'd abandoned them with the stroller in the street below.

Her stomach had also growled during their hours on the roof, though it seemed a trivial issue compared to leaving their temporary safety for food and water.

Only for so long if we want to stay alive.

"Mommy, I'm scared."

She peered over her shoulder and gave him her serious look—the one usually reserved for refusing him McDonald's if he didn't pick up his toys. Their survival likely depended on his silence. However, there was no way of explaining the gravity of their situation to a boy of his age and expecting him to understand.

Joey covered his face with his dirty hands and quietly sobbed.

That was marginally better than talking.

Karen's heart broke for him, but her priority was both of their immediate survival. She continued her crawl and reached the edge of the roof.

On Lombard Street below, everything remained still. To the right, the static logjam of battered cars. Corpses spread around them, deathly still among the bushes or on the sidewalk, all in gruesome twisted shapes. Some were unrecognizable as human beings.

The left end of the street painted a similar picture.

The *Norwegian Pearl* cruise ship aimlessly floated in the golden bay. As it was preparing to depart the dock, creatures must have attacked and slaughtered the passengers. Earlier that morning, Karen had spoken to a few excited passengers who were boarding the same ship. Apparently it was a comedy cruise, organized by the guys from a popular cable TV show. Nobody would be laughing now.

She squinted her eyes at the sign of movement in the water.

A lone swimmer. One survivor.

His arms desperately cut into the gentle swell as he attempted to swim away from the ship and back toward the wharf. The man eventually reached it and climbed to the concrete. Bald head, wearing a soaked black T-shirt and gray jeans. He hunched, rapidly looking in all directions, then sprinted out of view. Moments later, a Tesla driven by the same man roared past as he made his escape. Perhaps there would be one survivor of the cruise after all, if he managed to escape the city.

An earsplitting shriek broke her from watching the Tesla wind its way through the static cars. She immediately flinched. Looked down.

Directly below, a massive creature stared up at her from the street, tail wafting from side to side, talons opening and closing. Bloodstained teeth bared.

In the blink of an eye, it bolted inside the apartment building entrance.

Oh shit.

The creature saw her on the roof. That's undoubtedly where it was headed now. They had to hide somewhere else, fast. They had been compromised and staying here spelled a brutal end.

Karen scrambled to her feet.

"What's wrong?" Joey asked.

She didn't reply. Instead, she scooped him up into her arms. He protested, but Karen shushed him and patted his back while she sprinted across the roof to the door.

A primal scream rang out from the lower floors. She caught the edge of a black figure powering up the stairs at an unbelievable speed.

Her body trembled. She could barely breathe. Joey wriggled in her grip.

They had to move.

Karen raced down a single flight of stairs and found herself on the top floor of the building. All four apartment doors were hanging on their hinges, having been previously battered open.

The creature would reach this point in seconds.

An acrid stench filled her nostrils as the monstrosity approached.

Sacrificing myself to give Joey time to escape won't work. He's too small, too young. I'll only prolong his death for a few painful seconds. He'd watch me get cut to ribbons in front of his eyes, so his last sight would be a nightmare.

Still, she wasn't left with many options. She could hear the creature racing up the stairs. Karen dove into the first apartment, turned, and kicked the door closed behind her.

The lock had been smashed and it wouldn't shut.

Footsteps hammered on the floor directly below.

Snarls.

She turned and headed along the hallway into the main living area. The stench of copper mixed with burning food hung in the air.

"Don't look," Karen whispered in Joey's ear.

He buried his face into her shoulder.

She took a second to get an appreciation of her surroundings, searching for a place to hide. It was their only option. She wasn't sure there was any point, but she was a mother and this was her son— she'd do everything in her power to protect him.

Still, the thought of hiding in here was almost too much to bear.

Pools of drying blood covered the wooden floorboards. A young man sat upright on a leather couch, butchered. His dead eyes stared upward. His chest cavity had been sliced open. The bottom half of his left leg rested against a Persian rug. The waist and legs of a woman, perhaps his wife, lay slumped over an open window. Maybe she had tried to jump for her life. Her upper half had made it, at least—it lay twenty floors down, smashed on the street.

A kitchenette lay to her right. Something black burned in the oven. If the window hadn't been open, the apartment would be filled with smoke. As it was, a murk lingered everywhere.

Outside the apartment, the creature hesitated for a second, and she stiffened. But then it bounded up to the roof and smashed the door open. She could hear its pounding footsteps above the ceiling, could hear its guttural breaths as it hunted its prey.

As it hunts me and Joey.

Karen spotted a door to the left. She quietly moved across the kitchen to it, grimacing as she turned the handle, scared of making any noise.

The door quietly opened up to a bedroom. The bed was a queen-sized, wooden, IKEA-style frame. Hiding under it would make them easy to see. A dresser. A set of drawers.

And built-in cabinets.

Karen moved across to them and slid the door open. She quickly swiped dresses to one side, stepped inside with Joey, then closed the door behind them silently. Light radiated through the slats, casting white lines across their bodies.

The frustrated creature on the roof above slammed its feet down hard, causing the plaster in the ceiling to crack.

Her son looked into her eyes and opened his mouth. Karen cupped it before he could say anything. His rapid breaths warmed her palm. The tears streaming down his face rolled over the back of her hand.

Her own tears fell unimpeded.

The creature had reentered the building's stairwell and approached the very apartment Karen was hiding in. The footsteps stomped closer. She was sure the creature had entered the apartment.

Karen's body trembled with fear. Her slow breaths seemed too loud, even against the sound of the alarms coming through the living room's open window.

The hanger for the dress she was leaning against shifted along the rail. She winced at the low, metallic scraping sound. Tried her hardest not to move a muscle.

A black figure moved past the doorway.

A moment of silence followed.

The silence was smashed by furniture crashing in the next room against the walls. The sofa crumbled against the kitchenette. A glass coffee table shattered to pieces. The creature was systematically tearing the place apart, looking for them. It would not stop until the hunt was complete.

And that meant they were dead.

She almost gave in then. Almost just opened the door and let the creature take them. End this dread and misery that was almost as brutal as the pain they were sure to suffer. But she held firm. She held Joey, and because of that, she held on to hope.

The creature appeared in the bedroom doorway, filling the space with its muscular frame. Its chest heaved. Its beady black eyes darted around, scanning every inch.

Karen gulped.

Effortlessly, the creature lifted the bed with its talons and flipped it into the air. The bed came crashing back down to the floor in pieces.

It tore apart the dresser. Clothes and particleboard flew everywhere.

There was only one place left to check.

The creature slowly turned toward the cabinet. It took a step forward and reached out an arm. Hot breath came through the gaps in the slats.

Karen squeezed Joey tight. She prayed for a miracle.

This is it.

I love you, she said to Joey in her heart, still afraid to make any noise. The slats darkened with the bulk of the creature—

Suddenly, a deafening screech filled the room.

The ink-black nightmare stopped, its talons only inches from the cabinet door. Inches from Karen's sweat-drenched face.

Then it inexplicably turned its back on her as a new, smaller creature—perhaps half the size of the larger one—came in.

The small creature bellowed again, and whatever it communicated sent the bigger one bounding out of the apartment. Shortly after, the smaller creature left the bedroom and followed its companion outside. The sound of claws down the stairs echoed in the otherwise silent building.

She still didn't dare move an inch.

For the next half hour, Karen and Joey stood in the cabinet, both straining to hear any ominous sounds in the building.

None came.

While waiting, she tried to process what she had seen. It was as if the larger creature was taking orders from the smaller one, like a soldier follows a general's orders to fall back in line. It was the only thing that made sense, considering the circumstances.

But these are animals . . .

Aren't they?

The thought of their coordinated intelligence sent a shiver down Karen's spine.

But for now, they were still alive. A small trickle of relief had now turned into a torrent. Joey had calmed down, too. He played with a coat hanger while mumbling his favorite tune.

Darkness had now enveloped the city and the apartment. Whether that was good or bad remained to be seen.

Whatever the situation, the lack of creatures in the near vicinity meant she could give Joey some food and water from the kitchenette.

Karen hoped it wouldn't be their last supper.

CHAPTER NINE

President Amanda Brogan stared at the monitors in the conference room of Air Force One in disbelief. She'd been intently studying them for the last few hours. A dozen screens displayed a dizzying array of satellite and drone footage, air traffic, live feeds from cities, and global communications. The Joint Chiefs sat around the table, digesting the latest information.

Despite the cool air-conditioning, she dabbed her forehead with a handkerchief. They were airborne and safe for now, but with nowhere to go.

Vice President Webster and General Robert Emmer both gazed up at the largest screen in the conference room. It displayed a green map of the United States, covered in misshapen red blotches, like tracking the spread of a contagious disease. But in this case, the disease was the creatures, and she knew each red mark undoubtedly meant millions of Americans dead.

"Updates, General?" she asked.

"Most of our ships have now made it to sea, Madam President," General Emmer said. "Bases away from the big cities are still operational. The air force is at eighty percent strength, and most of our fighters are airborne. The overseas recall is under way."

"How long can the fighters stay in the air?"

"They refuel every two hours. We've identified sites away from the outbreaks for them to land."

"Excellent. Thank you."

"I'd say we were lucky that the creatures targeted mostly the big cities, but *lucky* isn't the right word," Emmer continued. "Especially for the inhabitants."

"No, *lucky* isn't the word I'd use. How long before this map is all red?"

Emmer let out a deep sigh. "Tracking their current spread, I'd estimate one week, Madam President."

"*One week?*"

"Again, if we're *lucky*."

Brogan felt sick to her stomach. She watched the heat map as she crossed the room, and a chilling thought crossed her mind. Each of the engulfed cities previously had a bomb planted underneath it by the Foundation for Human Advancement. Planted by Van Ness.

The bombs would've killed millions. But they would have also destroyed the nests in the process, effectively stopping the current genocide with a genocide of their own. What Van Ness called during his court case "acceptable collateral damage, killing millions to save billions," now appeared on the money.

Did we have time to evacuate the cities and carry out the same strategy? Were we arrogant fools to discount him as insane?

Brogan shook her head. *No, I can't think like this.* No president in history would sanction the evacuation and nuclear bombing of so many American cities. Hindsight was an unproductive vice in the current global disaster. Dwelling on the ifs or buts wouldn't change a damned thing. Her hope was that if Albert Van Ness truly had intelligence to see this coming, then he'd also put a contingency in place. Because right now all she could think of was bombing the cities from above and hoping that did enough to destroy the creatures.

Because it would surely destroy the country.

"How close is Cafferty?" she asked.

"Madam President," General Emmer replied, "the SB-1 Defiant helicopter is approaching Albert Van Ness' prison rig as we speak."

"Thank God."

THE TURBULENT AIR ROCKED THE CHOPPER'S BODY. RAIN hammered against its windows. Below, the Atlantic Ocean roared. Flashes of gray appeared on top of the angry swells as waves formed and crashed in the howling wind. Bile rose in Cafferty's throat again. A string of saliva swayed from his bottom lip. Thankfully, this endless, vomit-inducing flight was nearly over. They were heading for a dim set of lights in the distant darkness, marking the prison rig's location.

Not that the thought of landing on a rig in the middle of a hurricane—or whom he was supposed to meet on that rig—brought him any comfort.

"We'll be there in two minutes," one of the pilots said through Cafferty's headphones. "Hold on tight."

The switch from the military plane to the chopper at Cherry Point Marine Corps Air Station had been so very fast, Cafferty and his team had barely gotten any sleep. He rubbed his temples to try to force clarity into his mind.

He grabbed a bright red waterproof jacket from storage and quickly put it on. Van Ness would enjoy him walking in looking like a drowned rat. That wasn't happening.

The chopper hovered over a bright yellow *H* on the listing platform for a brief, rocky moment before unsteadily lowering. When the wheels touched the ground, Cafferty whispered, "Thank God."

Diego and Sarah nodded at him, and Ellen squeezed his hand. He nodded back. This was both an affirmation that they'd all made it and a temporary farewell to Tom—this was a meeting only he was invited to.

He flipped up the jacket's hood.

One of the crew opened the side door and shouted above the engines, "Good luck, sir. See you shortly."

Cafferty gave a thumbs-up.

He jumped out into the biting wind. Rain lashed his waterproof jacket, followed by a drenching, foamy sea spray. An entrance opened from the main building, sending a shaft of light across the platform. He jogged across to it, careful not to slide on the slippery metal grates.

A marine officer stood in the doorway and encouraged him inside. "Welcome to V.N. One, Mr. Cafferty."

The officer shut the door and a welcoming warmth returned.

Cafferty took off the jacket and shook the raindrops onto the entrance grid. He turned and peered down a long, thin corridor, several solid doors lining either side. All the steel walls had been painted gunmetal gray. It was as if they'd figured out a color that was a visual mute button. The other thing he noticed was no sound, only the wind whistling outside and the roiling sea.

"Van Ness' cell is at the end, sir," the officer said. "Access code is 5760."

"Copy," Cafferty replied.

He walked slowly down the corridor, leaving the officer behind, moments away from seeing the man who had brought the world to the brink a year ago. Anger welled up inside him once again. If he had the opportunity, he'd punch the maniac in the face again to remember how good it felt.

Cafferty continued past a room full of bunks, a kitchen, a communications room, and other closed doors until he reached the final one. A white plastic sign on the door read ALBERT VAN NESS. He peered through the small, square Perspex window.

And there he sat. The butcher of Rapid City, Lincoln, and countless other places. The man who had ordered the destruction of the Z Train and killed hundreds of New Yorkers in the process. The man whose lack of action saw the creatures creating new ruins in the gleaming cities of America and beyond.

Cafferty clenched his teeth. Every instinct told him to punch in the code and finish what he should have done in Paris.

I should've left him to the creatures.

But he reminded himself that that wasn't why he'd come. The world was falling fast. He had to rapidly ascertain if any useful intelligence actually existed.

And then I can kill him.

Van Ness sat upright with his back to the door, facing an antique record player. An untouched food tray sat on a table to the right of his wheelchair, a neatly made bed on the left. Van Ness' hair was perfectly combed, and from this angle he appeared clean-shaven. Nothing like the last photo Cafferty had seen, where the old man sat slumped in his wheelchair with an unkempt beard that was caked in vomit.

Cafferty took a deep breath.

Here goes nothing.

He entered the code on the pad.

Multiple locks snapped open.

The door slowly swept outward with a pneumatic hiss.

Van Ness didn't turn to see who had entered. Instead, he waved his remaining hand around as if he were a conductor to the strains of Johannes Brahms.

Cafferty glanced around the walls for security cameras. None was visible, but then again, they were in the middle of the Atlantic Ocean. There was no means of escape, so who cared what a deranged old man could do?

"Hello, Thomas," Van Ness said without turning around.

Hearing his German accent again, the familiar sound of his voice, made the hairs on Cafferty's arms stand at attention.

"They allowed me to watch your speech at the United Nations," Van Ness said in a cool, confident tone. He twisted a controller on his wheelchair. It spun around until he faced Cafferty. He stared directly into his eyes. "How'd all your bold plans work out, Mr. Mayor?"

"How's the hand, Albert?" Cafferty shot back.

Van Ness grinned, glancing down at the stump at his wrist where his number two, Edwards, had betrayed him and severed the appendage.

"I do miss our repartee, Thomas. But I have things I need to do, and no amount of wit is going to make up for lost time. Now, shall we commence with our business?"

"Tell me, Albert, what business do we have together?" Cafferty asked.

"Why, the business of saving humanity. If it's not too late already. If you haven't already ruined my plan. By now, I assume the creatures are flowing out of the cities, killing millions, killing those I would have saved without your interference."

"It never should have gotten to that point in the first place. You could have destroyed them another way. Or you could have told us about this timeline, that a mass attack was imminent. But no, Albert. You needed to play God. Your greed led you here, led humanity here. Not me. To put it more bluntly, you're nothing but a genocidal asshole," Cafferty snapped back.

"Now, now—don't test me with your language, Mr. Cafferty," Van Ness coldly replied. "It is *you* who has failed humanity. This happened on *your* watch, Mr. Mayor. *You* are unsuited to the task, which is why *you* came here today."

"Go to hell. I'm leaving." Cafferty turned and opened the door to exit the cell.

"Do you want to know how to stop the creatures?" Van Ness called out.

Cafferty paused, teeth gritted.

"Because, my dear fellow," Van Ness continued, "*I know how.* It seems destiny has brought us back together again, Thomas."

Everything inside Cafferty screamed at him to just leave and let the old man rot in this cell for the rest of his days. But images of Las Vegas flashed through his mind. San Francisco. Washington. Chicago. And so many more cities, falling by the hour.

Cafferty stopped and turned back to face Van Ness with an icy look in his eyes. "Tell me what you know," he said coldly.

"Better than that, I'll show you. Now, we'll need a long-range military plane—"

Cafferty let out a bellowing laugh. "You think you're ever getting off this rig? You're going to die in this place, Van Ness. You can either do that knowing you helped your fellow man or just sit here and rot for the last of your days."

"True, I might die here," Van Ness replied. "But it will be quite some time before that happens—unlike you. No, I'll be safe and sound in this cell long after you and your friends have been exterminated. Or you can ask for my help." He paused for a second. "No, not ask. *Beg.*"

It took all of his strength not to jump forward and strangle Van Ness. But the truth in his words struck Cafferty. Humanity was being wiped off the face of the earth, and there was nothing Cafferty could do to stop it.

"How is Ellen, by the way?" Van Ness asked. "And your son?"

"Fuck you, Van Ness," Cafferty replied, clenching his fists.

A smile crept across Van Ness' face. Cafferty knew that could mean anything. A nervous reaction. Amusement at the outburst. Confidence in what he had to say next. It didn't matter.

"That temper will be the end of you, Thomas," Van Ness said. "Either that or the creatures. One way or another, you're dead without my help. As is your beloved wife. And your friends. And your son."

Van Ness lifted the needle off the record and placed it in its holder. Silence filled the room as the two men stared at each other with equal hatred in their eyes.

"Now, shall I continue?" Van Ness asked. Cafferty stayed silent. "Good. One year ago, I watched you walk through my cryo-chambers in Paris. The place where I've been crossbreeding our species. I'm sure you observed the empty chamber at the end of the row. Did you ever wonder what became of that *final* experiment? The final hybrid?"

"My wife sliced it in half in your command center."

"Oh no." Van Ness laughed. "No, no, no. That monstrosity was not my masterpiece. That was more *creature* than human."

"What are you saying?" Cafferty asked, confused.

"You see, Thomas, I've perfected the design. And I'm more than happy to share what I've created in order to save humanity. But . . ."

Van Ness turned toward the record player, took the disc off the turntable and delicately put it back in its sleeve.

". . . there is one simple condition, you see . . ."

"Let me guess, you want half the U.S.'s gross domestic product," Cafferty quipped.

"Haha, no, no, Thomas," Van Ness replied. "We're far past that. No. What I want is much more personal than that. I want a gentleman's agreement, if you will, solely between you and me, for only you and I to know . . ."

Cafferty shifted his weight, suddenly uncomfortable. "And that is . . . ?"

Van Ness turned his wheelchair to face Cafferty again. "At the end of all this, *if* we win the day, only one of us—either you or I—will be alive to claim the victory. Winner takes all, so to speak. To the victor goes the spoils. What was it I told your wife last year? One must live, and one must die."

Cafferty could not believe what he was hearing, but Van Ness' expression and tone told him he was serious. If they defeated the creatures once and for all, one of them would live, one of them would have to die—presumably at the hands of the other. He was playing a game of Russian roulette with a madman. One who almost certainly knew where the bullet would be in advance.

"So, my friend. Are you willing to play my one final game?" Van Ness asked.

Cafferty thought of Ellen, of David. Of Diego, of Sarah. He was literally gambling with his life. What would keep Van Ness from trying to kill him at any moment? How could he possibly trust him to see this through?

Then Cafferty thought of his fallen friend David North, standing there in the subway tunnel, fighting the creatures to his very last breath, willing to sacrifice his life to save the remaining passengers on the Z Train. To save him.

And finally, Cafferty thought of Albert Van Ness, sitting there smugly while the world burned.

Him or me. Defeat the creatures, then kill Van Ness. Or die trying . . .

"So, Thomas," Van Ness said, "I'll ask one more time. Are you willing to play my one final game, putting our competence and honor on the line?"

"I am," Cafferty replied confidently, although the pit of his stomach dropped. "At the end of this, one of us lives, the other dies. Let's see what fate has in store."

Did I just sign my death warrant?

"There's the spirit, Thomas," Van Ness replied. "What fun! Now, as I said, you and I will need a long-range plane to take us immediately to Antarctica."

"Antarctica?" Cafferty asked.

"And one more thing. Have your president send every carrier strike group to the West Coast of America and all other world leaders send their cargo planes and ships to the coordinates I'm about to give you. They need to leave immediately."

"Which planes? Which ships?"

Van Ness leaned forward and stared at Cafferty. *"All of them."*

CHAPTER TEN

Thin dawn light streamed through the San Francisco apartment's blinds. Joey snuggled in Karen's lap, fast asleep on the wrecked bedroom floor. She pulled the blanket back over his body to protect him from the cool early-morning air.

There was nothing she could do about the faint odor of decomposing bodies. That'd only grow stronger as the day wore on.

She hadn't slept a wink. Images of Danny's death had repeatedly spun through her mind. The gratuitous, barbaric nature. He hadn't stood a chance, just like the thousands of corpses littering the city.

Also, she'd been afraid the creatures would come back. That their respite had been a fever dream, and it was only a matter of time.

Because by now, the sinking realization hit her that no immediate fight against the creatures was coming, no cavalry descending to save the day. She had prayed for the sound of tanks grinding on concrete. Weapons firing. Anything to give her a sign that this current terrifying world wasn't the future.

Nothing came.

Through all the thinking, though, it was still a struggle to wrap her head around the events.

Creatures from below rising to the surface?

How many cities had fallen?

Karen remembered the former mayor of New York City's speech to the United Nations a year ago. People had taken notice and it was all the newspapers and TV programs could talk about for a few months, but the news moved on, people moved on, and it had taken on the status of bogeyman like so many other things in politics: guns, opioids, global warming. They were all real, but they didn't affect *her* reality.

Now it had become everyone's reality.

It was clear San Francisco had fallen. Alarms had gradually stopped during the night. Buildings with backup power had fought on against the darkness, only to systematically go out one by one from east to west. No doubt at the hands—or claws—of the monstrosities that had blitzed the city before the sun had set.

The eerie silence outside chilled her more than the temperature. No car engines. No horn blasts from boats. No rumbling trams. Only the sound of seagulls in the bay. It'd taken Karen a while to shed the paranoia that the shrill cries of the birds were the creatures and even longer to eventually calm Joey, clean him up as best she could (since the water stopped working soon after she'd taken a shower), and finally get him to sleep.

Regardless of their gloomy prospects, she wouldn't give up. She'd fought for everything in her life, everything in her son's life. Danny had fought for them both to his dying breath.

Karen strained to hear any signs of the creatures' return. But mostly she just heard her own thoughts.

Danny.

Mom and Dad.

Great-Aunt Lillian.

Maybe everyone I know . . .

She choked back the tears. Forced her trembling lips together to avoid letting her emotions become audible. For the sake of her son and for the sake of their safety.

Joey's eyes flickered open. He stifled a yawn and then nearly jumped out of her arms. "Are they back?!"

"Easy, easy, baby," she whispered. "We're safe. We're waiting here till help arrives."

Thankfully, Joey settled down quickly, believing his mother's lie.

They had devoured the orange juice and cold cuts in the lifeless refrigerator while they had the chance. The owners had cans of food in the kitchenette, so they had supplies to last a few days.

Her phone had provided light when they'd needed it. The battery had dropped to a meager 9 percent on low power mode. Although with all cellular communications down, the device had no use beyond illuminating their immediate surroundings.

Sooner or later they'd have to move to avoid the stench of the rotting corpses. Or move the corpses. But even then, it would only be a brief respite before the potential diseases that so many dead bodies clogging the city air would create.

But when?
And where?
And how?

A distant shriek rose above the cries of the sea-gulls, breaking the silence. Long. Menacing. The first she'd heard for several hours.

"I'm scared," Joey said.

Karen wrapped her arm around him. Both sat in silence.

Then a cacophony of distant shrieks echoed through the streets, like a frightening ancient battle cry. At best, she guessed, it was the sound of the creatures announcing their victory. At worst, a portent for a fresh attack on the remnants of the city's decimated population.

As the chilling noise grew louder and seemingly closer, her chest tightened, along with a sense of doom. A sharp pain pulsed below her sternum, making it feel like her heart was about to explode. Sweat beaded her brow. She leaned forward and gasped.

Joey's eyes widened. "What's wrong?"

"Nothing," she choked out. "It's okay, sweetie."

Karen took extended, steady breaths. She had always kept herself fit. A heart attack? No, it wasn't that. She guessed the symptoms were caused by anxiety. She'd treated a few patients who'd displayed a similar set of problems. A panic attack. Or maybe even PTSD.

Pull yourself together, she told herself.

But it was easier said than done. Because with every passing minute, slowly but surely, the creatures closed in.

She had to know if they were coming down Lombard Street again and, if so, what they were doing. The only way of finding out was going back to the rooftop and not making the same mistake as last time.

Karen rose to her feet. Her thighs ached from the inactivity, sitting in the same position for hours with Joey on her lap. She stretched her back. Mentally prepared herself to move, maybe into more danger, but they had to take the risk.

"We're going back upstairs," she said quietly. "Be a good boy and follow my instructions. Okay?"

Joey nodded.

The boy was usually unruly, difficult to control at the best of times. But he took her hand, obeying without question, and they both crept toward the bedroom door. She reckoned his young mind had at least pieced together that they were in severe danger and that following her lead was the best and only way out.

Karen circled the upturned couch. Thankfully, it had landed on the apartment owner's body, shielding the corpse from Joey's view. She picked her way past the shards of glass from the smashed coffee table and neared the apartment entrance.

The collective creature noise sounded a few blocks away. It was impossible to tell from here.

Or closer . . .

They could be silently stalking any survivor.

Already on Lombard Street?

That thought propelled her out the door and up the stairs, which remained lit with emergency battery lights on the exit signs.

Neither she nor Joey glanced down the staircase at her fallen husband and his father. Karen shuddered as she stepped through the pool of his drying blood. She swallowed hard and continued up the stairs. Joey gripped her hand tightly. He had his eyes squeezed shut, and he stumbled every few steps.

Once outside on the roof, the hairs on her arms prickled. Not from the temperature. The heat from the rising sun had brought warmth and cast long shadows across the bay. No, the shrieks—even closer now than before—caused this reaction.

They sound right on top of us.

Karen dropped to all fours on the asphalt. Joey did the same.

She crawled to the edge of the roof silently.

A few hundred yards down Lombard Street, five small creatures stood in the middle of the road on the roof of a white delivery truck, staring at the tall buildings to their immediate left and right. Bone-chilling howls emanated from the shattered windows of the lower floors and reverberated through the buildings. Windows exploded outward on the higher floors, the bursts of fragmented glass slowly rising until they reached the top.

"What's happening, Mommy?" Joey asked. "Are they coming here?"

"I hope not . . ." Karen trailed off, not sure what to say next. Because she had no idea what was happening, either.

For a split second, nothing seemed to move.

Until hundreds of creatures rushed out of the entrances of both buildings. They surrounded the small group on the truck, swelling the street with their ranks. Tails thrashing. Beady eyes darting everywhere. Snarling. Moments later, they moved up to the next buildings in sequence on the street and siphoned through the smashed doorways.

Once again, the frightening process continued.

Corpses smashed through windows and their dead weights crunched against the sidewalks. The first floor. Second. Third. Fourth.

They are going building to building, killing anyone who's left . . .

Joey attempted to raise his head over the edge of the roof. Karen gently forced it back down. He didn't need to see this. She could barely look without wanting to vomit. Her knees trembled. She balled her hands into fists to avoid her son seeing her shake like an old washing machine on a fast spin cycle.

It only took a few minutes for the vast throng of creatures to return back outside. Then they moved on to the next buildings. Only two buildings away from Karen and Joey's refuge.

A piercing scream rang out.

A man.

Someone still alive.

The scream stopped as abruptly as it started.

They're clearing the area.

Annihilating us.

Karen crawled to the left edge of the roof, toward where the creatures were continuing their work. The building below, which she guessed was the next target on her side of the street, looked like offices. Its roof lay a story below the one she was on, with a six-foot gap between the buildings. The rooftop held a glass structure containing a trendy break room. Sunshine glinted off its surface. Coffee and vending machines lined the wall. Bright red chairs surrounded circular tables. A Ping-Pong table. A billiards table. It opened out directly below Karen to a patio filled with garden furniture.

Back on the street, creatures flooded from their now-searched buildings, teeming between the cars. The five smaller creatures that seemed to be in charge bounded up the street to a battered SUV and hunched on the hood and roof. One of them bellowed. A heartbeat later, creatures rushed into a building on the opposite side of the street and the office building right next door.

Karen pushed back her internal terror and focused. Within two minutes, the vicious army would be done with its current buildings and then storm through these apartments. She guessed this time, there would be no hiding during an uncompromising search.

She looked at the office break room on the roof once more, seeing the creatures swarm through.

Only one option came to mind.

Jump.

After the creatures had cleared the office building next door and headed back out, she and Joey had to jump across the six-foot gap and hide in a place that had already been purged.

Joey won't make the jump.

Unless I hold him in my arms.

Then we both might not make it.

But there was no other choice.

It was a fifty-fifty shot at life—maybe better, maybe worse. They make the other roof and possibly live, or they plunge to their deaths trying. Either way, they had to try.

She sucked in a deep breath. Tried to imagine succeeding at the jump in her mind, time and time again. Tried to believe she and Joey could make the leap. It was a silly technique she'd heard during a team-building event, when a life coach came along as a guest speaker and attempted to fill their heads with hocus-pocus. It had failed to elicit optimism in her back then, and it failed to bring her comfort now. It didn't matter, though, and she shook the silly exercise from her head. The more she thought of the leap, the more she realized it was a do-or-die moment she couldn't avoid.

A window shattered below her.

She craned her head over the lip of the roof.

A lone creature stood inside the break room of the office building. It had hurled a dead woman into the patio area. She lay facedown, surrounded by broken fragments of glass. Pale legs and arms with purple blotches. Blood pooling below her skin as rigor mortis set in.

Seconds later, the creature tore out of the room.

Karen glanced toward Lombard. Hundreds of the nightmarish creatures flocked into the street once again. Then they systematically rushed into the apartment building she and Joey were in.

A collective earsplitting shriek filled the stairwell.

Windows below her smashed out, on higher and higher floors.

There's no time left. We have to jump now.

Karen rose and picked Joey up in her arms. She moved to the edge of the roof, to the gap between the buildings. She kept low to avoid being spotted from the street.

"What are we doing, Mommy?" Joey asked.

"We have to jump across."

"We won't make it!" Joey said in a panicked voice.

"We'll make it, baby," she lied, but she had no other choice.

The carnage below her feet reached within two floors below. The sounds of the creatures' rapid approach came loud from the external roof door: Heavy feet pounding the steps of the stairwell. Growling. The building shook below her.

Karen glanced down, first to the ground below. She hoped that wasn't their next destination. Then she identified her landing spot on the neighboring roof: a clear area of paving next to the walled edge of the building.

Within seconds, the creatures would burst onto the roof. She couldn't delay and risk them seeing her. It was jump now or die regardless.

Karen crouched down and summoned all of her strength.

She thrust forward and leaped.

Joey tried to scream, but she slapped her hand down over his mouth in the nick of time.

Their bodies flew through the air off the edge of the roof.

Halfway across the gap, their forward momentum slowed and gravity took over. They began to fall.

Karen flung out an arm to catch the edge of the roof.

One arm wouldn't give her enough strength to hold them both.

Or herself for that matter.

But her sneakers hit the patio of the office building. She landed and collapsed to her side, turning Joey to avoid him slamming against the ground. Pain shot through her right ankle.

Karen lay on her back, momentarily dazed from the impact and the experience.

Then her training kicked in, reacting to an immediate emergency situation when many others froze. She grabbed Joey and rolled them flush against the walled edge of the building, biting her tongue as agony tore up her leg from her ankle, praying their bodies were not visible from the other roof. She clutched her hand over her son's mouth again and held her breath.

Above her, from the apartment building roof, a metallic crack signaled the door slamming open from the stairwell.

Karen prayed the creatures didn't notice her.

She prayed Joey and she had remained unseen.

A massive creature rushed to all edges of the roof, scanning every inch for any signs of life. Karen could hear its heavy breathing only a few feet above their heads, a few feet away. If it wished, she knew the creature could easily make the same jump.

Karen's whole body shook from fear and adrenaline. She squeezed her eyes shut and waited for the sound of the creature crashing onto their roof to finish the job.

Silence.

Nothing.

Minutes ticked past. The creatures had left the apartment building, and the sound of shattering windows had moved farther up the street.

They were safe. She and Joey had survived for now.

But the question remained: How would they get out of this living nightmare? And even if they did, was anybody else around to join their quest for survival?

CHAPTER ELEVEN

After two refuels, the massive C-130 Hercules airplane powered toward Albert Van Ness' coordinates in Antarctica, past the Weddell Sea. Cafferty sat on a red bench inside the back of its bright green rectangular interior. He stared across to the opposite bench where Ellen, Diego, and Sarah were catching up on some well-deserved sleep. They all realized that if Van Ness truly had some kind of weapon to fight the creatures, this might be their last chance to rest in the fight against extinction.

An armed soldier sat between Cafferty and Van Ness, mostly focusing on the old man. His wheelchair had been secured next to the bench, and Van Ness sat with his eyes closed, though he was clearly awake.

Cafferty peered out the window. The glistening deep blue ocean stretched for miles from east to west. Directly ahead, icy peaks jutted into the sky-line. As Cafferty stared at the foreign land ahead, the implication of his deal with the devil at last started to sink in.

He had probably sacrificed his life for humanity's survival. That also meant Ellen becoming a widow and David becoming fatherless. On one hand, he would gladly give his life to keep those two alive. On the other hand, though, this wasn't that. This was playing a demented game at the behest of a narcissistic sociopath.

This wasn't sacrifice. This was suicide.

He looked back at the meditating Van Ness, studying the man.

As if he could sense Cafferty's stare, Van Ness opened his eyes and returned the look. And then the old man grinned.

This is insane.

The copilot exited the cockpit door and made his way over to the group. "We're passing Mount Tyree."

"Lovely," Van Ness replied. "We're so very close now, aren't we?"

"Close to what, Albert?" Cafferty asked. "What's out there?"

"Sir, there's nothing out there," the copilot replied. "Palmer Land is a barren ice sheet. I've seen it with my own eyes. There's no secret base there."

Anger welled up inside Cafferty.

If this is a wild-goose chase . . .

"Before you lose that famed temper, Thomas," Van Ness replied, "I never said the base was on top of the ice, did I?"

Could Van Ness have built something below *the ice in the most remote part of the world?*

Cafferty knew anything was possible, after seeing the Foundation's secret underground lair built inside a creatures' nest underneath Paris. He hated to admit it, but Van Ness was capable of anything.

"Simply land at those coordinates, Lieutenant," Van Ness said. "I will take care of the rest." With that, he closed his eyes and continued to meditate.

Cafferty followed the copilot past the twenty soldiers on the plane up to the cockpit. The plane crossed over a steep mountain range and descended toward a barren icy plateau.

"Can this bird land on ice?" Cafferty asked.

"Yep, no problem," the copilot replied. "But . . . you sure we want to? Radar shows nothing down there, above *or* below the ice."

Cafferty knew Van Ness was not to be trusted, except when it came to one thing: bragging about his accomplishments.

"Land the plane at the coordinates, Captain," Cafferty said.

"You're willing to bet your life on this?"

Though the question was hypothetical, it gave Cafferty a sinking feeling in the pit of his stomach. He'd already bet his life in the last twenty-four hours, and it only served as an unwanted fresh reminder—not that he required reminding of anything.

"Land the plane, Captain."

Cafferty returned to his seat, squeezing Ellen's hand before sitting and buckling in.

The massive airplane descended quickly and, within moments, touched down onto the frozen wasteland. The pilots reversed the engines and the plane slowly drifted to a stop.

The copilot stood from the cockpit and walked back to Cafferty's team. "Um," he said. "Now what?"

"Van Ness?" Cafferty asked.

"When I'm done meditating, please . . ." Van Ness replied, eyes still closed, oblivious to the question.

His silence enraged Cafferty.

"*Van Ness!*" Cafferty shouted, pounding his fist into the bench. "*Now what?*"

Slowly, Albert Van Ness opened his eyes and fixed his gaze on the former mayor. "Now what, indeed . . ." he replied.

Suddenly, the cracking of ice shook the plane, and Cafferty could feel it dropping downward. The copilot raced to the cockpit. The ice sheet they were resting on was descending into Antarctica itself. The plane lowered downward until the sky above disappeared entirely.

Cafferty bolted to the front to watch the spectacle unfolding. They were literally disappearing into the ice into an unknown abyss below. His eyes widened in disbelief.

What the hell?

"What's going on?" Cafferty shouted back into the plane.

Van Ness smiled. "We're here."

CHAPTER TWELVE

Munoz and Bowcut scrambled to the windows and stared openmouthed at the scene before them. The plane continued to descend on a perfectly square block of ice, plunging at least a hundred feet below Antarctica's surface. But it wasn't a free fall—it was definitely a controlled descent.

And as they lowered, a distant mechanical whine came from beneath the C-130's body. The plane's lights illuminated a thick layer of cobalt-blue ice—and something more. Huge steel girders supported the walls, with electrical units attached at regular intervals.

This is some feat of engineering, Munoz thought. *The strength and technology to hold back the powerful shifting ice.*

This is more awesome than if the Death Star was on Hoth . . .

As the plane descended farther, the ice opened up into a massive hangar, carved into the bedrock. Its metallic concertina doors were open, revealing another internal space roughly the size of four football fields. Giant, dazzling globes of light, like the ones that held the creatures at bay in the Paris caverns, blazed down from the steel vaulted ceiling.

Van Ness built a cathedral in the ice . . .

A central path led deeper into the complex. Hundreds of tall steel racks lined the route, each packed with enough supplies for years of underground survival.

"How . . . is this possible?" Munoz uttered, staring out the side windows of the plane.

"I'm afraid I cannot take all the credit," Van Ness replied. "The Foundation for Human Advancement *inherited* what you see here. Naturally, I expanded it greatly."

"Inherited?" Sarah asked.

"Learn your history, my dear," Van Ness replied cockily. "The Third Reich built the initial fortress in the forties. Surely your government knew and tried to find it. I believe they called it Operation Highjump. The United States futilely scoured the continent for this base in 1946, even launched missiles to try to destroy it. Naturally, they never found it. But surely your president told you this already?"

The silence on the plane answered the question.

"Clearly not," Van Ness said. "I wonder what else you haven't been told."

Munoz had heard of Operation Highjump. The official line was it was a training mission: the U.S. government testing personnel and equipment in frigid conditions, to determine the feasibility of establishing and maintaining Antarctic military bases. He had always suspected it had other motives, but none had ever been credibly established.

"And let's not forget," Van Ness continued, "your country's Operation Deep Freeze in the fifties that also failed to find this base. Needless to say, I improved on the design since then and, of course, dramatically expanded and modernized the facility."

Once again, Munoz knew the code name for the American mission to the region, but to his knowledge, no government had built a military compound in Antarctica.

Until he had seen this . . .

"If you'd like, I can send your team a few books to read up on all this," Van Ness added. His arrogance grated the team.

"What now, Van Ness?" Cafferty asked, coming back from the cockpit.

A slight jolt shook the plane, and the platform came to a stop, finally level with the icy fortress. Munoz estimated they had descended at least three hundred feet.

No wonder why no one detected this former Nazi base . . .

"May I suggest we open the cargo bay doors and go for a stroll?" Van Ness replied.

The U.S. soldiers on the plane suited up and grabbed their AR15 rifles and laser pistols.

"Oh, you won't need weapons," Van Ness said. "Your soldiers would be far outmatched anyway. And besides, we are on the same team, are we not? Why would I want any of you dead? Isn't that right, Thomas?"

Munoz caught Van Ness shooting an odd look at Cafferty.

What the hell is going on?

Munoz suspected something was said between the two men back on the prison rig. But that would have to wait. He, like everyone else, remained acutely aware that the outside world was falling fast. What he had seen so far in Antarctica provided a glimmer of hope that the Foundation had something substantial here. Whether it was enough to beat back the creatures was yet to be seen.

The last time he felt this uneasy was when they were climbing down a rope into a nest beneath London, not realizing it was all a trap.

Van Ness pointed a bony finger toward the windshield. "My head of combat strategy, Franco Roux, will join us on a tour of the facility."

A stocky figure strode toward the hangar entrance. He was dressed in dark combat fatigues with lasers holstered on the sides of his chest. He rested his hands on his hips, grim faced, and glared toward the cockpit. From the looks of his blond hair, blue eyes, and fair complexion, Munoz gathered Roux was Dutch or the like.

"Looks like a pleasant dude," Munoz said sarcastically.

"Franco Roux is my blueprint," Van Ness replied. "What he lacks in charm he makes up for in brute force and brilliant combat planning and execution."

"Blueprint for what?" Diego asked.

"Shall we?" Van Ness said, ignoring the question. "Every minute wasted amounts to an untold loss of life."

Munoz could not argue with that.

Cafferty instructed the pilots to open the rear cargo doors. Then he headed toward the plane's rear, closely followed by Van Ness, Munoz, Ellen, and Sarah.

Bowcut kept her rifle slung by her side with her hand on the grip. Munoz had seen her adopt this stance before. In the blink of an eye she'd be firing, if required.

"What's the situation?" she asked.

"We're getting a grand tour," Diego whispered.

"Any clue what he's got here?"

"Well, it's either a really big ice-skating rink or another evil lair."

"You can say that again." Sarah smiled.

The cargo doors fully opened, creating a ramp to the icy surface. Freezing air rushed through the cabin, as well as a steady collective hum coming from electrical units mounted on the frozen walls.

Cafferty trudged down the ramp.

Van Ness descended by his side to the bottom, and the wheels of his chair crunched over the ice as he spun it to face the hangar entrance.

By the time Munoz and Bowcut had joined them on the ground, Franco Roux, looking even meaner up close, stood in front of them. He had scars on his forehead and right cheek. His muscles bulged against his clothing. And his piercing light blue eyes darted from person to person as his breath fogged in the frigid air.

"Mr. Roux," Van Ness said, now sounding as if he was completely in command. "It is excellent to see you again."

Roux replied with a slight nod of his head.

"Lead the way, if you will," Van Ness continued. "Let's show our guests most everything."

Roux gestured the team forward, spun on his heel, and headed toward the base.

"Some tour guide," Munoz whispered to Bowcut. "We didn't even get headphones."

He winked at Sarah, and she winked back at the joke. But her eyes were constantly moving, taking in everything. Munoz bit his lip as more jokes got ready to spill forth—a defense mechanism for when he was nervous. He needed to focus, to see if he could learn anything here that might help.

The team followed the burly Dutchman, stony-faced and focused.

Munoz wrapped his arms around himself, attempting to stem his shivers as he followed Roux toward the base's entrance, toward a mystery solution that could stop humankind's genocide.

BOWCUT KEPT ROUX FIRMLY IN HER SIGHT. SHE INSTANTLY recognized the look in the Dutchman's eyes. He was a stone-cold killer. Somebody who acted without remorse and saved questions for later. She'd met people like him before: mercenaries and murderers she'd busted while with NYPD SWAT. These types of people lived outside the confines of civilized society.

Which made sense considering how far away from civilization they were . . . and how close they were to having no society at all.

The group headed through the hangar doors.

Roux stopped by the first set of shelves. He extended a palm toward Cafferty, Munoz, and Bowcut, gesturing for them to halt. Roux swept his hand across the vast indoor space. "This warehouse contains supplies for the base. Constant expansion has led to daily runs by the Foundation's underground trains to our docks at Pine Island Bay—"

"Wait," Bowcut interrupted. "You've built underground trains here?"

"How else would you suggest we transport supplies from disguised survey ships?" Van Ness replied.

Bowcut peered at the hundreds of shelves lining the massive walls. They held thousands of sacks labeled as corn, barley, various vegetables. Electronic devices. Lasers. Water purification systems. Pretty much everything she could think of that could feed and equip thousands of people for a very long time.

"I don't get it," Bowcut whispered to Munoz and Cafferty. "How has all this gone undetected?"

"He built a fortress under Paris and no one noticed," Diego said. "When's the last time you looked at Antarctica on Google Maps?"

"But you personally scoured the Foundation computers," Cafferty said. "Zero mention of this base."

Van Ness spun his wheelchair to face Cafferty, having overheard his comment. "Makes you wonder what else you do not know, doesn't it, Thomas?" Van Ness replied smugly. "Kindly let me know when you no longer feel up to the task."

Munoz could see the silent anger on Cafferty's face as he bit his lip. He could not imagine the intensity of what the mayor was feeling at this moment.

"This way," Roux said matter-of-factly. The big Dutchman moved along the walkway with purpose. His boots pounded the smooth stone floor as he briskly made his way through the area.

The group passed Foundation guards who eyed them with suspicion while they advanced. The strangeness of the moment and the lack of backup kept Bowcut on a high state of alert. She had a round in the rifle's chamber and the safety off. She didn't expect a battle, but if one came, the only option was going down shooting.

But it can't end like this. We've come too far. The Foundation still needs us. Needs our ships and planes. Van Ness didn't bring us out here to die.

She kept telling herself that, her head on a swivel.

They followed Roux to the end and inside a grated industrial elevator. He slammed the metal gate shut and slapped his palm against a red button.

The elevator beeped, then slowly rose above the rows of shelving, giving Bowcut a breathtaking overhead view of the massive scale of the warehouse. It was beyond belief that the Foundation could build something so impressive without being noticed. But it had. Just like in Paris.

If only it had put that engineering ingenuity to stopping the creatures all those years ago.

The elevator bumped to a stop in front of a brightly lit, long white corridor.

Roux opened the gate. "These are our laboratory facilities."

The first room was full of glass-and-steel cryochambers, now empty, as if the experiments inside had escaped. Bowcut cast her mind back to the freak-show experimentation room in the Paris underground lair. Human and animal experiments. Cryo-chambers full of mutated monstrosities, stomach churning to the core.

"What happens in these labs?" she asked.

"I design the future," a man said from the other side of the lab. The unknown voice took the group by surprise.

From behind one of the glass chambers, a man in a white lab coat walked out and promptly tripped over a waste bin. The metal container ricocheted off the wall loudly, and after a few seconds, the clanging stopped. He looked disheveled, shirt half untucked, and wiped sugar off his face, presumably from a jelly doughnut.

"Sorry," the man said, and approached the group. "Um, I was saying I design the future."

Van Ness looked visibly disgusted by the man. "This is Dr. Cornelius Liander, head of this Antarctic laboratory."

"Oh, hey, Mr. Van Ness," the doctor replied, quickly tucking in his shirt. "Um. How are you?"

"Show us what you've been working on please, Cornelius."

"Sure thing, boss."

Bowcut could tell by Munoz's face that he liked this guy.

Liander cleared his throat. "Well, as you know, the creatures are stronger than us, probably smarter than us. So I was like, what if they weren't, you know?"

Bowcut spied Van Ness, who looked like he was moments away from slapping the good doctor across the face.

"So, you know, I combined different, um, combinations of DNA to try to level the playing field, as they say in some sports."

"What sports exactly?" Munoz asked.

"I don't know, I was never into sports."

Undoubtedly a solitaire guy, Bowcut thought.

"It took some time, but you know, we finally got it right," Liander continued. "Let's see the creatures fight *them*!"

"Fight who?" Cafferty asked.

"Wanna show them, Mr. Van Ness?" Cornelius asked proudly.

Van Ness nodded, visibly annoyed.

The doctor led the group to a set of black double doors at the end of the lab. When he reached within a couple of paces, the doors automatically parted to reveal a dimly lit, wide metal bridge, thirty feet in length, with pitch black all around. At the far end, a console cast a weak glow onto the grating.

The doors closed behind them, shutting out all artificial light from the laboratory. To Bowcut, it seemed like they had entered a void and stood over a massive black abyss with nothing below. She strained to see anything in the darkness. Tried to listen for any noise above a low roar from what sounded like the largest air-conditioning unit in the world.

Is it a nest? Another show of supposed dominance over the creatures, like Van Ness' Paris lair?

Wherever they had entered, the nature of it sent a chill down Bowcut's spine.

Van Ness approached the console. A smile stretched across his wrinkled face as he locked eyes with

Cafferty. He hovered his index finger over a button. "I'd like to introduce you to my army that's going to save the world . . ."

Van Ness pressed the glass pad.

A row of fifty brilliant globes thumped on above the group.

Then another fifty ahead of them.

Rows blazed on in sequence until they stretched forward to a distance of roughly a mile. The enormous underground warehouse suddenly blazed with light in all directions, illuminating every inch.

Cafferty leaned over the railing and sucked in a sharp breath. *"What the holy hell?"*

CHAPTER THIRTEEN

Over an hour had passed on the roof of the San Francisco office building. The merciless mid-morning sun beat down on Karen and Joey, uncaring about their situation. Her son squinted up at her and smiled. The wall they'd ducked behind shaded his arms and legs. He finally seemed calm after their leap for survival. After what he'd experienced, she had no idea how.

Sweat trickled down Karen's back. Her heart still pounded against her chest and her mind raced at a million miles per hour. Added to her scrambled mental state, her stomach fluttered every time a creature's cry echoed through the streets. She hadn't dared to enter the building to grab some snacks.

But that jump . . .

It was almost as unbelievable as the creatures.

Joey and she had come inches from certain death, then hidden from the same fate. Karen's ankles and knees ached from crouching against the wall. She didn't dare raise her head in case of catching a crea-ture's beady eye.

The shrieks had gradually receded as the creatures stormed their way through buildings farther up Lombard Street. The sickening sounds of bodies being hurled through windows and hammering against the road had waned.

She was taking nothing for granted.

It doesn't mean all the creatures have gone. Lone ones might be still searching here, or have tracking skills beyond human comprehension.

The final conclusion struck her as odd. But this was the horrific, unforeseen, and unpredictable world they were living in right now. All the normal rules she knew had vanished. Conventional wisdom had no answer to the onslaught.

Karen slowly twisted around and stared at the break room behind them. At the far end, two bloodied corpses—or maybe three; it was impossible to say, as it resembled a mound of hacked body parts—kept an elevator's doors wedged open. She guessed the poor souls tried to escape when creatures attacked the top floor. A futile move, as descending would only have taken them to the same brutal end. Tinted windows lined the wall on each side of the elevator.

The fire escape door, which almost certainly led to a staircase, was ajar. A quick way down for Joey and her, but a fast way up for the creatures.

She peered across to the neighboring building on the other side. Like the apartment roof she had jumped from, it was also a story higher than the office building. There was no way off this roof if another wave of creatures swept through again. Karen couldn't risk waiting for too long.

The simple, gut-wrenching, yet compelling answer was to move when they had a chance. She realized that meant stepping out of their hiding place, realized it was a huge risk. But it was a risk that could further preserve their lives.

But where do we go from here?

Out of the city center . . .

The countryside.

Finding refuge away from urban areas appeared like a logical option.

Farmland?

No, the creatures might begin hunting animals.

But they seem only intent on killing people.

A cabin or a beach house? Somewhere remote with views of the surrounding area?

But she figured it would only be a matter of time before the creatures spread outward, decimating the rural areas. A total annihilation demanded that course of action. And from what she had witnessed, that seemed to be their intent.

We're being exterminated.

Karen recalled her last view of the bay. Sure, the cruise liner had been attacked in port, though it could've drifted from the wharf after creatures boarded. Perhaps the captain tried to set sail in a desperate attempt to get clear of the falling city. The lone survivor who'd swam from the *Norwegian Pearl* had no trouble making it to shore. Whether he made it out of town was another matter. But he survived . . .

The monsters cannot swim.

A boat!

Once the immediate area was clear of creatures and the city free of their screeches, Karen decided they'd risk moving to the relative safety of the water, or, at least, a safer place than here.

"Mommy," Joey said. "What's that smell?"

"It's nothing, baby."

It wasn't nothing, though. The stench of death in San Francisco had grown stronger by the hour. Karen's paramedic experience told her it would happen any time between twenty-four and thirty-six hours after death. Even faster for corpses rotting in the sun, and thousands of the slaughtered clogged the streets. Despite her familiarity with dead bodies, it was never on this scale, and the smell was starting to get to her, too. And that was without thinking about how it would all become a breeding ground for diseases to cut down any remaining survivors.

A single screech came from a few blocks away.

They're still here.

After another half hour of waiting, San Francisco eventually fell deathly silent. A gentle breeze whipped over the buildings, providing some relief from the sun and the stench of death. It also carried a faint buzzing sound with it, some distance away.

What sounded like a helicopter . . .

Somebody was alive in the area.

Searching for survivors?

She scanned desperately in every direction, but couldn't locate the chopper in the clear cobalt sky.

The buzz gradually faded, along with her hopes of rescue from this nightmare.

Dammit. We can't just wait to die.

"Be a good boy and stay right here," she said. "Stay quiet, too."

"Okay. The monsters won't see me."

"You're my hero, Joey. Dad would be proud."

Joey smiled, trying to be brave, just like when he had his first flu.

Karen took a deep breath and listened intently for a few seconds.

Nothing. Still no heavy footsteps. No guttural breaths. No snarls.

Her body shook with fear as she rose to view the edge of the apartment building.

No monstrosities stood on the adjacent ledge.

Karen immediately spun and set off at a crouching run toward the break room. She raced past the pool table, ignoring the sharp pain in her ankle. Stepped around the billiard balls scattered across the parquet floor, careful not to hit any. Leaped over a butchered victim, ignoring the puddle of congealed blood. Then skidded to a stop by the tinted windows.

Dammit.

Below, on the opposite side of the street, a single creature stood outside the entrance to every building. It appeared like they were on guard, ready to pounce on anyone escaping or waiting for any sounds that gave away the location of a survivor.

For now, she and Joey remained trapped.

A creature in front of a battered garage door glanced upward.

Her heart skipped a beat, though she forced back her paranoia. Unless the creatures had x-ray vision, the glass was impenetrable to the naked eye.

What do I know about them that might help our escape?

The smaller ones appear to give orders.
But what else?

She had to know, so she crept forward again. Thankfully, the tinted window had saved them from another attack.

The creatures were focused, static. Fixed to their apparent jobs, like well-trained soldiers.

Karen glanced back at Joey.

He responded by defiantly sticking up his thumb. She waved him over.

Joey raced to her position, keeping one eye shut, the other focused on her.

"Watch out," she whispered loudly.

Too late.

He slipped on the pool of blood and skidded facefirst through it, coming to a rest a few yards from her. His outstretched palms dripped with glistening crimson.

Joey scrambled to his feet. The front of his pale blue T-shirt and shorts were soaked. He looked down at himself and his mouth opened.

"*Shhh!*" Karen whispered loudly, stopping her son before he said anything. "Come here, baby," she continued quietly. "It's okay."

Joey stumbled toward her, lips quivering.

Karen reached out her arms. "Come and gimme a hug."

He staggered forward a few steps and threw his arms around her. She didn't care about the blood. But as the sickly warmth soaked through her T-shirt as well, it was difficult not to wince. Joey was her immediate priority, despite the overwhelming odds they faced.

"It's okay, Mommy," he said in her ear. "We're fighters."

"Damn right we are, little buddy."

Karen turned her head to view outside. Before she could focus on the street, a shrill blast split the air, deafening, like a foghorn. The floor below her feet rattled. The window shook.

Karen cradled Joey and peered downward.

The creatures outside every building suddenly raced away at lightning-fast speed toward the park at the bottom of the road. Thousands of them. All seemingly attracted to the noise. They created a circle around a grassed area, like they had raced to watch something.

In the center, a huge area of the turf exploded upward. Chunks flew through the air and rained down on the surrounding area.

Joey looked over Karen's shoulder. "What's happening?"

"I don't know."

More dirt flew skyward, until a wide, spherical black hole lay in the middle of the baying mob.

Then the ground rumbled again, even stronger this time.

Something was rising out of the newly formed hole in the ground.

Something clearly of great importance.

Something bigger than any creature Karen had already seen.

CHAPTER FOURTEEN

Van Ness studied the expressions of Diego Munoz, Sarah Bowcut, and the Caffertys. All stared down wide-eyed at what they were witnessing in the massive warehouse. The color drained from their faces. The awe remained fixed.

Van Ness smirked, impressed with what he had built.

Below their feet, more than one hundred thousand identical soldiers stood perfectly lined up in rigid, crisp rows, dressed in identical black-and-gray camouflage clothing. All breathing deeply, slowly. They were most definitely human, but with an ever so slight green tinge to their skin. Rank-and-file warriors, standing indefinitely at attention, ready for the command to battle.

And every soldier looked identical to Van Ness' head of combat operations, Franco Roux.

The planet's—no, my *ultimate creation.*

Van Ness took no pleasure in this moment. These supersoldiers were never meant to be used in this way. They had been for *after*. Had he not been defeated underneath Paris, the creatures would already have been exterminated, and the world would have been his. But as the months ticked by as he sat in his ocean prison rig, Van Ness knew he'd eventually be back here, mobilizing these supersoldiers to save the world.

If there was anything good to come out of the past year, it was the look on Cafferty's face in the prison cell, asking Van Ness for help with his tail between his legs. Even if it meant doing something that should have been finished long ago, if his nukes hadn't been disrupted.

"Allow me to introduce you to my supersoldier program," Van Ness said to the group, breaking the silence. "Thanks to Dr. Liander, they are the perfect combination of human and creature DNA, creating what you see below. The loyalty and intellect of a human, the strength of a creature. And they always follow my orders, unlike some of my human colleagues from the past . . ."

Van Ness looked downward at the stump on his arm, reflecting on the betrayal of his number two, Edwards. He snapped out of the memory.

"So, Mr. Mayor, *this* is how we win this war. *This* is how we take back Earth."

Nobody replied. He'd expected motormouthed Cafferty to have a response, though the majesty before the failed mayor seemed to have shut him up for a change.

It didn't matter. Van Ness' point had been proven when the lights had thundered on. What irked him more than anything else was that it didn't need to come to this. Millions of lives had been lost because of the ragtag team standing in front of his wheel-chair. The fools didn't seem to grasp this simple fact, despite the world collapsing at this very moment.

But the former mayor will eventually grasp the magnitude of his errors.

Mr. Cafferty's time on this planet will be ending so very soon . . .

Van Ness watched the looks of concern spread over the mayor and his team's faces. Only now must they be realizing they were not in charge, that they were never in charge, that Van Ness was now hold-ing every single card—as it always had been.

"Now, now, why such nervous looks?" Van Ness asked, addressing the group. "Without our words, we are just like the creatures—merely animals. Don't you think?"

Van Ness looked down at the thousands of super-soldiers and smiled to himself.

"I gave you my word I will see this all the way to the end," Van Ness continued. "And I will. Perhaps the right question is this: Will you know when the end is upon us, Mr. Cafferty?"

Van Ness eyed Cafferty for a long moment, studying his impact on the man, seeing the anxiety spread across his face. Truth be told, he could order the mayor's execution right now, in this moment, in this place. All it would take was one look at Franco Roux, and the mayor's life would be snuffed out before he even had time to react. The entire team could be cut down in moments by the supersoldiers.

It was so very tempting.

No, no, a swift death is not a fitting end for Thomas. His team will watch him die.

After *he's witnessed me break the backs of these creatures once and for all and my victory is complete.*

Van Ness was, if anything, a man of his word.

"Perhaps a little demonstration is in order," Van Ness said. "Dr. Liander, can you be of assistance?"

Cornelius Liander poked his finger against his glasses. "No problemo. Follow me."

The doctor strode along the bridge, arms locked by his side. He appeared to Van Ness like an annoying teenager, despite his advancing years.

Van Ness had sent him down here twenty years ago because of his irritating, quirky behavior. It turned out to be a masterstroke. Liander was a genius at genetic manipulation. What he sorely lacked in social graces he made up for with scientific imagination and lack of moral boundaries. Precisely the man Van Ness needed to create these supersoldiers.

"How is all this possible?" Cafferty asked the doctor, as they followed him across the bridge.

"You built an army of adults?" Munoz added. "How?"

"Oh, DNA sequencing, amniotic tanks with enhanced growth conditions, brain-computer interfaces, and some WD-40," Liander replied, making himself laugh.

"Are they . . . human? Self-aware?" Munoz continued.

"Oh, they're human . . . kinda. Eighty-seven-point-two percent human, to be exact. Any less . . . whew, no good. Self-aware, not quite. They are essentially clones of each other. I added some things, took a few important things out as well. And now . . . well now, they behave very nicely."

"Did they *not* behave nicely in the past?" Munoz asked.

"That's enough, Doctor," Van Ness said, cutting him off. "The demonstration, please."

Liander punched in a code on a panel and the doors slid open.

Van Ness pushed the joystick on his wheelchair forward. "Follow me," he commanded.

Van Ness rolled into a pristine laboratory with a transparent wall at the far end. An unusual cylindrical glass tube containing a syringe with a glowing green barrel caught Cafferty's attention.

"What's in that syringe?" he asked.

Van Ness stopped for a moment to study the green liquid inside the needle.

"More creature than human—" Dr. Liander began to say.

Van Ness immediately cut him off. "That would be our last resort. Pray to whatever god you believe in that we never need to use that, Thomas."

Van Ness continued to the glass wall at the end of the room. Everyone fanned around him. Munoz and Bowcut kept having a whispered conversation. He would soon have their attention.

Dr. Liander stood to the side, a tablet illuminating his face. "Mr. Van Ness, I'm sending in Timothy. The elevator is ascending."

"Stop giving them names, Cornelius," Van Ness replied. "It gives them a level of humanity that they don't deserve. They are a creation. They are soldiers."

"Um, okay. I'll send him in."

"*It*. You'll send *it* in."

The doctor nervously nodded and fingered his tablet. The lights in the lab faded out, leaving the room dimly lit.

The glass to their front illuminated, highlighting a basketball-court-sized room several feet below them. White walls. Varnished wooden floorboards. A solid steel partition in the middle, splitting the room in half.

On one end, a lone supersoldier stood at attention, stoic, expressionless, breathing steadily like the thousands of supersoldiers they just witnessed below.

On the opposite side of the partition, a two-meter square opened in the floor.

Much like the Colosseum in Rome, Van Ness thought. *A gladiatorial fight for the modern ages.*

A creature's muffled screech came through the reinforced window. On the other side of the partition, the soldier tensed instinctively. The creature bounded through the square hole and hunched in anticipation.

"My God," Ellen muttered.

"Bad memories, Mrs. Cafferty?" Van Ness replied, referring to the exact test he put her through in his lair one year earlier.

"Not for me," she shot back defiantly. "I seem to recall killing that creature in Paris."

Cafferty smiled at Ellen and squeezed her hand.

"True, true," Van Ness said. "One important difference, though. Can anyone spot it?"

"That soldier has no weapons," Cafferty replied. "He'll get slaughtered in seconds."

"Thomas, my supersoldiers don't need weapons," Van Ness replied. *"They are the weapon."*

The steel partition slowly descended, revealing the opponents to each other. The creature let out an ear-piercing screech and bared its serrated claws and three rows of razor-sharp teeth. Its tail crashed into the ground with tremendous force, preparing to attack.

With lightning-fast speed, the creature rocketed across the floorboards. It leaped in the air, over the top of the soldier, and its massive black tail swung down to tear him to shreds.

THE SIGHT OF TENS OF THOUSANDS OF HYBRID SOLDIERS HAD stunned Cafferty earlier, but he was finally regaining his composure. He watched the scene unfolding before him with intense scrutiny. He moved closer to the glass wall, expecting to witness the super-soldier's senseless slaughter at the hands of the monster below.

The creature's tail whipped toward the unmoving soldier's neck. In the blink of an eye—faster than the creature itself—the soldier's arm reached up and grabbed the tail, stopping its momentum dead. Then he drove the tail into the center of the creature's torso, ripping right through its rib cage. The tip penetrated through the back of its body, impaling the creature midair.

Yellow blood spattered the floor in every direction.

The creature crashed to the ground, gripping its chest in agony.

The soldier circled over the writhing black body. He smashed his boot down onto the creature's skull with incredible force, caving it instantly and crushing its brain stem and vertebrae.

The lifeless carcass lay at his feet, and the soldier stood at attention again, barely out of breath, seemingly oblivious to the carnage.

The entire encounter appeared unhuman.

Cafferty, Ellen, Diego, and Sarah stared through the glass in complete shock, unable to process what they had just witnessed.

"My God," Bowcut said.

Cafferty's hatred of Van Ness suddenly overwhelmed him. He hated witnessing this demonstration. Hated knowing that Van Ness' supersoldiers were the only way they had a chance at winning. And he hated the deal he had made with the devil. It was clear Cafferty was a dead man at the end of all this, and Van Ness was just teasing him along.

To make matters worse, Ellen gripped his arm. She still didn't know Van Ness' terms for humanity's survival, didn't know the secret deal Cafferty had made with him.

One must live, and one must die . . .

The supersoldier's success surely meant Cafferty's eventual death. Van Ness would make him watch as he conquered the world and then dispose of him once and for all. When he agreed to the deal, Cafferty thought he had a shot at surviving all this. Now he realized Van Ness had baited him the whole way.

I never had a chance . . .

Dr. Liander pressed his finger on the tablet again, and the lights in the lab brightened. "Here endeth the demonstration."

Bowcut turned to Van Ness. "So what's the deployment plan? Where do we even start?"

"Cut the head off the snake, of course. We'll take five thousand of my soldiers to San Francisco first."

"Why San Francisco?" she asked. "And why only five thousand?"

"Because, my dear," Van Ness replied, "it's all we require to kill the queen."

CHAPTER FIFTEEN

All Karen and Joey could do was stare in silence at the gaping hole in the middle of the park. The thousands of creatures surrounding it stopped screeching, almost in unison. The mass appeared focused on what was about to rumble from the ground.

Sweat beaded on her forehead, partly from the nervous anticipation, mostly from the stifling heat in the break room on the roof of the building they were in. The lack of power had turned the place into a giant greenhouse. Even with the doors open and some of the windows smashed out, the breeze wasn't enough to mitigate the soaring temperature.

Back in the park, the massive black head of a creature rose from the depths below with what looked like a crown of thorns on top. Karen squinted to get a better look. Two glowing red half-moon eyes cleared the hole, and massive claws clutched the edges, pulling the creature up farther. This monstrosity had to be the size of a truck.

Suddenly, it let out a deafening screech that even from the break room sounded earsplitting.

Joey covered his ears quickly from the terrifying noise.

Karen quickly followed suit.

Windows in buildings around the park shattered into a million pieces.

The throng of smaller creatures backed away several yards.

"My God," Karen muttered.

Is this their leader?

How could it not be?

The giant monster climbed out of the hole and stood on the grass, towering over the surrounding thousands of creatures by at least twelve feet. Its scaly body glinted in the late-morning sunshine. It looked in all directions and screeched again.

The surrounding mass obediently organized itself into a thick corridor that led down an adjacent street. Even the smaller ones who'd appeared to have previously given the orders had now fallen into a deferential line.

The giant creature strode between them, moving smoothly on its muscle-ripped legs, until disappearing from view. The rest promptly followed until the park emptied.

Karen peered at the hole in the ground.

Are they taking it on a tour of their devastation? To show their leader what they've accomplished?

"What was that thing?" Joey asked.

"I'm not sure, little buddy."

The only thing she was sure about was the street below them was clear of the living nightmares. And this presented them with a chance to head in the opposite direction of the mass.

To head for the wharf. To save ourselves.

It may be our only opportunity.

"Baby, I need you to listen to me carefully," Karen said, stroking her fingers through her son's hair. "We're gonna leave this building and head for a boat, okay? I want you to stay close to me. Stay quiet. Can you do that for me?"

"Like a boss!" he said, making her smile.

Karen took a deep breath. Joey gripped her hand.

She headed for the fire escape, pushed the door farther open, and entered the stairwell. Everything remained silent, apart from the moan of a gentle breeze rising up the flights. Karen peered down the gap toward the ground level. Natural light flooded in from the emergency exit.

A single human arm protruded from several floors below her, absolutely still, caked in blood.

Heading past mutilated bodies was unavoidable, and she guessed the carnage would only get worse as they made their break through the tourist spots on the streets. She wished there was a way to protect her son from seeing all this. He had already witnessed the attacks. Seen his father butchered. Slipped in blood. And yet, she wanted to keep him from experiencing more. It was almost certainly impossible, though. This trip would likely further scar him, but it was too late to worry about that.

Karen and Joey descended the stairs. She moved at a fast but careful pace. Listened carefully for any creature sounds. Kept her vision focused on any dark corner or open entrance.

Three levels down, they passed an open-plan office with around forty workstations. The fire door had been ripped clean off. A pile of corpses lay in the corner, women and men of different races and ages. The creatures didn't discriminate. Blood spatters decorated the pristine white walls behind them. She guessed they'd backed into a corner before the killing commenced.

Like an execution by firing squad.

She and Joey continued down the stairs past the severed arm. Karen looked only long enough so they could step over it. The years as a paramedic had gotten her used to grisly scenes, which helped. However, no training existed for anything like this, for something of this scale and magnitude.

They reached the ground level, and she breathed a sigh of relief until she realized that was probably the easy part.

She slowed to a stop by the entrance and forced back the fear building inside her. They had to commit to this plan. They were getting on a boat and getting away from these creatures.

They *were* going to do all that.

We are . . .

Karen craned her head outside.

Once again, no creatures. Only the quiet yet constant buzz of flies coming from around the dead. She picked up Joey and headed outside.

Three blocks of weaving around dead pedestrians on the sidewalk took her to Columbus Avenue. She turned left onto the tree-lined street and moved past rows of independent restaurants, cafés, and stores, all now torn apart at the hands of the creatures. The ground was littered with shards of broken glass, torn clothing, handbags, bloodstained jackets.

And, of course, corpses.

The slaughtered bodies lay thicker here than on Lombard Street. Some had been thrown out the windows above the stores and lay slumped on the hoods of the stationary cars. Others had been cut down while likely trying to take refuge in the buildings. A French bistro had upturned tables, several dead beyond the counter.

No one was spared. Everywhere she looked was carnage.

It would have been numbing, but there was always a fresh atrocity, some new horror she'd not yet seen. Weirdly, that probably kept her sane, kept her thinking about where she was and where she needed to go.

Karen continued her fast walk past a park containing a statue dedicated to the city's firemen. She avoided looking at the children's playground and shielded her son's eyes as they passed.

They were making good progress, though Karen knew they were only one creature away from bringing their attempt to a swift end.

Joey kept his head nestled in her shoulder. She could feel his little heart beating fast, but he was acting like a trooper. A heavy little trooper—even in this moment, she marveled at how big he'd gotten, and her love gave her more energy to get him to safety, continuing to ignore the pain in her ankle.

A yellow trolley sat dormant in the center of the street. Dark red stains concealed the horror inside, though the slight incline on the street had caused blood to run out the battered back door and drip onto the pavement.

Karen moved to the center of the road, keeping low, and scampered from car to car. She turned right along Leavenworth Street and neared the wharf.

So very close . . .

Excitement rose inside her.

We're gonna make it to a boat . . .

She picked up her pace to a jog.

Suddenly, a piercing screech caused her to skid to a stop.

She turned to look back.

Roughly three hundred yards behind her, a single creature stood in the middle of the road, staring at them.

Then another joined it. In the blink of an eye, the two creatures leaped forward, bounding over cars toward her location.

Karen desperately scanned the immediate area. She'd never outrun them in time to get to Pier 45, much less make it to a boat.

She spotted an ambulance on the corner of Leavenworth and Jefferson, back and front doors open. She immediately rushed for it and circled to the driver's side.

A dead paramedic lay by the front wheel. She stepped over him and placed Joey on the passenger seat. The keys were in the ignition. She prayed the battery hadn't gone dead and attempted to start it.

As the engine rumbled to life, shrieks filled the street, mingling with the siren that had been switched on by the previous EMTs. She switched it off so as not to draw more attention, though the shrieks had grown louder. Closer.

Maybe seconds away.

Karen slammed the ambulance into drive. She punched the accelerator, the wheels momentarily spun, and they shot forward.

She drove between the vehicles spread to her front. The edges of the ambulance crashed against a few of them, ripping side mirrors off entirely. Joey clung to his seat as the pier came into sight. Maybe only twenty seconds away, but she calculated there would be no time to stop the vehicle and get onto a boat.

Her mind raced with what to do.

Suddenly, something crashed on top of the ambulance roof, causing Karen to swerve and struggle to stay in control.

A razor-sharp black tail stabbed into the cabin from above.

Karen pushed Joey to the edge of the seat to avoid the creature's tail. She slammed the accelerator down as far as it would go, barreling toward the wharf.

"Get on the floor, baby!" Karen shouted out, as she scrambled to click the seat belt into place.

She swerved the ambulance left and right, trying to break the creature free from the roof.

"*Come on, dammit!*" she shouted, and cut the wheel hard.

The tail ripped out of the metal above, and the creature's body flung off the ambulance, leaving a gaping hole above their heads.

There now appeared only one course of action that might save them . . . or kill them . . . but she had no choice. The lack of time dictated her decision.

Karen sped directly for the water at the end of the pier.

The ambulance crashed through a metal barrier, just as another creature leaped into the open back doors of the vehicle. Its bellow resonated through the cabin.

She swerved the ambulance left and right, causing the creature to slam hard against the sides. But it was no use—the monster still advanced toward them.

Only seconds left . . .

"Take a deep breath and hold it, Joey!"

The speeding ambulance destroyed everything in its path on the pier, and Karen screamed as they approached the water's edge.

Let's see if this son of a bitch can swim . . .

The ambulance flew off the edge of the wharf. The front end crashed nearly headfirst into the water, plunging her world into total darkness.

The sudden change in momentum caused the creature behind them to fly forward uncontrollably, smacking hard against the backs of their seats.

The front windows shattered instantly and a massive wall of water rushed inside, shocking Karen's senses. She reached out for Joey but couldn't locate him.

The water slammed into the creature's body behind them, and it thrust its tail forward into the dashboard, trying to gain any grip. The force of the water was too strong, though, and the creature shot out the back of the rapidly sinking ambulance. The frantic creature flailed its claws and tail desperately, tumbling to the bottom, drowning in the abyss.

Karen took her last breath of air as water instantly consumed the entire cabin. She struggled to undo her seat belt and, once free, reached into the murky water to her right, trying to find her son.

Her hand clutched his shirt near the passenger side. He had been on the floor, curled in a ball. She grabbed her son and knew they had seconds before they would be dragged down to the bottom of the bay with the creature.

She kicked off the dashboard toward the back doors of the ambulance, Joey's limp body clutched tightly under her left arm. She swam desperately to escape the now fully submerged vehicle, fighting her way through the dark, murky salt water, eyes stinging, lungs burning for more air, muscles aching as they worked against the descent and the weight of her son in her arm.

The surface of the water was so close . . . she could see it brighten up ahead.

They cleared the sinking ambulance out the back, but her muscles began to betray her.

She could fight no more.

Her right hand stretched out toward the surface, but their bodies began to sink.

We're not gonna make it . . .

I'm so sorry, Joey. I'm so sorry. So . . .

Suddenly, a hand grabbed her right arm tightly and yanked her and Joey upward.

A second later, they broke the surface of the water, and Karen frantically drew in deep breaths of air.

An HH-65 Coast Guard helicopter hovered above them with a rope and harness dangling from it. The diver who'd pulled them to safety held them firmly in his grip above the water.

Karen's EMT training kicked in and she immediately opened her son's mouth, forcing air into his lungs.

Nothing.

She did it again.

Joey coughed hard, ejecting the seawater from his lungs. He clutched his mom close as he drew in life-saving oxygen.

The diver attached the harness around their three bodies. Karen and Joey held on to his body tightly. The diver gave a thumbs-up, and they lifted out of the water. The helicopter winched them upward, while slowly moving away from the pier.

They were safe.

As Karen looked back at the wharf, in shock at what they had just survived, a lone creature stood at the edge, eyes fixed on them, watching its prey escape.

They were safe . . . for now.

CHAPTER SIXTEEN

A million questions raced through Sarah Bowcut's mind after what Van Ness had just said.

The creatures have a queen? If we stop her, do we stop them all?

Can the supersoldiers kill her? If not, what then?

But that last question seemed to be allayed for the time being. The supersoldier had efficiently dispatched the creature. Swiftly and concisely. Effortlessly. The kind of direct action the world sorely needed to combat the ongoing decimation. As much as she despised Van Ness, it was clear his army gave them a ray of hope.

The simple fact is that we can now fight back.

Bowcut studied her unusual colleagues. She never thought she'd be fighting a war alongside a madman, a crazy scientist, and a hundred thousand clones. Not to mention the imposing figure of Franco Roux, who stood next to her, expressionless. He'd been silent during the entire display. Relaxed, even, with no signs of the aggression she'd initially expected. The Dutchman appeared to be all business with no ax to grind.

But we'll see about that.

Van Ness spun his chair toward the group.

"Surely there are many questions," he said. "May I suggest we head to my situation room to speak with your president Brogan so that I only need to explain myself once?"

Without waiting for an answer, Van Ness proceeded to exit the laboratory, followed by Dr. Liander, Cafferty, Ellen, and Diego. Bowcut hung back for a moment with Roux. It might be her only chance to size the man up, to get a sense of where his loyalties lay and what his mission was.

Bowcut and Roux exchanged glances.

"I am aware of your actions in New York, London, and Paris," Roux said curtly. "You've been trained well, and your actions were commendable."

"Thank you," Sarah replied, surprised by his comments. "Unfortunately, I'm not aware of any of your past actions, so you have me at a disadvantage."

"We are here with a common purpose," Roux replied. "I am a soldier. My goal is to defeat the enemy and save lives."

"And that's it?" Bowcut asked, studying the man's face for the slightest deception.

"That is it."

Bowcut was a highly trained NYPD SWAT team member and came from a long family line of cops, and, most important, she was a New Yorker. She could tell when people were bullshitting her.

He's not bullshitting. He's telling the truth.

Roux's stern expression softened. "When the battle for San Francisco begins, I'll need you to command along with me. You are certainly capable."

"You want *me* to help lead the supersoldiers?"

"As I said, we are here with a common purpose," he replied.

As Sarah considered his proposition, a slight smile crept across her face. Roux matched her expression, the first crack she'd witnessed in his steely exterior.

"I'll take that as a yes."

ELLEN FOLLOWED TOM AND VAN NESS INTO A BRIGHTLY LIT conference room, along with Munoz. A few moments later, Bowcut and Roux caught up to the group and entered the room as well.

A video screen at the front took up the entire wall and showed a tranquil image of the alpine countryside. It seemed oddly corporate for this kind of clandestine base, which had been built in the harshest climate on Earth and had gone undetected for years. But after seeing the chilling feat of engineering Van Ness had secretly built under Paris, nothing surprised Ellen anymore.

Van Ness wheeled to the head of the oval conference table.

"Kindly take a seat," he said. "I will connect us with President Brogan on Air Force One. I hope she is more receptive this time than when we spoke last, one year ago."

"Something tells me she won't be," Ellen replied.

The last time Brogan and Van Ness conversed, he was literally holding the world hostage and had set off nuclear bombs in two American cities. People don't forget things like that easily.

"We shall see," Van Ness said. "The difference now is she and I both want the same thing. We all want the same thing. Don't we, Thomas?"

Cafferty replied with an uneasy nod.

Ellen reached over and squeezed Tom's arm. He was trying to keep his cool, but she'd known him long enough to realize that something was going on between the two men. Of course, she understood their animosity toward each other. For both her husband and Van Ness, this battle . . . everything . . . was always personal.

But this is deeper. There's something more he's not telling me . . .

It was impossible to figure out without her husband actually saying. For now, it would have to wait until they had time to talk privately.

Van Ness pressed a button on the table.

On the video screen, the alpine scene vanished. In its place, a map of the world flashed up on half the screen, showing different-sized red hotspots. The other half brought up a videoconferencing satellite interface.

Ellen couldn't take her eyes off the hundreds of hotspots around the world. These were cities where the creatures had already attacked—hundreds of cities worldwide, in nearly every country. Curiously, she noted, no attacks were present on various islands around the world, such as Hawaii, though Great

Britain obviously hadn't been spared. The events in London last year had already told them the creatures had infested that island. Still, most nests seemed to be landlocked under the continents . . . for now.

Her thoughts drifted, as they so often did these days, to her son, David, and her parents. Thank God they were alive and safe, in the hands of the U.S. military, off the coast of Virginia. She was acutely aware that she and Tom may not survive, orphaning her son. But if he lived, wasn't it worth it?

Because one way or another, we have to finish this . . .

Munoz pointed out the hotspots on the screen.

"It looks like the creatures' expansion has slowed in the past twenty-four hours. Why would that be?"

"Excellent question," Van Ness replied. "Now that they control the major cities around the world, it is possible that they are consolidating their gains and planning a second wave of attacks soon to come. What is your expression? The calm before the storm."

"What would the second wave of attacks be?" Munoz asked.

"Our complete annihilation," Van Ness replied.

A long, loud tone pumped through the speakers on the walls as the videoconference call connected.

Seconds later, the image of President Amanda Brogan appeared, sitting behind a long conference table inside Air Force One. Vice President Webster was to her side on a bulky brown leather seat. Both had dark shadows around their eyes, likely exhausted and frazzled by the past twenty-four hours.

Ellen was pretty sure she looked the same to them.

"Madam President," Van Ness said. "I feel the last time we spoke was less than cordial. Shall we call it water under the bridge?"

"Water under the bridge?" Brogan shot back defiantly. "You assassinated the president of the United States!"

"In fact I did," Van Ness replied confidently. "Yet here we are, Madam President, at a crossroads. Fate has brought us back together, you see."

"Fate? Are you mad?" Brogan retorted.

"Now, now, Madam President. Shall I be more blunt? I have the means to win this war. Without me, you're already dead."

"What exactly *do* you have, Van Ness? By our estimates, there's already been close to a billion casualties worldwide."

"One-point-four billion, to be exact," Van Ness countered. "Double that by next week, but I'm sure you already know that. I am not one to gloat, but it needs to be said. Perhaps you should have taken my deal a year ago."

"Enough!" Brogan shouted, leaning forward over her desk. "Tell me what your solution is."

Van Ness told her a brief history of the Antarctic base. How the Foundation had created a hundred thousand hybrid supersoldiers, ready for deployment. Cafferty confirmed what he had witnessed in the demonstration area.

"I don't see how a hundred thousand supersoldiers, as you call them, can possibly turn the tide of war," Brogan said. "We're vastly outnumbered."

"First rule of warfare, Madam President. Kill the leader, and the soldiers fall into disarray. In this case, we need to kill the queen."

"The queen?" Brogan asked. "These creatures have a leader?"

"I have long since suspected, yes," Van Ness replied. "I've been hunting the queen for decades, analyzing every nest around the world, tracking its size, its growth, its expansion. And I've come to believe the queen is nestled safely inside the largest nest in the world. The scene of the very first attack, which kicked off *all* the attacks around the world minutes and hours later."

"And where is this nest?"

"Madam President," Van Ness replied, "it's time to take back San Francisco. Kill the queen, and we decimate the entire command and control structure of every nest around the world."

"Let's say I believe you," Brogan said. "*If* you're able to fight your way into San Francisco, *if* you're able to breach the nest, *if* you find the queen, can your supersoldiers defeat her?"

Van Ness paused, considering the question carefully. He pulled a handkerchief out of his pocket and dabbed his forehead lightly. "We're going to find out, aren't we?" he replied.

A sickly look came over the president's face. That was clearly not the answer she'd hoped for. But it was the only answer she got.

"Tom, your thoughts?" the president asked.

"Madam President," Cafferty replied, "it's the best and only chance we've got."

President Brogan looked at the vice president.

He nodded in agreement. "All right then, let's hunt down and kill that queen, no matter the cost. What do you need from us?"

"May I introduce you to my head of command strategy, Mr. Franco Roux?" Van Ness said, deferring to his master strategist.

"Mr. Roux," she said.

"Madam President," Roux replied. "We have enough C-130 airplanes here to transport the necessary five thousand supersoldiers to the United States. While our planes have much-extended range, we will still need a complete refuel at NAMRU-6, the U.S. Navy military command center in Lima, Peru, which is approximately halfway."

"The U.S. does not have a military base in Peru," Brogan interjected. "That is a medical facility."

"Tut-tut, Madam President," Van Ness replied. "This is no time to lie about the true purpose of your 'medical facility.'"

Brogan looked away silently.

"Carry on, Mr. Roux."

"Including refueling, we will land in approximately twenty hours at the Naval Air Station North Island off the coast of San Diego. Satellite images show your navy has already protected the island from the creatures."

Ellen caught Bowcut admiring Roux as he spoke. The man was well prepared.

"Once off the coast of San Diego, we will transfer the supersoldiers onto the USS *Nimitz*, which will promptly set sail for San Francisco. In the meantime, you should send as many carrier strike groups as possible to rendezvous with us. Once in San Francisco Bay, we will launch our coordinated counterattack, utilizing both your forces and ours. I will be strategizing the offensive with Sarah Bowcut. Also, in the meantime, every country should already be sending their ships and planes to our coordinates"—he typed something into his computer—"here. We will transport all remaining supersoldiers around the world, along with weapons and technology that will be helpful in the fight."

"Excellent, thank you, Mr. Roux," Brogan said, clearly impressed with the man. "Is there anything else?"

"Yes, ma'am, one more thing," Roux added. "Madam President, we *will* find that queen and we *will* kill her."

For the first time in a while, Ellen felt like she might actually see her son, David, again.

CHAPTER SEVENTEEN

Bowcut and Munoz walked with Dr. Liander and Roux down a wide internal ramp toward a stark staging area with smooth bedrock walls and concrete flooring. *Nothing cosmetic included*, Munoz thought. Small white vehicles—like the ones that buzzed around an airport—drove past them in a regular stream, each loaded with various supplies. Their electric engines filled the corridor with a continuous whine, along with the distant beeps of reversing industrial transport vehicles.

Dr. Liander cheerily greeted most of the drivers when he didn't have his eyes glued to various measurements on his tablet. He ambled along like he was in a park on a sunny day.

This guy's acting more like Norm from Cheers *than a scientist at the end of the world.*

Bowcut remained locked in conversation with Roux about his time in the Korps Commandotroepen, the Dutch army's special forces. He'd served in Iraq and Afghanistan, then was recruited by the Foundation in Mali. Munoz knew she was getting a feel for the man. So far, she appeared increasingly relaxed in the big man's presence.

In fact, everyone in the whole place had that vibe, save for the lone supersoldier that singlehandedly dismantled the creature earlier.

Who wouldn't be comfortable here? It's probably the safest place on the planet.

But aren't we all about to leave this haven?

He was pretty sure he didn't want to leave. No, if anything, Munoz had realized the logistics to this base must be huge after seeing the warehouse and supersoldiers. He reminded himself that this was humanity's best shot, regardless of the Foundation's past murderous history. The more he saw, the more it impressed him for two reasons. First, the scale, of course. But mainly for something else. Despite years of studying conspiracy theories and discussing them online with fellow enthusiasts who knew their shit—and sifting through the evidence recovered from Paris—not a scrap of information pointed in this direction. And the secret base had been running for decades. There was something so much more real about secrets you never knew about than the ones everyone thought they did.

"Hey, Doc," he called over to Liander. "How big is this place?"

Liander stepped across to him, brushing his shoulder in the process. The man evidently had no idea about personal space. "Oh, it's about two-point-seven square miles, or roughly two Central Parks. We're expanding as production ramps up."

"Production?"

"No need for armies anymore once we bring more supersoldiers online."

Munoz squinted his eyes at the doctor.

Did he just reveal something he shouldn't have?

"Got it. How do we command these soldiers? Do they understand English?" Munoz continued, trying not to draw attention to the comment.

"To a basic extent. They follow simple commands, but language really isn't necessary."

"And why's that?"

"Well, I hardwired their DNA to do one thing: hunt down and kill creatures. As I always say, the DNA leads the way." The doctor cackled at his own joke, slightly too loudly. He peered forward. "But of course, Foundation staff can control their actions. Okay, we're here."

They walked around a sweeping bend and came out in the cavernous area they'd seen from the viewing deck. Thousands of grim-faced soldiers faced Munoz, steady in their positions. He stopped abruptly at the sight. Close up, and knowing their capabilities, he sensed their aura, and his right leg began to tremble. But none of the supersoldiers paid him the slightest bit of attention. An odd aroma invaded his nostrils, like the smell inside of a carpet store mixed with detergent.

The doctor grabbed his wrist and pulled him forward. "Don't sweat it, Mr. Munoz. They won't hurt a fellow human. Well, at least something with a higher percentage of human DNA."

"They can tell that?"

Dr. Liander cackled. "They know a creature when they see one."

And I know a monster when I see one, he thought, staring at Liander.

CHAPTER EIGHTEEN

The Coast Guard chopper thumped over the water at low altitude, its downdraft blasting a foamy trail in the shimmering blue Pacific. A cool wind rushed into its open side door. Karen wrapped a blanket around Joey and pulled him closer. He sat holding his knees, still shivering, his hair dripping after their near-death experience.

Their savior, the diver, gave her a reassuring smile. "Don't worry, guys. You're going to a safe place."

"Thank you. For everything."

Karen couldn't muster anything more than those stuttered words. The events of the last twenty-four hours had started to properly sink in. She finally found the time to process the horror. Their lives hanging by a thread. The gruesome scenes on the streets. Their hair-raising escape. It made her shudder, but it beat constantly worrying about immediate survival against seemingly impossible odds.

She viewed the San Francisco city center as they flew away. It looked dead, apart from several thin wisps of smoke that coiled into the air. Every skyscraper had shattered windows. Ferries listed in the wharf. At least the sound of the chopper's blades blocked out any remote screeches.

The chopper banked left, giving her a view of the Dwight D. Eisenhower Highway, whose overwater sections connected San Francisco to Oakland.

But no longer.

A huge section of the Bay Bridge had been destroyed. The lengths of road on either side sagged into the water like two mighty drawbridges that'd collapsed. Support cables hung loosely from the tall concrete pillars. At the foot of the collapse, close to a hundred creatures floated facedown in the gentle ocean swell.

The sight took her breath away.

She peered beyond Yerba Buena Island toward the Oakland side. A section of the bridge had been destroyed there, too, marooning the former from the mainland. The conjoined Treasure Island was cut off as a consequence, and that's where the helicopter descended. The island, now completely separated from the mainland, was apparently the safe haven the diver was referring to.

They powered over a neighborhood of small houses on the island. She'd been here once as a child to watch a game of Gaelic football, and they headed directly for those sports fields. Hundreds of tents covered the area, the old green Base-X type used by the military. People milled between them. Other survivors. Each likely with his or her own harrowing story to tell. She wasn't ready to share her experiences just yet. She sighed with relief at the sight of a functioning part of civilization.

Somewhere Joey could recover.

Somewhere I can recover.

Karen's experience told her that the worst suffer-ers after traumatic events were not the dead; they were beyond pain. It was the injured and the family of the victims. Hearts ruptured by the agony and loss. Knowing that the worst things in life could *actually* happen. Some never recovered and spent the rest of their lives as hollow shells. She hoped her son didn't fit into that particular bracket.

The chopper bumped down on a road next to the busy fields.

The diver pointed at the far end of the grass, to-ward a larger open tent with a table inside. "Head over there, ma'am. They'll familiarize you."

She nodded in acknowledgment. "We're alive because of you. I won't forget it."

"Just doing my job. Let's hope we all live long enough to remember."

"You can say that again."

He clearly had an important job, retrieving any-one left alive in the city. He'd already proven that in a selfless and assured manner. Karen decided it was better to avoid engaging him with questions about what the hell was happening. Others in the camp would know more than her. She picked up Joey, disembarked, and turned to give a smile of appreciation.

Joey waved his little right hand. "Thank you, Mr. Helicopter Man."

"You were the brave one, kiddo."

With that, the diver closed the door, and the helicopter ascended again.

Karen turned and walked along the road. As she did, she peered across the field.

Tent doors gently rippled in the breeze. A young couple gazed toward her and Joey with pity and sorrow etched across their faces. She avoided eye contact.

Just how many people are left alive in San Francisco? This surely can't be it.

Steam drifted out of an open set of garages at the far side. Possibly a makeshift cafeteria. A teenage boy, dressed in a Warriors jersey, walked out. He had a steel mess kit plate in one hand and a sourdough roll in the other. This confirmed her suspicions, and her stomach growled at the thought of hot food. It also made her realize that Joey hadn't complained about not eating since scarfing down cold cuts in the smashed-up apartment. That was unusual for him.

The diver was right.

My brave boy.

A forklift truck carried a stack of blankets out of a warehouse. Farther along, outside a rusting warehouse, a group of people ripped open boxes of toiletries and sorted them into individual piles.

It had all the hallmarks of a refugee camp, something she'd witnessed only on the news or in documentaries.

Never thought I'd be in a place like this in my own country.

But I'm glad I am.

As Karen neared the larger tent and peered in, a grim-faced soldier looked up from behind a desk.

Maps lined the wall behind him, showing both islands with plans scrawled across them in permanent marker.

"Hey, little guy," the soldier said to Joey. "I've got something here for you."

He reached into a box and pulled out a Kit Kat. Joey ran the final couple of paces to the desk and grabbed it from the soldier's hand.

"What do you say?" Karen ordered sternly.

"Thank you, sir," Joey replied. He peeled off the wrapper and took a hungry bite.

With her son distracted by his tasty treat, she turned her attention back to the desk. "I'd ask what's been going on, but . . ."

"Call me Jim," the soldier said to her. "I know you've been through a lot—"

"We all have."

He nodded. "That's true."

"How many more safe places are there like this?" Karen asked.

"Locally? This is it, I'm afraid."

"For the entire city?"

He nodded again. "Just over a couple of thousand people. Survivors were placed in the houses until we ran out of space. A tent is the best we can do for now . . ."

"How far has this thing spread?" she asked.

"You really wanna know?"

"Yes."

She had family all over California. Danny's lived in Ontario, Canada. All were close to her heart. The tone of his voice and his forlorn expression already told her that it wasn't just San Francisco.

"It's global," Jim replied. "Most major cities. Some smaller ones. We don't know exactly because they've been slowly taking out all forms of communication."

"San Bernardino?"

"Gone."

"Sacramento?"

He let out a deep sigh.

"Ontario?"

"Canada?" He glanced down at a map for a moment. "Ottawa and a stretch of land reaching from Toronto to Hamilton."

"My God."

She wanted to ask how many dead, but what was the point? That number must be growing by the minute. Millions? Billions? It was also evident that pretty much everyone on the island had lost someone close, including the soldier in front of her, who was doing his best to appear calm and helpful.

She took a deep breath to stiffen herself. "What now?"

"For now, we assign you a place in the camp. It'll give you a chance to rest and eat. Be patient, we're still organizing everything, which I'm sure you appreciate." He gazed beyond her at another descending chopper. "More people are coming in by the hour. I'll put you in a tent next to another mother and child, Stacy and Taylor. It'll give the little man a playmate, and she'll familiarize you with the camp. What are your names?"

"Karen Green, and that's my—"

"Joey," her son called out, wafer spraying from his mouth.

Jim scribbled their details into a ledger and peered

up. "The Green family. Got it. Stay strong for us and be patient, little man. I promise we're gonna do our best."

Joey saluted the soldier in response.

"One last question," Karen said. "Is any help coming?"

The soldier looked down and wiped sweat from his exhausted face.

Karen knew the answer. She gently touched his hand. "Thank you for the help," she said.

The soldier looked back up at her appreciatively. He pointed to the left edge of the field. "Your tent is the second row along. End tent. If you need anything, just ask and we'll try our best."

Karen turned to look outside. Already, four more disheveled people had disembarked from the chopper and were trudging toward her location. She still had a million questions. Who wouldn't? But despite the confusion and sorrow that plagued her mind, she was self-aware enough to understand that now wasn't the best time.

"Hang in there," the soldier added. "I know this might seem like the end of the world, but those monsters will soon realize that they've screwed with the wrong guys."

As she took Joey by the hand and they wandered toward their allocated spot in the dazzling sunshine, Karen wondered whether those final words were just bravado. Something to keep her spirits up until they were inevitably attacked. To keep her from thinking that this place, seemingly one of the last enclaves of people, wasn't a bastion of resistance but merely a dying ember of humanity.

CHAPTER NINETEEN

Cafferty peered across a huge underground hangar. Ten C-130s were parked in two lines. Light gray in color. Numbered on their tails from FFHA01 to FFHA10. All with their four mighty propellers stationary.

The stench of aviation fuel clogged the frigid air.

Each plane had its rear gates down. Foundation members spread around them, dressed in dark blue coveralls, thick coats, and chunky earphones. Engineers. Cargo handlers. Loadmasters. Maybe pilots. It was impossible to say as none wore insignia on their uniforms.

A tracked container handler drove to the back of the closest aircraft. It carried what looked like a transparent dumpster with a sealed lid. Thick green liquid sloshed around inside.

"What's that?" Cafferty asked, more out of curiosity than surprise. After spending a few hours here, he'd grown numb to anything that might have previously shocked him. The only question on his mind was *What's next?*

Van Ness turned toward him. "All of the essential nutrients our soldiers require, until they're on the ground. An army marches on its stomach, as they say."

Four long lines of supersoldiers stomped in, led by a man and woman in the same black-and-gray camouflage clothing. They headed to the farthest plane, boots pounding the stone floor in synchrony. The sound reverberated around the hangar as the soldiers swiftly ascended the ramp. Shortly after they filed in, the tailgate closed.

Cafferty stood watching in awe as five hundred supersoldiers efficiently boarded each plane in a matter of minutes. The execution was perfectly choreographed, like they knew this day was coming and had practiced the maneuver until attaining complete perfection.

This rehearsed parade was all in stark contrast to the chaos they were about to face. Cafferty couldn't imagine exactly how things would go down. Those moves had been taken out of his hands, and he had little doubt about who was calling the shots now.

Roux looked on with pride as the hangar cleared of vehicles and the soldiers finished loading onto the planes.

Bowcut stared at the slickness of the operation with an expression of amazement.

"You see, Thomas," Van Ness explained, "although I never wanted the world to come to this, I'm sure even you appreciate by now that I don't prepare for failure."

Cafferty stood motionless. He was still to be convinced that such a small force could take on and eliminate so many creatures. Sure, the creatures had met their match in a one-on-one fight, but they numbered in the millions. How could one hundred thousand supersoldiers possibly stand a chance?

A bearded man in the same blue coveralls as the other workers approached Van Ness' chair. "We're ready and loaded, sir. Comms are established with Lima. They'll be ready to refuel upon our arrival."

"Very good," Van Ness replied. "Have we opened up channels to the U.S. Navy?"

The worker checked his watch. "We sent our crypto . . . half an hour ago. Should be going through radio checks as we speak."

"Thank you, Craig."

"Hey," Munoz said. "My research stuff is still on our plane."

"Mr. Munoz," Van Ness replied, "you'll find that all your equipment has been relocated onto FFHA01, the very plane I will be on, along with the rest of your team."

"Wait, so we're not going back in our bird?" Munoz asked.

"I leave the choice to you," Van Ness replied coldly. "We've made a few enhancements to our fleet that improve the likelihood of success. Whereas your plane . . . well. So, shall I put your equipment back?"

Diego looked at Van Ness' pristine C-130s and the dilapidated U.S. Air Force plane he flew to Antarctica in.

"Um . . . no, I'll take your plane," Munoz replied.

"I thought so," Van Ness replied smugly. "I must say, I am interested in hearing about your research at some point, Mr. Munoz."

Diego shifted uncomfortably at the sudden attention. "Err . . . okay," he replied awkwardly. "I think I might have an . . . um . . . PowerPoint or something."

Cafferty watched Diego lower his head at the idiocy of what he had just said. Munoz had been working on theories related to how the creatures communicate. He had been studying the various frequencies of their shrieks for some time, trying to discern some kind of pattern in them. So far, he hadn't produced any worthwhile results. And time was something that nobody had to spare. But he'd definitely done more than put together a slide show.

A few more weeks and a few more raids, and Diego would have almost certainly cracked their language.

On the far side of the hangar, a giant steel door slowly opened, cranking from left to right. Cold wind rushed down along with a slither of natural light from above. Moments later, a white drone, armed with a missile, powered down the sloping runway. It turned to the left and parked alongside three others.

The bearded worker pressed his hand against the device in his ear, attempting to listen over the noise in the hangar. He eventually looked back to Van Ness. "Conditions are good and the ground is clear, sir. We're ready to go."

"Very good," Van Ness replied. "Shall we, team?"

Team. Cafferty almost spat the word back out. He remained under no illusion about his own use from here out. He was simply a spectator to the Foundation's main event. The same went for Ellen and Diego. At least Sarah seemed to have found a place working with Roux.

Van Ness wheeled toward the first plane in the fleet, the lead aircraft in their journey toward what Cafferty hoped would save humanity. Save his son. Save Ellen. Provide a future free from the creatures' barbarity.

Even if that future most likely wouldn't include him.

ELLEN TRUDGED UP THE C-130'S RAMP, FOLLOWING TOM AND Van Ness into the cargo hold. The supersoldiers parted, shuffling to their left or right, and they formed a corridor that led to the front of the plane.

"They're packed in like sardines," Munoz uttered from behind.

"They do not require personal space," Van Ness replied, and wheeled past them straight for the cockpit.

She tensed as she walked between the soldiers. It would take only one of these things to eliminate all of them. If just one went rogue—forgot an order, had some kind of psychological meltdown and mistook her for a creature—that would bring a fast and brutal end.

They didn't even look at her, though. They just seemed to stare into nothing, oblivious to those around them. The plane remained in near silence.

Eerie, she thought.

Hot breaths brushed against her face, though all of their eyes remained looking up. She wondered what kind of awareness the supersoldiers had.

There's no doubt they are sentient. I've seen them walk and fight. But do they possess even the faintest scrap of free will?

What happens if the battle doesn't go as planned and we need to improvise? What if we need a bridge built, or a generator rewired, or a communications tower set up? Are they capable of anything beyond killing creatures?

All valid questions, she considered. But the nature of their whistle-stop tour around the base, coupled with the necessity for their quick departure while some semblance of civilization still existed, meant nobody had had any real time to reflect on the mind-blowing things they'd seen since landing. And while she respected the urgency, she also worried if things were moving too fast. This was Van Ness, after all, and his creations. He'd never been a plain dealer, and even as he talked about the supersoldiers as his contingency plan, she couldn't shake the feeling there was another plan hiding deeper under the surface. With Tom so distracted by . . . well, by whatever it was that preoccupied him, Ellen was left to puzzle this on her own.

Roux directed them to a set of seats behind the cockpit and they buckled up. By now, Ellen was used to the complicated military buckle and wondered how her life had changed so much in just a short space of time.

The plane's engines roared to life.

Ellen stared out the small window at the propellers spinning to a rapid blur. It was amazing to think that, despite all the advances in science and technology sitting inside this plane, the machine itself was basically the same design that had been used by the U.S. military for decades. There was something comforting about the fact that as the world progressed—and possibly progressed into complete meltdown—constants remained. Yes, this plane. But also family. Love. Hope.

A sense of anticipation rose inside her as they taxied out of the hangar and gradually picked up speed toward moonlight. The C-130 burst into the wide-open whiteness of Antarctica, roaring along the ground on a flattened section of ice until its nose lifted and the wheels left the ground.

Ellen grabbed Tom's hand and squeezed. He returned a nervous glance.

"What's going on, Tom?" she whispered.

"What do you mean?"

"You know what I mean. I've known you long enough to know when you're hiding something from me."

Cafferty's eyes darted away from her gaze. Ellen hadn't meant it this way, but she realized her husband undoubtedly was thinking about his marital infidelity a few years prior. She had known he was hiding something then, too.

"I mean," she clarified, "I get that you and Van Ness despise each other. That's fine. But there's something more you're not telling me."

The C-130 hit a pocket of turbulence in the cloudy sky. Its body shuddered several times during the bumpy climb to cruising altitude, but the plane was built to withstand it. For all her adventuring, though, Ellen was not a big fan. She grabbed on to Tom's arm. He patted her hand, even as he didn't answer her question.

He looked back and was surprised—but also not surprised—that the supersoldiers remained standing each time the plane encountered some turbulence, swaying in unison to maintain their balance. All seemingly unperturbed.

As it climbed higher, the plane hit smoother air and quickly gained altitude.

Ellen turned her attention back to her husband. "This is more than just a personal grudge and you know it," she continued.

"Let's try to get some rest, baby," Cafferty said, looking away.

Sleep was the last thing on her mind. Although it had been over twenty-four hours since her last decent rest, the idea of Tom doing something reckless kept her firmly awake. She squeezed his hand harder. "No, Tom," she pressed on. "I'm your wife. Your partner in this. In everything. I need you to make a better choice here."

A sickly look spread over Cafferty's face.

"Now, what's going on?"

Cafferty let out a deep sigh. "I made a deal with Van Ness."

"What kind of deal?"

"It was his one condition to help."

"What was the deal, Tom?"

"It was my only chance to save you, to save David, Sarah, Diego, everyone. The entire planet."

"Tom, what was the deal?" she asked sternly.

Cafferty swallowed hard, then finally spoke. "Only one of us survives this war, either him or me. No matter what. Winner takes all."

Her eyes widened. "Have you lost your mind?!"

"It was either that or we all die."

"That's ridiculous!" Ellen replied. "One way or the other, he needed to get off that rig to show off these supersoldiers and try to regain whatever power he once had. Can't you see he set all of this up? He baited you, knowing that he had his army all along. He knows he's going to win."

"Don't you think I know that?" Tom growled. "What choice did I have, Ellen?"

"You tell him to go fuck himself. You threaten to lock him up and throw away the key. Seriously, Tom, you think if you didn't agree, he'd just sit there and let the creatures destroy us all? That the Foundation would have just left its soldiers in Antarctica until there was nothing left to save?"

Munoz and Bowcut were both looking across from their seats.

"Please keep your voice down," Cafferty pleaded.

"Why, so you can keep this secret from everyone else, too?" But she lowered her tone. "You've been like this ever since Paris. Ever since the UN. Thinking you need to do it all on your own. Why didn't you talk to me first?"

"Because we didn't have any time! I don't know what he would have done. All I know is the options I had in the moment. Besides, it might take years to win the war. We might not even find this queen he's talking about. We might even lose. This is all on me, Ellen. It's all my doing. I'm not prepared to sign humanity's death warrant."

"Your ego is out of control right now," she hissed.

"What?" Cafferty looked down, forlorn.

"You should have spoken to me first, Tom. What you think was selflessness is actually the worst form of selfishness."

Cafferty was at a loss for words. All he could mutter was "I'm sorry."

"'Sorry,'" she whispered. After his revelation, that was all he had to say.

Everything Ellen had suspected was proven true. She resisted the temptation to slap Tom across the face. She needed to think this through, to process what she had just heard.

She closed her eyes, ending the conversation abruptly.

Perhaps he was right—it was time to get some rest. *Time to think.*

Her mind spun with ideas about how she could stop this deal from going ahead if the supersoldiers came out victorious. She imagined a humiliating execution of her husband, a gruesome spectacle with his head in a noose and Van Ness excitedly pulling the trapdoor lever.

That wasn't going to happen on her watch.

The most obvious course of action was this: during the heat of the battle, when nobody was looking, Ellen could put a bullet in Van Ness' brain.

Will he predict this move?

Will the supersoldiers defend Van Ness to the death?

The sound of an electric wheelchair hummed toward the seats.

Ellen opened half an eye.

Van Ness sat in front of the group, fingers steepled, appearing deep in thought.

"Is there a problem?" Roux asked.

"I'm afraid Lima is under attack," Van Ness replied.

"Is there anywhere else to refuel?" Cafferty asked.

Roux shook his head. "Nowhere safe between here and San Diego."

The big Dutchman's voice didn't seem alarmed. Maybe it was just his accent, but it seemed like he truly wasn't capable of panic. As much as he scared Ellen—especially with his face repeated in the Xeroxed versions of him that filled the plane—it was reassuring that he was cool under pressure.

It didn't get more pressure packed than this.

As Roux considered alternative plans, Ellen quickly considered the consequences. The super-soldiers would never make it. The battle might never be won. And her last thoughts around a solution to her husband's problem now appeared redundant.

"What do we do?" Cafferty asked.

Van Ness stared along the row of seats. "We proceed as planned, Thomas. Nothing will stop me from seeing this through to its absolute conclusion."

The pit of Ellen's stomach dropped, knowing now what Van Ness meant. She tried to disguise her panic to not reveal what she had learned.

Van Ness rotated his wheelchair back toward the cockpit and wheeled away.

"Captain," Van Ness said, "creatures or not, we are landing these planes."

CHAPTER TWENTY

An hour had passed since all contact from the U.S. Navy base in Lima had stopped. From what Cafferty could make out during the transmission, the people on the ground had fought bravely and initially held back a small wave of creatures with conventional weapons. No small feat, considering the lack of impact bullets had on the creatures and the even more disconcerting minimal impact of a missile on a large group of creatures. Then, an hour before the planes were due to land, a larger second wave was reported, advancing on the perimeter fence at breakneck speed. Silence followed shortly after.

He imagined it was like a fast-forward version of the Battle of the Alamo, the initial onslaught repelled until a larger force attacked, leading to a retreat into the buildings. From there, it was just a case of the survivors being picked off in brutal fashion.

This, it seems, is game over. An end to the task force's plans.

We have no way of refueling, no way of making it to San Francisco.

So we can't take down the supposed queen . . .

And, he concluded, a possible terminal blow to everyone's survival. If the theory held true that destroying the queen would paralyze the creatures' rank structure, and they had no way to reach the queen, all was lost.

But Cafferty guessed he was missing something. He had to be for a simple reason: the man to his front.

Van Ness sat behind the pilots as the C-130 swept over the Pacific Ocean and headed toward the smoking remains of the Peruvian capital, silhouetted by the pink early-evening sky. He didn't seem the least bit perturbed by the recent news. He just stared through the windshield as they descended to take a look at the base at low altitude.

Hundreds of tall, light-colored buildings lined a cliff edge overlooking the shore. Once over them, the devastation in the city became chillingly clear.

Just like my first view of Vegas.

Stationary cars, jammed at odd angles on the roads. The tiny figures of corpses surrounding them.

Everything deathly still.

Cafferty visually searched for any signs of the creatures. He couldn't see any, but it remained obvious they'd been here no less than an hour ago. Probably still were, perhaps underground or crammed somewhere in the shattered ruins.

"We'll be over the airstrip in a minute," the pilot said.

"Thank you," Van Ness said, and nothing more.

A heartbeat later, a mass of creatures came into view—thousands of them, swarming a western neighborhood. They filled the wide streets, rushing in and out of houses, clambering over rooftops. Windows shattered. Human bodies went flying, got trampled, were tossed to the side like pieces of garbage.

The sound of the C-130s' approach made hundreds of creatures stop dead. All eyes went up. Cafferty felt like they were all staring directly at him, and his soul shriveled just a little under their black gaze.

The pilots continued their course directly toward the distant runway, not deviating a degree. The plane sailed straight over the top of the neighborhood.

Cafferty edged across to the left side and peered down.

Predictably, the onslaught below had changed focus.

The creatures now followed the ten aircraft.

"Dammit, Van Ness, what's your plan now?" Cafferty snapped. "You see them all down there. Don't we need to find a safe place to land?"

Van Ness returned his glare. "We don't need a new place. I've told you my plan already."

"The base was overrun by creatures, thousands of them. We'll be slaughtered."

"Will we?" Van Ness asked rhetorically.

Cafferty glared at his nemesis.

"I suggest you strap in, Thomas. I'm expecting a bumpy landing."

Tom wanted to say something, but realizing the futility of it—the plane was landing whether he argued or not—he rushed back to his seat and buckled in.

"Why is everything so goddamn secretive?" Cafferty said to no one.

But Ellen, sitting beside him, answered. "Because he gets off on it. It's all a game to him. A game he thinks he's best at. He thinks he's playing four-dimensional chess while the rest of us push a hoop with a stick, and he can't imagine explaining anything to us will make the slightest difference."

She smiled at Tom.

"Put bluntly, he's an asshole."

Cafferty couldn't help a short bark of laughter. He returned Ellen's smile, but it didn't last long. Something she'd said reminded him of the moves Van Ness was somehow planning: this was a game, and the winning move for the maniac was Tom's death. He gazed back out the window.

Damn him.

The C-130s put at least three miles of heavily urbanized area between them and the chasing creatures. How much time that would actually buy them, he couldn't possibly know. But despite all the tricks Van Ness had so far pulled off, he didn't think it was going to be enough.

The pilot banked over the base's flattened perimeter fence, littered with a few dead creatures, and powered past the runway. The rest of the fleet remained higher in the air, in a holding pattern until the first plane had landed.

At least one thing seemed to be in their favor: as promised, the fuel trucks had been readied for their arrival. Of course, dead ground crew members lay around them. Pools of blood and spatters of viscera stained the tarmac. Most of the windows of the several official-looking square buildings had been shattered. Corpses lay outside a few of them in gut-churning, twisted shapes.

Cafferty let out a deep sigh. They had all the visual evidence they needed to flee this place, and if that wasn't enough, they knew more creatures were swiftly returning to the site.

"We land now," Van Ness commanded the pilots. "Tell the rest of the fleet. Only the supersoldiers on our plane will deploy."

The pilot immediately spoke through his mic. The rest of the planes acknowledged in turn, no fear in their pilots' voices, only cold acceptance of the order.

Cafferty couldn't believe his ears.

The plane arced around and descended toward the base, smooth and fast. No hint of panic in any-one's face. Well, almost everyone. He glanced back to Ellen, Bowcut, and Munoz. The three's expressions matched his inner dread. All had their laser weapons out, preparing for the inevitable battle they'd soon be facing.

"As fast as you can, please, Captain," Van Ness said.

"You got it, sir."

"Are you insane?" Cafferty exclaimed. "You've got to call this off—you've seen what's coming for us."

"I've seen what's been coming all along, Thomas."

"I meant landing here. Thousands of creatures against a few hundred soldiers from only one of the planes? Send them all out at least!"

"Yet again, you've proven yourself the typical government employee, Mr. Mayor," Van Ness replied. "Send ten men to do a job it only takes one to do."

"What if it isn't enough?" Cafferty asked. "You're consigning us all to death." He no longer cared that he now sounded increasingly desperate. The opposing force and theirs seemed utterly imbalanced to the point of the supersoldiers being sent out on a suicide mission.

"There's only one death I care about, Thomas." Van Ness' eyes thinned as they rapidly closed in on the runway. He grabbed the arms of his wheelchair in preparation for landing. "Why, the creatures, of course," he continued, shooting Cafferty a look.

The aircraft wheels screeched on impact and the plane shot along the runway. It gradually slowed and turned toward the fuel pumps.

Cafferty shuddered as the C-130 bumped over something. It didn't take a lot of imagination to guess what . . .

He peered out the window again. First, at the unmanned pumps.

Nobody to operate them.

If *they still work.*

Second, at the other planes landing in quick succession.

Are they just going to sit there and watch?

And third, at the narrow roads beyond the flattened fence that led back to the infested neighborhood. They were quiet for now. Soon, in perhaps a minute or two, a horde of creatures would once again descend on the base.

We're exposed from all sides, and the only way is up.

If we even have that chance.

Each C-130 landed successfully and stopped in two formal lines alongside the four mobile pumps as if this were all routine. The planes were precariously close together—a small target for the incoming creatures.

We're sitting ducks . . .

"Ramp lowering," Roux bellowed from somewhere in the back. "Stand by to exit and take up a 360-degree defensive position."

Humid tropical air rushed into the plane's body, carrying the stench of death.

Undeterred, the supersoldiers disembarked in quick succession, boots hammering against metal.

Van Ness spun his chair toward the back of the plane and wheeled toward Cafferty. "Thomas, if you and your team would care to join me outside while our engineers refuel."

Cafferty spun to face the back of the plane, now empty. Munoz, Bowcut, and Ellen stood staring toward the lowered ramp, lasers raised.

Van Ness continued forward. "Keep up. I'd hate for you all to miss this."

The plane was now empty except for Cafferty and his team.

"This is suicide," Cafferty said.

"I'm not so sure," Bowcut replied. "He seems pretty confident."

"But are we confident?" Ellen added.

"No," Munoz replied. "I'm shitting bricks, but what's new?"

"I haven't been sure about anything since we landed in Antarctica," Bowcut replied.

Something in Cafferty clicked then. Ever since New York, he had been tired of sitting on the sidelines, waiting for others to do while he watched. He didn't abandon his fatalistic thoughts, but he also couldn't stem his curiosity, nor his desire to do something. "If the supersoldiers fail," he said to the group, "we're dead anyway. At least let's go down shooting."

Munoz shrugged. "So, basically the same plan as the last three years. Ready, boss!"

Exactly.

Bowcut glanced outside. "Roux isn't a madman. He didn't come this far to get slaughtered before the real fighting starts."

"She's right," Ellen said. "Neither did Van Ness. Say what you will about that a-hole, but he's a born survivor."

"And it's definitely better to fight out there than cower in here," Bowcut said to the nodding group.

Cafferty took a deep breath. "All right," he said. "We're all in agreement?"

Everyone nodded.

"Then let's light this place up!"

The team turned and walked together toward the back of the plane. Cafferty's previous words about going down shooting had come out naturally, without even thinking. He had subconsciously slipped back in his fighting zone, a place he never thought he had in him, until the Foundation had forced him into action. The problem was he liked it. The adrenaline made him feel alive. He reveled in the acclaim of taking down Van Ness in Paris. Wanted more. Jumped into the Foundation's place as fast as he could to fill the void.

But things were different now, and he could feel it. Things were out of his control, and the team had put their lives in Van Ness' hands.

Yet, maybe things were never in his control to begin with. And maybe that was part of what he liked, too.

Cafferty quickened his pace to catch up to Van Ness and joined him on the runway. He wiped a sheen of sweat from his brow as he surveyed the immediate surroundings.

The supersoldiers had fanned out in a circle around the planes, within an arm's length of one another. They all stood motionless but ready, chests breathing deeply, slowly rocking on their heels.

So few, he thought. *There's just not enough.*

Deploy the other soldiers! he wanted to scream.

At the same time, engineers had disembarked from one of the planes and were already working lines from jet fuel trucks to four of the planes.

Distant screeches approached. They could be from halfway across the city. They could be from less than a mile from the base. It was impossible to tell. The increasing loudness announced that the creatures were coming, and fast.

"You look nervous, my friend," Van Ness said, smiling.

"When's the last time you were on the battlefield, Van Ness?" Cafferty asked. "Not safe and sound in your underground bunkers or fortified towers? We're about to get hit by the most vicious things on the planet, and all we've got between us and them is a single ring of soldiers."

"Wrong again, Thomas," Van Ness replied.

"What—"

"The creatures are about to get hit by the most vicious thing on the planet."

It was the kind of bravado that put Cafferty's teeth on edge. The assurance of the master of the self-proclaimed master race that brooked no argument. It didn't lack for a response, though—only it wasn't Cafferty or any of his team who spoke. Rather, as Van Ness made his condescending pronouncement, his voice became increasingly drowned out by deafening screeches. Beyond the base's flattened perimeter, clouds of dust burst out of five streets, all directly in front of the runway.

All coming straight at them.

Roux strode around inside the ring of supersoldiers, yelling something at them. Cafferty couldn't make out what. He wasn't even sure it mattered.

If it were just a matter of numbers, Cafferty was pretty sure they were doomed. But when he remembered that the creatures had numerical superiority in terms of limbs—that their deadly tails gave them a further advantage—he didn't think there was any way out.

How can they even be sure of the apparent kill ratio? We don't even know the number of creatures coming to kill us. It's reckless, considering what's at stake.

Because everything *is at stake.*

The only thing he could hope for at this point was that he lived long enough to see the smug self-satisfaction wiped off Van Ness' face.

"I'm begging you," Cafferty shouted above the earsplitting noise. "At least unload another one of the goddamn planes."

"I do love to hear you beg, Thomas." Van Ness ignored Cafferty's plea and turned back toward the oncoming creatures.

Cafferty raised his laser, preparing for the impending massacre.

Bowcut dropped to one knee, and Munoz, Ellen, and Cafferty followed suit. Back to back. Pistols raised.

Van Ness pulled a cigar out of his pocket and calmly cut the tip off. He lit it and pulled in a deep breath. "Any moment now."

Surprisingly, the one thought that flashed through Cafferty's head at that moment was how much he wouldn't mind a cigar right now.

Several creatures rocketed through the dust clouds. More appeared behind them in the haze.

Only three hundred yards away.

In an instant, two hundred yards.

At this speed, the task force had roughly ten seconds before the hand-to-hand fighting started.

Cafferty swallowed to moisten his parched throat. He didn't dare believe this was the end. Van Ness wouldn't have planned something like this.

But here they were, ready for impact, against what he considered impossible odds. *Then again*, he thought, *if the supersoldiers can't win here, what chance did they have once arriving in San Francisco?*

If the answer was none, everyone would die on the runway. And with it, humanity's best chance at salvation.

CHAPTER TWENTY-ONE

Bowcut swallowed hard and raised her pistol skyward through the cloying humidity. A bead of sweat trickled down her temple. Sure, it was warm, but nowhere near how humid the New York City subway was in August.

She leveled her laser's sight above the heads of the supersoldiers. Squinted as the cloud of dust hit the group, moments before the front ranks of creatures would with devastating force. Hundreds of dark figures rapidly dropped down from their final leaps, letting out deafening screeches as they closed within a breath of first contact.

The early-evening sun shone down on the dusty air, surrounding the area in a thick orange haze. The adrenaline surging through her body had the effect of slowing the world down. It always did during the moments before action. Just like when she used to storm into a house as an NYPD SWAT team member.

But this time, her vision fogged in the haze and dust. Clear visibility was near impossible. She shielded her eyes with her left hand.

The soldiers all rocked on their heels, ready for action, unflappable. Intimidating obstacles the creatures had yet to meet. The first and last line of defense. Roux confidently prowled a few feet behind them. He looked poised, ready.

Immediately to her left, Munoz's pistol shook in his hand. She couldn't blame him. This situation had ripped all of them firmly outside their comfort zones, if such things even existed anymore in this world on the brink of obliteration.

Van Ness remained still, relaxed, with a neutral expression. Chin on his knuckle, cigar between his thin lips. Acting as if he were about to watch a game of croquet, rather than a battle to the death.

I just wish I knew what he did to be as confident in this reenactment of Sparta's battle against Xerxes as he is. Even with two hundred extra Spartans . . .

Glints of the attacking creatures appeared through the haze, descending on the task force like a living hell. Deafening screeches closed in.

She wiped the grit away from her eyes and blinked, attempting to improve her vision.

Suddenly, eight thick laser beams shot from the cockpit roof of every C-130 and swept the ground beyond the supersoldiers. The shots cut down hundreds of monsters, but their advance continued unabated. Where creatures fell, other dark figures appeared in their place. A seemingly endless supply.

To her front, dozens of razor-sharp tails lashed down simultaneously toward every soldier. The collective action created a chilling *whoosh*, signaling that the battle had commenced in earnest.

Immediately, every supersoldier in Van Ness' army sprang into action, moving at incredible speed, and Bowcut blinked once more, unsure of what she was seeing. In a flash, they had repositioned themselves to deal with each individual creature. It all seemed so absurd—posturing for the sake of posturing so that their deaths would look more impressive. But nobody from the Foundation betrayed that kind of body language. Roux stood tall, alert. Van Ness sat, smoking, eyes twinkling with excitement.

And the supersoldiers . . .

Soldiers snagged tails in their thick-gloved hands, stopping engaged creatures' momentum dead. In an instant, they rammed the serrated tips through scaly black chests, turning the creatures' own strength against them. Just like in the lab, but this time en masse.

Then the soldiers moved on to the next creature. And the next. And the next. All while seemingly dancing between the lashing tails of the creatures they had yet to deal with. It looked preternatural to her, like they had some sort of innate sense of where the attack would come from and where to move before a blow was landed.

The spectacle was mesmerizing.

Viciously beautiful.

Pools of yellow blood spilled across the concrete as the initial monstrosities fell. Shrieks turned to gurgled screams. Writhing black bodies piled around the defensive ring. Not a single creature was breaking through the line.

And the four of them hadn't even fired a single shot.

Bowcut took a moment to scan the runway. For the first time, she dared to wonder if the creatures' attack methods were somehow predictable. She knew they had many different forms of attack, but the soldiers efficiently dealt with assaults from tails, teeth, and claws in an equally detached, efficient way. Again and again. Moving faster to combat every move.

They were outmaneuvering and outthinking the enemy.

However, the main body of creatures was still coming. She couldn't see them through the thick haze, but she could feel them coming and could certainly hear them. The shaking ground and deafening noise told her that. The force had dealt with only the very first to arrive. The vanguard. Thousands more were about to join the fray. This would surely put Van Ness' amazing military specimens to the test.

As the final thought crossed her mind, one of the soldiers collapsed, fast and hard. His back slammed against the ground only a stone's throw from her position. A creature had its teeth clamped around his neck, its claws sunk into the sides of his head. With his dying breath, the soldier punched at a wound on the creature's black torso. His fist rammed inside the creature's chest cavity, ripping out its still-beating heart. Slimy blood oozed down the soldier's forearm and the creature collapsed on top of him.

Bowcut aimed down at the carcass. Munoz and the Caffertys did, too.

Before any of them could shoot, Roux calmly stepped across and fired a laser through both bodies, slicing them in two. He then returned to the inner edge of the soldiers and barked orders. They inched back, tightening their defensive formation to close the gap while continuing the fight.

Another creature bounded to the top of the black corpses and tried to vault over the defenders toward Van Ness. A single soldier jumped up to meet it, grabbed its leg, and dragged it down. The creature's body hammered against the runway. Before it could move an inch, the soldier gripped both sides of its head and spun it 360 degrees.

The deafening screeches that had swamped the immediate area gradually reduced to snarls. The initial fight against the creatures seemed to have had an effect.

And it had all happened in seconds.

Now, the creatures no longer purposefully charged forward.

This provided only slight relief, though the situation was still perilous. It would take only one section of the ring to fall for the creatures to reach the planes. And the engineers were still filling the first four.

What happens when the creatures come all at once? Why does Van Ness not bring out reinforcements? And if not him, why not Roux? Surely a military man of his experience knows they'd have a better chance with more men.

But maybe that wasn't true . . .

Sarah's experience as SWAT had shown that a tight, elite group—one that had each other's back and trained ceaselessly to avoid mistakes—could be just as powerful as a large, unorganized opponent. She'd raided drug dens where there were way more guns against her, and never once did she doubt that she and her team would win.

So why do I doubt now?

Because with my team, I know I can trust every person around me.

These supersoldiers—they were strangers to her. She hadn't seen them train, still didn't know what they were truly capable of doing.

The approaching mass of creatures slowed, cautiously stalking around the supersoldiers as if looking for the weakest point, weighing their options against a previously unknown opponent.

She wasn't the only one who didn't know what to expect from the supersoldiers.

They remained facing outward, toward the creatures. Focused on anything that came their way. Chests heaving, but perhaps not as much as she might have thought, considering their exertions. Uniforms drenched in creature blood. Bowcut reckoned they had killed at least three hundred of the monsters, perhaps more. It was impossible to say because of the poor visibility and the tangled pile of black bodies surrounding the formation, melding into a single mass.

This pause in action threw her. She'd never seen the creatures shy away from an attack.

Maybe it's the first time the creatures have encountered overwhelming resistance. A force to be reckoned with.

"Why have they stopped?" Diego asked, echoing her thoughts.

Van Ness glanced across to the team. "Because they're smart."

"Meaning what?"

"They don't understand what they are facing," Roux said. "They are trying to figure it out, calculate any weaknesses we might have."

"Of course, they won't find any," Van Ness quipped. "But I don't think they are simply assessing us. I believe they are waiting for reinforcements. Surely you don't believe there are not many, *many* more creatures headed this way?"

"So we just wait?" Bowcut shouted.

"No."

"Then what?"

Van Ness shook his head, enjoying her exasperation, and returned his focus to the defensive ring. He nodded to Roux, who in turn shouted out an order.

The supersoldiers drew lasers from their thigh holsters. Each one aimed into the haze and fired. Hundreds of red-hot beams speared through the dusty air—extended shots that all swept from left to right, up and down—carving through the creatures.

Screeches engulfed the base again.

Several creatures raced forward, seemingly more out of desperation than any coordinated move. Every one of them fell before reaching the supersoldiers, lanced by the searing shots.

But one creature leaped over the ring of soldiers and bounded straight at Cafferty. He frantically swung his laser in its direction, as it raised its claws to tear him apart. Bowcut could see the weapon would not discharge in time to stop the attack.

"Tom!" Ellen shouted out.

Suddenly, a supersoldier put both his fists through the creature's body and slammed it backward, away from Cafferty, a split second before it took his life. The creature wriggled in agony on the ground as the life quickly drained from its body. The soldier—just as quickly as it had saved Cafferty—moved back to his place in the line, once more indistinguishable from his brethren.

Cafferty looked visibly shaken by the close encounter. Bowcut swung to look at Van Ness, who had watched the entire scene with amusement on his face.

"That was awfully close," Van Ness finally said. "Wasn't it, Thomas?"

That son of a bitch, Bowcut thought. But she wasn't sure if she was thinking of Van Ness or the supersoldier at the moment.

The main body of creatures stalled their attack once more. They could not break through the line, no matter what tactic they tried. They slowly withdrew, hissing at their failure, and backed away toward the distant neighborhood. They were still close, but the lightning assault had lost all momentum. The Caffertys and Munoz appeared lost for words. Bowcut attempted to understand what she'd just witnessed.

Five hundred—no, 499 supersoldiers, rebuffing an assault. Aboveground. Against thousands. First unarmed, then with lasers. The result was undeniable.

But against millions? We're still only a force of five thousand.

Every minute the planes refueled felt like hours. After some time had passed, one of the Foundation team members sprinted over to Van Ness and informed him that the planes had sufficient fuel to reach San Diego.

Bowcut didn't look back at the planes. She'd heard the pumps working until the creatures had drowned out their low, rhythmic hums. All she wanted right now was to board and get the hell out of here. A much larger and more ferocious attack could come at any second, and she hadn't seen enough yet to convince her that being over-whelmed wasn't still a distinct possibility.

Van Ness wheeled over to the group. "My friends, don't think we've got the upper hand for a second. We can't stay in Lima to finish this fight. It'll allow them to learn from us."

"Good with me," Munoz replied, then pointed toward the flattened fence, still shrouded by the orange haze. "But I don't see any of these mother-fuckers reaching San Fran before we do."

"You of all people must know they have a vast communications network that we still do not under-stand, Mr. Munoz," Van Ness replied. "I suspect our element of surprise in San Francisco died when we crossed swords with their southern forces."

"When we try to take off, what's to keep them from tearing the planes to pieces before we hit the air?" Bowcut asked.

"The soldiers from our vessel will stay here to ensure our smooth departure," Van Ness replied.

Cafferty stepped toward the wheelchair. "Don't we need them for California? For this supposed queen?"

"The majority is still coming with us. But these will stay here to expand my foothold in South America—"

"*Your* foothold?" Ellen snapped.

Van Ness gave her a wolfish smile. "Our foothold, my dear. Our foothold."

Ellen and Tom looked at each other then back to Van Ness. Bowcut knew what they were thinking, but if it saved humanity, the time to deal with Van Ness' ambitions would come later.

Van Ness wouldn't be the first in history, and probably not the last, to try to exploit war and societal unrest for his own gain.

The C-130s' engines roared to a louder pitch as their propellers spun to a blur. Every plane turned in the tight defensive circle, and the pilots skillfully lined them up on the runway for takeoff.

The creatures remained distant.

Sweat poured down Bowcut's forehead. She gulped in the stale air while searching for any signs of attack. From here, she expected the creatures to fall silent at any moment. Their telekinesis was a typical strategy deployed from afar. She briefly wondered if their collective power could pull a plane from the sky, or if the supersoldiers were immune, or if the creatures could drag everyone from inside the line to their deaths.

The last idea made her shudder. She pushed that thought to the back of her mind as she scanned the ground in front of the defensive ring.

A minute passed and still nothing came.

"Let's load up," a voice yelled from the runway.

Van Ness spun his wheelchair toward the back of the first C-130. "Ladies and gentlemen, while this has been a lovely layover, I'm afraid we have to continue on our journey. If you'd care to join me?"

Tom, Ellen, and Diego didn't need a second invitation. All followed.

Bowcut hung back for a second. She considered how to say good-bye to Roux as he headed over. Flecks of creature blood had spattered on his face and shirt. He appeared cool and composed, completely in command of the situation as he purposefully strode toward her.

"Impressed?" he asked.

"Are you kidding me?" she said. "That was incredible. But you'll be under attack again in no time."

"I'm coming with you all," he said.

"You're not staying to command?" Bowcut asked.

"Of course not," he replied, as if it were the most natural thing in the world—he must have learned that from his boss. "The supersoldiers know their mission. They won't need my command to execute it."

Roux's statement haunted her.

If *we win the day* . . .

If *we stop these creatures* . . .

Who's going to stop these supersoldiers?

"Stand by," one of Roux's cohorts yelled. Hundreds of black figures rocketed through the haze toward the defensive ring.

No, not hundreds. Thousands. From all directions. Heading straight for the runway toward the departing planes.

The supersoldiers quickly lined the runway and took up hunched positions, preparing to fight once again.

"Time to go," Roux said.

Both jogged toward the back of the C-130, ascended the ramp, and entered the body of the now empty cargo hold. The ramp immediately swung shut with a mechanical grind.

Seconds later, the plane jerked forward, picking up speed as it raced along the runway.

Bowcut glanced out the window. A seemingly endless swarm of creatures frantically attacked the supersoldiers, trying desperately to get to the planes.

It was no use.

The supersoldiers dispatched every one in a similar fashion, snapping creatures' necks, impaling them with their own serrated tails, slicing them to pieces with lasers. The creatures were fast. The soldiers were faster.

Tom, Ellen, and Diego had strapped themselves in the seats at the front of the plane. The edge of Van Ness' wheelchair was visible in the cockpit, between the two pilots. A sense of relief washed over her as she headed toward her team. Events had been hard, if not impossible, to process, but they had survived.

The plane's nose rose and they took to the sky, on their way to San Diego to meet the USS *Nimitz*. Bowcut continued to peer out the window at the battle raging below.

The lines of supersoldiers remained in position on the runway, surrounded by a huge black mass. The creatures' numbers grew by the second as more raced to join the fight. Before she could see if the supersoldiers were capable of holding out against what now appeared like impossible odds, the C-130 entered the clouds, shrouding the air base from view.

Bowcut let out a deep breath and crouched against the wall.

Was it relief she felt? She wasn't so sure.

Maybe it was the disappointment of not being able to see how the battle played out below.

CHAPTER TWENTY-TWO

Karen lay supine on a sleeping bag, hands behind her head, staring upward at the tent's pitched canvas ceiling. The flaps were partially open to let in the cool breeze coming off the coast. Natural light was fading, though she was no longer scared of the dark. This island provided enough comfort to sleep because of these creature-free hours. Regardless, she'd tossed and turned without managing to drop off for more than a few minutes. Events continued to stay indelibly forged in her mind like a mental manacle.

Danny. Dead. Butchered.

Possibly all of our families.

By creatures that rose from the deep.

The more time she had to think about the monsters, the more her current situation staggered her. Karen puffed her cheeks. The life she knew merely two days ago was long gone and would never ever return. The enormity of that fact had finally forced its way through her numbness. Only now did she finally accept the cold reality. She didn't have any other choice.

Joey slept soundly by her side. His face looked so pure and innocent, showing no visible scars from the last twenty-four hours. At least for now, he was safe. She wasn't sure what the future would bring— for his physical well-being or his mental health— but she would take this image for as long as fate willed it. He, at least, was a touch of beauty in the now ugly world.

Footsteps approached outside.

She tensed.

A woman around Karen's age, dressed in a track-suit and with short peroxide-blond hair, crouched in front of the entrance.

"Can I help you?" Karen asked.

"Sorry. Didn't know if you were asleep. Jim said I'd find you here."

"You're from the next tent over?"

"Yep. I'm Stacy, and this is . . ." She waved an encouraging hand to her left. A little girl, maybe a year older than her son, stepped across and shyly peered inside. "Taylor. We were lucky enough to get here yesterday, which is more than I can say for you."

"Tell me about it." Karen groaned to a sitting position. "We were—"

"I know you've been through a lot, and there's no need to explain. All we can do is make the best of it here until help arrives."

"So help is coming?"

"I meant if, not when. Who knows what's going on out there."

Karen gave a solemn nod in acknowledgment. All she knew was that this wasn't confined to California, but Joey and she remained alive. That was good enough for now. Good enough for the foreseeable future if they could stay out of the creatures' path of destruction.

The quiet conversation must've disturbed Joey. He rolled toward her and stared at the woman and her daughter. "Mommy, are these our friends?"

"Of course. Meet Stacy and Taylor."

"A pleasure to meet you, Joey," Stacy said.

Joey shook both their hands. His politeness, even after everything they'd been through, made Karen proud.

"Lemme guess, you're thirty-eight years old?" Stacy continued.

Joey let out a huge laugh.

"I'm four!" he shouted.

"Ahh, I knew you were either thirty-eight or four."

The grin on Joey's face made Karen well up with tears. His laughter was the best thing she'd heard in a long time.

The sound of an approaching chopper, thudding through the darkened sky, cut through that laugh, catching both Stacy's and Karen's attention. It slowly lowered and landed near the hundreds of tents. The side door rumbled open.

Two of the crew, dressed in olive coveralls, carried a stretcher out. A woman lay on it, a bloodstained bandage tightly wrapped around her right leg. Then another stretcher was carried out holding a man. His arm had been cut off at biceps level. A leather belt was wrapped just below his armpit, acting as a makeshift tourniquet.

Karen's instincts kicked in. She guessed the crew had run out of supplies or perhaps didn't have the training to realize that the belt wouldn't be effective enough to stem the flow of blood.

"Do you mind keeping an eye on Joey?" she asked Stacy.

"Sure, where are you going?"

"I'm a paramedic."

"Go for it. Your son is safe here."

Karen turned her attention to her son. "Baby, Mommy's gonna go help those people, okay? I'll be back in no time."

Joey nodded, understanding.

"We've got some toys in our tent," Stacy said to the boy. "Wanna go play?"

Joey scrambled to his knees and crawled toward the entrance. Taylor led her son into the neighboring tent.

"Taylor's good with other kids," Stacy said. "He'll be fine."

"Thank you."

Karen headed quickly in the direction of the helicopter. The crew carried the two stretchers past the admin tent, toward a road that ran the length of the island. Karen glanced down at the tents. Part of her didn't want to leave her son after what they'd been through. But she had to trust Stacy. There weren't enough people left in the world to start getting paranoid, especially as her assistance might help some survive.

We all have to help each other. If nothing else, that's what makes us human.

Karen rushed over to the road as both of the injured were loaded onto the back of a flatbed truck. Now closer, she stared at the injuries, trying to ascertain which one needed treating first. Both the man and woman were conscious, pale faced, eyes full of terror. The woman had no visible wounds apart from the single bandage, though she looked like she had gone into shock.

"Can I help you?" one of the crew asked, a serious-faced man with the stress of the situation etched all over his face.

"I can help *you*," Karen said authoritatively. "I'm a paramedic. Where are you taking them?"

He pointed toward a grim-looking warehouse nearby. "We've set up a field hospital right there. Listen, we need to head straight back out. There're a few more people holding out in the same place as these two. Hopefully we reach them in time."

"No problem," Karen responded.

"The driver knows where he's going. Are you good?"

"I've got this."

The four crew members jumped off the flatbed and sprinted back to the chopper.

The truck's engine growled and it steadily made its way along the road.

Karen crouched between the two stretchers. The man's tourniquet gave her the greatest concern. Blood still seeped from the bandage, and the leather belt likely wasn't wide or tight enough to effectively stem the flow. She could change it now or wait for the short journey to the field hospital.

Experience told her that she had to act now. Every second was crucial in order to stop this man from bleeding out. She flipped open a green plastic box at the back of the truck. It contained basic medical supplies, including, crucially, a bandage and a pair of scissors.

Karen leaned over the man. He was in his forties, with salt-and-pepper stubble and a shaven head. Blood stained his pink polo shirt and cream shorts. Claws had gouged chunks of skin from his legs.

The man stared up at her. "How's it going?" he asked.

Karen smiled at him. She guessed the attempt to sound casual was for his own benefit as well as hers. He was probably relieved to have reached relative safety but scared shitless because of his missing arm and the consequences of his injuries.

"Hi, I'm Karen, a paramedic. I need to apply a new tourniquet; we've gotta whip you into shape here."

"Lemme guess, it's gonna hurt?"

She smiled again at him.

"Do your worst," he blustered.

Karen unwrapped the bandage and folded it to the proper width. The man hissed through gritted teeth as she raised his stump and wrapped the bandage in the space above the belt. Once snug, she attached the scissors as a windlass and started to tighten.

The man's eyes squeezed shut, and he let out several gasps.

Going slow wasn't an option. She had no morphine.

Karen grabbed another wrapped bandage and placed it close to his mouth. "Bite down on this. It won't take long."

The man crushed his teeth around the wrapper.

She twisted, harder and harder, until she couldn't turn the scissors anymore, then tied off the bandage and released the leather belt.

That would do for now.

The man's face finally relaxed.

"I thought you said that was gonna hurt," he said, fighting back tears.

"See? You got this," Karen replied, winking at him.

Karen turned her attention to the woman and elevated her legs while reassuring her that she was safe and that treatment was coming. Her words seemingly mostly fell on deaf ears as the woman simply stared skyward.

Her reaction was understandable.

The truck turned off the road and headed toward a huge set of open roller doors. Karen sharply inhaled at the sight beyond.

Rows and rows of camp beds filled up the large, brightly lit interior space. Hundreds of injured lay in various states of distress, with too few doctors helping. It looked like a scene from a World War I photograph. She thought they likely had more supplies back then compared with the situation in front of her now.

The truck hissed to a halt.

A uniformed officer looked up from a chart. He placed it on a desk and headed straight over. "What've we got?"

"I haven't had much time with them. One possibly going into shock. Another missing an arm with laceration on his legs."

"Okay, let's get them to triage." The officer looked down at the tourniquet. "Your work?"

"Did it on the truck coming over. I'm a paramedic, name's Karen. Arrived a couple of hours ago with my son."

He nodded. "We're shorthanded around here. I'm Scott Kohler, the camp commander."

"And doctor?"

"Not quite, but we're all wearing several hats these days. I'm glad you're here. Let's take the man first."

Karen jumped off the flatbed. She and Kohler slid the first stretcher off the truck. He took the lead and headed over to a room at the side of the warehouse. Two more of his team rushed over and grabbed the woman on the other stretcher.

Focused on her patients, it was easy to forget there were creatures out there. She had a job to do, and she put her all into it, happy for the opportunity to forget the monsters for a while.

CHAPTER TWENTY-THREE

The engines of the C-130 lowered in pitch as the plane descended toward the Naval Air Station North Island in San Diego harbor. Cafferty looked out the plane window at the small military base, which was nestled in the bay directly across from San Diego International Airport and the Gaslamp Quarter. The island was mercifully protected from the creatures' mainland onslaught by over two miles of water. Two massive aircraft carriers were docked at the east side of the island. One, Cafferty assumed, was the USS *Nimitz*, ready to depart for San Francisco with the supersoldiers once they landed.

The bridge that connected North Island to the mainland had been destroyed at its center, protecting the military base from the carnage unfolding nearby. To the south of the island, a thin sliver of land that connected another road to the air station was also no longer usable for the creatures. Cafferty guessed the armed forces must've used a bunker buster–type bomb to create a huge crater that flooded the access road with seawater.

Like Roux had said during the meeting with Brogan, the island had been completely cut off by protective measures and appeared safe.

But for how long? Creatures had no problem tunneling underneath the Hudson River. It'll only be a matter of time before they take the island too.

Cafferty looked across the bay to smoldering San Diego. The city was one of the last big American cities attacked, hours after the others had already fallen. This gave the U.S. military the critical time it needed to move as many soldiers and as much equipment as possible to the naval air station before severing it from the mainland.

Flames ripped through the city in the distance. There was no telling how many people were dead or dying in the city. What's worse was not knowing how many people might still be alive, in hiding, praying for help that may never reach them in time. Boats still packed the marina between the island and the city, but all remained motionless in the bay. If anyone had tried to escape by boat, they clearly never made it to the marina.

Rows of helicopters, fighter jets, armored vehicles, and soldiers lined the runways at the air station, armed and ready for Van Ness' planes to land.

"Looks like the navy is ready to give you a warm American welcome, Van Ness," Cafferty quipped, staring down at the scene below.

"Yeah, I think if you fart the wrong way, they'll shoot you on the spot," Diego added.

"Quite eloquent, Mr. Munoz," Van Ness replied, bristling at the crudeness of the man. "Their welcome is irrelevant. My mission is all that matters. Besides, actions speak louder than words. Your armed forces will soon witness what you've learned in Lima. My supersoldiers will not rest until these creatures are destroyed. Roux and I will make sure of it."

The pilots gained final clearance to land and approached the runway.

Cafferty glanced at his wife, who was still sound asleep, resting on his shoulder. His entire team looked physically and emotionally drained. The next twenty-four hours would decide humanity's fate. And his. This thought had kept Cafferty firmly awake.

Cafferty turned to Bowcut and whispered to her out of range of Van Ness. "This Franco Roux . . ." he said.

Bowcut looked at him. "Yes?"

"Do you trust him?"

Bowcut thought before she answered. "You know . . . for some reason I do. You know I trust my gut, Tom. And it says he wants what we want. Give him a chance."

Cafferty, too, had learned to trust Bowcut's gut. It never steered the team wrong. That was her years on the job as an NYPD cop. She had the best read of character he'd ever met.

The C-130's wheels screeched against the runway. The bump jolted Ellen awake, and she looked directly at Tom, expressionless. He guessed she was still thinking of his deal with Van Ness and the potential consequences. Regardless, he wasn't going to change his mind now that the task force was only an aircraft carrier ride away from launching its counterattack. The supersoldiers were needed, and he was the grease that was keeping that particular wheel turning.

Cafferty gave her a resigned nod.

The pilots gradually slowed the plane and turned from the runway. As they moved between the stagger of armored vehicles, the next C-130 landed. The other eight approached in a direct line, perfectly coordinated, just like the loading process in Antarctica, the robust defensive ring in Lima, and seemingly everything else Van Ness did.

On top of the smaller armed vehicles, soldiers peered through the sights of heavy machine guns. Cafferty wondered what was going through their minds. He, at least, had fought the creatures up close before. He had also witnessed the Foundation's genetic experiments in Van Ness' underground lair in Paris. Even armed with that knowledge, he'd still found the existence of supersoldiers a stunning revelation. The U.S. military was coming into this with briefings instead of experience.

The plane juddered to an abrupt halt in front of a large open hangar. Two officers in sand-colored uniforms stood at the entrance. Twenty marines surrounded them in a semicircle with their M27s shouldered, aimed at the aircraft.

"Will the supersoldiers perceive this as a threat?" Bowcut asked, concerned.

"*I* perceive this as a threat," Munoz muttered.

"They cannot harm another human being," Roux answered.

Cafferty spun to face Van Ness. "What happens if one of your supersoldiers *forgets* that?"

"My supersoldiers follow every order," Van Ness replied.

"That doesn't answer my question," Cafferty said.

"It's an irrelevant query. There have been no lapses in this version."

"Were there before?"

The tailgate of the C-130 lowered and light poured into the plane.

"We don't want to keep your officers waiting," Van Ness said. He unclipped his chair from the cockpit wall and rotated it toward the rear of the plane. "If you and your team would like to follow me, Thomas."

If I were being honest, I'd prefer to throw you into the bay and see how you fare.

But he said nothing as Van Ness eased the control lever on his chair forward and powered away. Cafferty followed, along with the rest of the team, who groaned from their seats. The group walked down the tailgate into the cool air and headed for the hangar.

Both navy officers had neutral expressions, cool and collected. One older, who had graying hair beneath his cap; the other around forty years old, stocky, clean-shaven, and square jawed. The type of person who wouldn't appear out of place in a UFC octagon.

Van Ness stopped a few yards short of the men. Cafferty did likewise. The marines' rifles, aimed in their direction, made Cafferty's heart hammer a little faster, even though he realized they wouldn't shoot unless Van Ness or his army did something to provoke them.

"Thomas Cafferty and Albert Van Ness?" the older man asked.

Cafferty nodded. "That's us."

"I'm Captain Paul Collingwood, commander of the USS *Nimitz*. This is my XO, Captain Nick Vasquez."

"A pleasure, gentlemen," Van Ness said. "This is my head of combat strategy, Franco Roux."

Roux nodded at the officers.

"Has President Brogan relayed our success in Lima?" Van Ness asked.

"She has," Collingwood replied.

"And has she conveyed your orders, Captain?"

"We're transporting five thousand of your soldiers to San Francisco on the *Nimitz* and launching a counterattack from there," Captain Collingwood replied.

"Four thousand five hundred, to be exact. And how many U.S. carrier strike groups will be joining us?" Van Ness asked.

"By the time we reach San Francisco, we will have seven carrier strike groups at our disposal, with a total of seven aircraft carriers, seven cruisers, fourteen destroyers, five hundred and twenty-five aircraft, thirty-seven submarines, and nearly a hundred amphibious assault boats."

Van Ness glanced away, lost in thought for a moment.

"Hmm. That should be enough for my plans," he finally replied.

"Enough?" Captain Collingwood asked. "That'll be the most powerful armada ever assembled in history."

"Precisely what we need to win the greatest battle of all time, Captain," Van Ness said.

The XO studied the planes' fleet as the next C-130 landed. "How much of a danger are these 'supersoldiers' to our crew?"

"None whatsoever," Roux interjected. "The soldiers are simply not capable of harming a human being. It's literally hardwired into their DNA."

"Uh-huh," the XO replied, unconvinced. "And what are their capabilities?"

"They are a tool at your disposal, Captain, and will listen to your every command," Van Ness added. "They are no different from a machine gun in the hands of your crew, except far, far more effective. Use them as you wish to protect your fleet from these creatures. But I might suggest you discuss tactics with Roux, as he knows their capabilities better than anyone."

The captain nodded. "We'll lower them on the aircraft elevators to the main deck. There's enough room for our marines to guard them. I must warn you: my orders are shoot to kill at the first signs of danger that these supersoldiers present."

Shoot to kill?

The U.S. military doesn't stand a chance against these supersoldiers anyway, Cafferty thought. *I wonder if bullets would even hurt them.*

"Understood," Van Ness said, checking his watch. "We should set sail quickly, Captain."

"Let me be very clear, Mr. Van Ness," Collingwood said sternly. "I don't trust you. You are a terrorist and a convicted murderer, and it is only out of presidential order and necessity that you are on my ship right now and not rotting in your cell for the rest of your life."

"What is your point, Captain?" Van Ness asked.

"My point is this: if you so much as blink the wrong way, I will personally put a bullet through your head. Clear?"

"Quite," Van Ness replied, smirking at the man.

"Now, board your soldiers onto the *Nimitz*," the captain replied. "Cafferty, you've seen these things in action. Do we have a chance?"

"We do," Cafferty admitted. "And the faster we move the better."

The group turned and watched the rest of the C-130s land, one after another. On command, the planes' tailgates lowered simultaneously, revealing the thousands of supersoldiers inside.

Led by Foundation members, each of the squads emerged from the planes in perfect unison. Boots thumped the runway until all the supersoldiers lined up together in four perfectly straight ranks. They stopped in sync and stared straight ahead at the aircraft carrier. None moved. None blinked. None flinched at the sight of the U.S. military's weapons aiming down on them. The supersoldiers were focused, expressionless.

Soulless, Cafferty thought.

It was as if the thousands of soldiers moved and

acted as one, perfectly choreographed, perfectly dis-
ciplined. No individuality whatsoever. They looked
human, but not quite. Because that was true—there
was part of them that was creature.

And that's what made them so goddamn scary.

As he got a closer look at the spectacle unfolding
in front of them, the XO's mouth dropped open.
"Wh-what the hell?" he stammered. "They all
look . . . the same."

The captain shook his head in disbelief at what
he was witnessing. He turned to Roux. "They all
look like *you*."

"They are clones," Roux replied.

"I gotta say, I've seen some crazy shit in my time,
but this one takes the goddamn cake."

But the XO had his orders and nodded toward
one of the marines, who in turn raised his handheld
radio.

Moments later, two light tactical vehicles at
the front of the supersoldier ranks powered forward at a slow pace, leading the army toward
the *Nimitz*. People peered through the windows
of the administration buildings, in shock at the
sight of the supersoldiers marching by.

As they approached the aircraft carrier, Cafferty
was taken aback by its sheer size. A huge gray hulk,
bristling with weapons and packed with fighter jets.
He guessed it was also armed to the teeth, with
enough missiles to surgically clear any area for an
amphibious landing.

Just as the supersoldiers began marching onto
the *Nimitz* gangway, a siren split the air, piercing,
long, and loud.

The captain stopped, rigid. His head snapped toward the distant city. A marine quickly approached, fear in his eyes.

"Sir, the creatures are moving en masse toward the marina, directly across the bay from us."

"As expected," Van Ness interjected. "They know my supersoldiers are here."

"What do you mean?" Captain Collingwood asked, surprised. "How the hell do they know you're here?"

"You are not fighting mindless creatures," Van Ness said. "Rest assured, they are smarter than you, Captain."

Collingwood looked irate at the dig.

"They will do everything in their power to stop us from reaching our target," Van Ness continued.

"But we're cut off from the mainland," Collingwood replied. "Surely this base is safe."

"For now. But rest assured, Captain—they *will* find a way to cross that bay. And they will find a way to slaughter all your men. So . . . may I suggest you follow your orders and we leave?"

CHAPTER TWENTY-FOUR

Justin Knapp leaned against the heavily barricaded door of the Sheraton San Diego Hotel's subbasement, along with a few dozen other hotel guests. Time seemed to be standing still down here, but they hadn't dared leave this relative safety after what they had witnessed. That would have to change because of their diminished supplies. And now a distant siren was blaring.

It spooked everyone into action.

He thought back to a few days earlier, when the world had been so very different. He had been working on his boat in the marina only a few hundred yards away from the Sheraton. He'd saved for three years for the boat, a Yamaha SX195. Compared with the mega-yachts in San Diego harbor, his humble, previously owned nineteen-footer wasn't much, but it sure wasn't bad on a mechanic's salary.

Hands full of grease and headfirst in the engine, he'd heard a few people shouting on the dock. He'd lifted his head to see what the fuss was all about. A few fellow boat owners went running toward the hotel. He scanned the rest of the marina and saw more commotion. Some people ran back toward their cars, some onto their boats and sped off quickly.

What the hell is going on?

He shouted to a nearby mariner, and the only reply he got was *"You gotta see this!"*

Curiosity got the better of him. And since he had just put the finishing touches on the engine anyway, Justin sealed the panels back up, wiped the grease off his hands, and followed other boaters toward the hotel.

When he entered the lobby, there were hundreds of people—hotel guests, employees, and fellow boaters—crowded around, watching the massive projection screen on the wall. His mouth dropped open at the sight on the local news. All he could mutter to the guy next to him was *"Is this for real?"*

Terrifying creatures stormed the streets of Chicago, Atlanta, San Francisco, and more. He could not believe what the news was reporting. Then the blast of an air-raid siren outside filled the air. Simultaneously, the TV network went dead, as did all the power in the Sheraton.

Within minutes, the creatures had reached the hotel and marina. He would never forget the sounds of their deafening screeches and of hundreds of people dying. Anyone outside the hotel got slaughtered. Most inside as well. In the panic, he followed a frantic hotel employee down the stairwell into a mechanical room subbasement and barricaded himself inside, along with thirty or so other strangers.

They stayed there in complete darkness and absolute silence for hours as the monstrosities tore apart the hotel above their heads floor by floor. By sheer luck, the creatures never discovered their hiding spot. Eventually, the horrifying combined sounds of screaming and screeching faded and hours passed by in silence.

That was two days ago.

The group had agreed on a plan. Since a dozen of them owned boats in the harbor, along with Justin, everyone would make a break for the dock and take off as fast as possible. They divided up who would go on what boats. Justin would take two hotel guests with him, Tim and Patricia, a young husband and wife on their honeymoon, both tanned with blond hair. Appearances made no difference right now. The rest of the hotel guests were partnered up with the other boat owners.

Once out to sea, they would head toward the two aircraft carriers in San Diego Bay—if anyone could help them, it would be the U.S. military.

Get to the boats, get to the help.

And pray to God those creatures can't swim . . .

As silently as possible, they removed the assortment of junk they had piled against the subbasement door and crept up the stairwell.

Justin nearly gagged when he entered the lobby of the hotel. It looked like a bomb had gone off. Mangled and twisted bodies littered the floor, pools of blood so thick the liquid had not yet dried, even after two days. It was a slaughterhouse, and the stench of decay overwhelmed his senses.

But no creatures in sight.

Justin stepped over dozens of severed limbs, cutting a path to the shattered glass entrance. The group followed and exited the hotel.

Outside, the scene was as gruesome. There appeared no escape from the carnage.

Stay focused.

Get to the boats, get somewhere—anywhere—else.

The marina was only a few hundred yards ahead. If they moved quickly, they'd be out to sea in under ten minutes.

Justin looked ahead at the docks. Thousands of boats still packed the west and east marinas. Many of them were sprayed with the blood of whatever occupants were on board when the creatures struck. He looked farther across the bay, and a wave of relief overwhelmed him.

At the North Island military base, the two aircraft carriers were still docked. And the *Nimitz* had thousands of people on the top deck, like they were preparing to mount an attack.

Thank God . . .

The wail of the siren was a lot louder once outside. The same one that had gone off two days earlier, moments before the creatures attacked.

Justin peered back toward the mainland of San Diego. In the distance, hundreds, no thousands of creatures sped toward the marina at incredible speed.

"Get to the boats!" he screamed.

The group sprinted toward the dock. His heart pounded in his chest as the horrifying screeches grew closer and closer by the second.

He estimated he'd have two minutes at best to free his boat and start the engine. He went through a mental checklist of what to do, what buttons to press.

Justin leaped on board. Tim and Patricia followed. He untied the ropes from the dock as fast as his hands would move and screamed at them to push the boat away from shore.

He slammed down on the button to lower the engine into the water. It descended, but not fast enough.

The creatures' screams filled his ears.

The black mass closed to within a few hundred yards of the marina.

There's no time left . . .

Justin put the boat in neutral and turned the ignition key. He drove the accelerator forward, making the engine blades whir to life while still in the air. The moment the blades hit the water, he wanted to be moving.

The creatures reached the dock and bounded toward them.

"Come on, goddammit!" Justin yelled.

The motor hit the surface of the water, and the boat powered forward at full speed just as the creatures reached the edge of his dock.

They crouched on their hind legs, ready to jump. But didn't.

The boat had now cut through the choppy water to around forty yards clear. No way the creatures could make that jump now. And it seemed that they didn't swim.

Justin and the couple were safe. He turned back and looked for the other boats. All had pulled away from the dock just in time. Everyone who had been trapped with him in the Sheraton made it safely away.

Justin let out a long, deep breath.

The twelve boats rode alongside one another in the direction of North Island, toward the distant aircraft carriers. Spray battered the windshield. Wind ran through Justin's hair. Exhilaration replaced the terror. A sense of freedom rose through him. He screamed out loud with joy, releasing the tension of spending the past forty-eight hours in constant fear.

Suddenly, his body jerked forward from a rapid change in momentum.

"Fuck!" he exclaimed, catching his balance.

The boat began to slow down for some unknown reason. But the engine still roared. It better, considering all the work he had put into it to fix it a few days ago.

"Why are you slowing down?" Tim asked.

"I'm not," Justin replied, confused.

He looked at the other boats alongside him, baffled.

What the hell?

They, too, were slowing down, all in unison.

A man behind the wheel in a boat to their right threw Justin a look of equal confusion.

Justin slammed the throttle down to full speed. It had no effect. The boat slowed to a complete stop, like the engine wasn't even there.

All dozen boats now bobbed in the water.

Justin twisted in his seat and looked back toward the shoreline. Hundreds of creatures had formed into a massive circle by the side of the hotel.

What are they doing?

Without warning, all twelve boats jolted and reversed direction toward the marina, as if they were being yanked backward like a yo-yo by some unseen force.

Desperate, Justin threw the anchor overboard. It snagged on the ocean floor, but immediately ripped right off the bow of the ship from the tremendous force pulling his boat backward.

Two people in the craft to his right leaped from their boat into the warm waters of the bay. But both, despite desperately attempting to swim forward, were dragged back in the same direction.

Back toward the dock.

Back toward the creatures.

Back toward their certain deaths.

CHAPTER TWENTY-FIVE

Diego Munoz peered out from the cool, air-conditioned bridge of the USS *Nimitz*. On the flight deck, the final two hundred supersoldiers lowered on a massive elevator to the hangar below, under the guidance of Roux. Bowcut stood by his side, taking in the proceedings. However, it didn't matter how impressive any of this was. All eyes were transfixed on something else.

Munoz, like Bowcut, the Caffertys, and the entire bridge crew, stared across the bay toward San Diego in absolute horror.

First, the sight of thousands of creatures rushing toward the coastline. Then seeing those brave people run for their lives and successfully make it to sea. But now, this . . .

The civilians' boats were being dragged back to the shore.

Diego could only imagine the panic they were feeling at the moment, having no clue why they could not escape.

But he knew why.

Munoz crouched, ripped open his backpack, and fished out his binoculars. The creatures had formed into a tight group in Harbor Island Park, a thin strip of grassed land in front of the marina's yacht club.

They must be focusing their telekinetic power. He'd seen them do this before in the subway tunnels of New York City and underneath Paris, but never like this.

Stopping speedboats dead in the water? Have their powers grown that strong that quickly?

"Captain, every moment wasted, countless scores perish," Van Ness said, dismissive of the drama unfolding on the water. "May I suggest we get moving?"

"Get moving?" Cafferty interjected. "Captain, we have to help those people!"

The captain watched the slow-motion slaughter about to happen with a sickly look on his face. "Just how powerful is that force they are using, Van Ness?" the captain asked, weighing his options.

"Their telekinesis?" Van Ness asked. "It grows stronger by the day."

"I mean, can enough creatures use it to stop this aircraft carrier?"

"Know this, Captain—your ships are their real targets," Van Ness replied. "They are baiting us. Might I suggest we not tempt fate?"

"Captain," Cafferty implored, "we can save those people. If we stop fighting for every single life, we lose everything. This is a risk worth taking."

Munoz could hear the passion in Cafferty's voice. That's what Diego liked most about the former mayor. Cafferty still believed, even after everything their team had been through the past three years, that they could actually *win*, that they would come out on top, that they would save everyone. Cafferty still believed, still hoped that redemption was possible. In the darkest of times, in the moments when Munoz thought all was surely lost, it was Cafferty's unflinching belief that good would ultimately triumph that kept him going.

Van Ness grinned at Cafferty's childish optimism. "Save twelve, Captain, or save the world. I leave it to you."

Collingwood dropped his head down, considering his decision carefully.

"Captain, an unmanned boat is drifting toward us," a crewman interjected.

Collingwood peered through the windows of the bridge at the listless speedboat approaching the aircraft carrier with the current.

Suddenly, a creature burst from the lower deck of the abandoned ship and leaped onto the side of the *Nimitz*. It clawed its way up with lightning-fast speed onto the main deck of the ship.

A single supersoldier instantly followed its path.

Crew members scattered in terror at the sight of the creature. But the creature ignored them, bounded up the deck, and scaled right up the structure toward the bridge. It crashed through the side of the glass, bursting onto the bridge, just feet from the commanding officers.

Munoz drew in a sharp breath, in shock at the sight of the captain moments from death. Not only that, the creature had made easy work of the strong protective glass. Every time he saw them again, they appeared to have gained strength.

But before the monster could strike, the chasing supersoldier entered the bridge and crashed a fist down on the creature's head.

The creature collapsed.

The soldier grabbed its tail and drove the razor-sharp tip right through its own skull, impaling the creature onto a metal table. Its carcass instantly went limp.

Collingwood staggered back, face etched with fear and confusion. He took a moment to compose himself, then said to the crew, "We are leaving, right now."

Munoz glanced back toward the marina at the desperate people fighting for their lives. All twelve boats were being dragged back to shore. It looked as if the creatures had pulled a giant plug from the edge of the water. The people who dove into the bay were being dragged back, too—two dozen arms and legs uselessly trying to swim against a force they knew nothing about. Some threw their hands in the air, waving toward the *Nimitz* for help.

The creatures onshore stayed in their tight formation, focusing their collective power on the task at hand. Cold and callous. Waiting for most of their prey to reach them. It would only be a matter of minutes before the boats reached shore and the people were slaughtered.

Munoz let out a long, deep sigh. If they were not going to help these people, then at least he shouldn't waste the opportunity at hand: the opportunity to study the creatures' collective telekinetic power from a safe distance.

He slung off his pack and grabbed a mobile spectrum analyzer and a portable frequency scanner from inside. It was a long shot, but he might never have the chance again to scan all frequencies while the creatures used their power. What it might lead to, he had no idea. But these creatures must have the ability to communicate with each other over great distances. That's the only way they could have organized a worldwide attack of this scale.

If I can just figure out how these sons of bitches chat . . .

He turned his scanners on and studied the displays carefully. Munoz prayed the creatures stayed in position long enough for him to make a discovery. Anything to help turn the tide in humanity's favor. He'd seen how badass the supersoldiers were in Lima. But the millions of creatures meant they might need an extra edge—an edge that he could hopefully provide.

The *Nimitz*'s engines roared to life, sending vibrations through the entire ship. The massive aircraft carrier pulled away from North Island and headed in the direction of San Francisco. As the boat gained some distance from the shore, Captain Collingwood rested his hand on Cafferty's shoulder.

"We'll never lose everything, Tom," the captain said quietly. With that, he addressed his executive officer, Captain Vasquez. "Nick, do me a favor. Target that yacht club with a RAM missile, would you?"

Captain Vasquez grinned widely. "Yes, sir," he replied.

Munoz and Cafferty smiled as well. As the *Nimitz* sped away from San Diego harbor and toward their mission that would decide the fate of humanity, sometimes it was the little victories that mattered.

"Ready," Vasquez said.

"Fire!" Captain Collingwood exclaimed.

An RIM-116 Rolling Airframe Missile rocketed off the deck of the *Nimitz* at incredible velocity. Within a minute, at a speed of over Mach 2, it reached its target: the very spot the creatures huddled onshore, harnessing their telekinetic abilities.

The twenty-four-pound blast fragmentation warhead hit the yacht club with shocking destructive power, tearing the creatures to shreds.

Instantly, the telekinetic force that had been dragging the boats back to shore faltered. The ships broke free, and the civilians resumed their course safely away from San Diego.

But a moment before the telekinetic signal went dead (along with the creatures), Munoz's frequency tracking equipment picked up an unusual, massive blip.

Could that be it?

CHAPTER TWENTY-SIX

Darkness had enveloped the makeshift military base on Treasure Island in San Francisco Bay. But in this relative safety, Karen still received constant reminders of the terror unfolding on the mainland. Haunting shrieks echoed across the water from the devastated city. A few of the tall buildings burned bright, sending smoke belching into the star-studded sky.

She had taken a short break from the field hospital to check on Joey. He ignored the noise from the city while he raced around the outside of their tent playing with little Taylor. The oversized fleece jacket she'd found, protecting Joey from the cool night air, dangled over his hands and went down to his knees. Seeing the kids laughing and playing gave her hope they'd pull through this all right. He showed no outward signs of the intense stress they'd been under. Taylor sped after him with a flashlight. The two had quickly formed a friendship that put Karen's mind at ease.

She scanned their immediate surroundings now that night had set in.

Other flashlight beams speared around the camp and glowed inside of tents. Artificial light shone out of a few of the surrounding buildings lucky enough to have generators to provide power.

Thank God it's not winter.

A small mercy in the current disaster.

The deep thwacks of a helicopter grew louder in the sky.

Karen looked up.

The rescue chopper sailed over the edge of the island. It slowed to a hover and lowered next to the camp. The rotor wash rattled the closest tents. As soon as it landed, the side door slid open.

"We've got six more here," one of the crew bellowed. "Five for the hospital."

Dark figures raced from the awaiting truck to the side of the chopper. One of the triage nurses had been waiting with the ground team to provide any urgent assistance before the injured reached the field hospital.

The arrival spelled the end of her break. Joey was in safe hands. She could go back to being of wider use. During the last few hours, the crews had brought in dozens of survivors, mostly injured. Those with a clean bill of health still had to deal with the mental scars of their experiences.

Karen knelt and grabbed Joey in her arms as he ran around the tent one final time.

"What's up, Mommy?" he asked.

"I'm going back to help more sick people, baby. Be a good boy for a few hours."

"Don't worry about me. Taylor's going to tell me a story. And I'm gonna tell her all my jokes."

"That's my little man."

Joey raised his hand for a high five. Karen slapped her palm against his. With that, her son and Taylor disappeared inside the neighboring tent.

She grabbed a bike that Scott Kohler had given her and cycled back down the dark road toward the hospital. The headlights from the truck briefly lit her way until she got in range of the light shining out of the warehouse.

Karen pedaled in to the sounds of moans and groans, dropped the bike, and immediately went over to Scott. He was making notes next to a patient with bandages covering his arms.

"Back so soon?" he asked.

"We've got five more coming in."

"You look exhausted."

"Right back atcha, Scott."

He smiled.

Karen looked at the hundred-plus occupied beds with patients in various states of distress. Every cot was occupied—they'd run out of room earlier in the evening.

"I've got two staff checking if anyone is okay to take a chair," Scott said.

"Any takers yet?"

He shook his head. "A few, but I doubt it'll be enough."

The sound of the truck closed in on the warehouse. Raised voices could be heard over the hiss of the brakes. Two stretchers came in shortly after. The teams efficiently placed them on the ground by the front of the warehouse and returned outside.

"What have we got?" Scott asked the accompanying nurse.

Karen recognized the nurse as Emma, who also looked like she hadn't slept for days. The young, redheaded woman looked back at the two patients on stretchers, both with bloodstained bandages on their legs.

"These are the two priorities," Emma said. "Deep lacerations. Both have morphine. I'll deal with the others."

"Thank you." He turned to Karen. "You take the left."

Karen grabbed a tray of medical supplies and went over to her new patient, a middle-aged woman in a shredded cream trouser suit. She carefully raised the bandages around her calves, revealing a deep gash across both, probably from the swipe of a creature's tail. To call this lucky seemed wrong, despite the numerous decapitations she'd seen on the streets of San Francisco.

Nobody is lucky.

She looked into the woman's glazed eyes. "What's your name?"

"Betty," she answered groggily.

"You're gonna be okay, Betty," Karen said. "But I need to close your wounds."

Betty nodded and gripped the sides of the stretcher.

Karen administered local anesthetic to her legs and comforted her while waiting for the area to numb.

"Where are you from?" Karen asked.

"Oakland. Is my husband here?"

Karen glanced over to the nurse, who shook her head.

"Please, I need to know if my husband is here," Betty repeated.

"I promise you I'll check right after we've closed up your wounds."

Karen didn't know what else to do but conceal the sad truth. The woman had already lost a lot of blood and was about to get her legs stitched up. She'd learned from experience that she had to choose the right time to deliver news to a trauma patient. Now wasn't it. She snapped on a pair of latex gloves.

"This'll only take a couple of minutes," Karen said.

"Thank you," Betty said. "I've been through worse. I'll make it through."

The bravery and defiance of the people flowing into the field hospital had come as a surprise. A few arrived in a state of shock, though most had a stoicism and strength about them that filled her with pride.

Humanity was being obliterated, but the human spirit was not being extinguished.

She grabbed the tweezers from the tray and clamped them around the already threaded needle. Next, she used a pair of forceps to expose the wound on the left calf to see the depth of the injury and the angle she needed to stitch.

Deep.

Not too bad, though, in the grand scheme of things. She'll recover.

Karen inserted the needle at ninety degrees, roughly half an inch from the gash. She threaded the wound, pulling until the knotted end hit flesh, and tightly stitched the entire length of the laceration. After tying off the loose thread and cutting it, she wiped away the excess blood and applied another bandage. She then repeated the procedure on the other calf.

Throughout this, Betty remained calm and composed. Karen knew her missing husband—almost certainly dead like Danny—played in her mind. This wasn't the time to compare experiences, though.

A man in a naval officer's uniform leaned out of an office at the side of the warehouse. "Captain Kohler, there's a call you need to take."

"I'll be a minute," he replied from the side of an injured man.

"It can't wait, sir." The junior officer's tone sounded urgent.

"Oh, for God's sake," he hissed. "On my way."

Scott finished with the injured man and jogged to the office.

Karen placed a blanket over Betty and leaned close. "Let any of the team know if you're experiencing pain. I'll be back shortly."

Whatever was happening with the call, Karen wanted to know. Any news would be helpful to reassure the victims or give an up-to-date assessment of the situation on the ground. She weaved between the beds to the edge of the door to listen.

Kohler had a phone planted to his ear. He nodded several times. As he did, his eyes widened and he slumped onto a swivel chair. Shortly after, he said, "Okay, we'll be ready, sir. Tell us if there's anything we need to do."

Then he spotted Karen outside. He encouraged her inside with a wave of his hand.

"Ready for what?" she asked.

"This information is—" the young officer started to say.

"To hell with that," Captain Kohler interrupted. "People deserve to know what's happening."

Karen moved into the room and closed the door behind her.

"U.S. carrier strike groups are heading en masse to San Francisco," the captain continued. "They'll be here by dawn."

Excitement and relief rose inside of her. This was the first good news she'd heard in days. But if this war was global in scale, it raised a question in her mind.

"Why San Francisco?" she asked.

"Apparently these creatures have a 'queen,' and command thinks she might be here in San Francisco. They intend to hunt her down and take her out. We need to prepare to receive wounded soldiers from the battlefield tomorrow."

Karen cast her mind back to the park on Lombard Street. The chunks of turf hurling into the air before that massively large creature rose from the abyss below.

She'd already guessed the creatures had some kind of rank structure, with the huge monster at the top of the chain. This seemed apparent when she witnessed the thousands of other living horrors protecting the giant creature as it walked through the streets.

"You look lost in thought," Kohler said. "What's on your mind?"

"I think I might know where the queen is hiding."

Kohler and the officer exchanged glances. "Really?"

"Yep, and I saw her with my own eyes while my son and I hid on Lombard Street. Saw how she behaved, how she controlled the other creatures."

"And you're sure this was the queen?"

"If *that* wasn't the queen, I'll eat my own shoe."

Kohler scratched his chin, lost in thought. "I think this is something the carrier group needs to hear firsthand. I'm gonna send you and your son out to the *Nimitz* when it gets within range. Are you okay with that?"

Karen frowned. "I'm needed here."

He circled around the desk to her. "This operation could mean the difference to our survival. If your information tips the scales, you'll have played a bigger part in our victory than any of us could've ever imagined."

"Why can't I tell them over the radio?"

"Because who knows how long we'll have a radio. And," he said somberly, "who knows how long we'll be safe here. You might be the key, and I'm not going to risk everything because you can't patch up some injured. It's not to say that isn't important," he said more gently, "but this is much, much more. Get your son and prepare—you're going."

She stood there, stunned by the information. Playing a part by treating victims had come naturally to her. This, on the other hand, by accident or design, had propelled her into territory she'd never thought possible.

"Tell them everything you witnessed," Captain Kohler said, fire in his eyes. "And then . . . help them kill that fucker."

CHAPTER TWENTY-SEVEN

The *Nimitz* plowed northward through the Pacific Ocean at top speed. On the flight deck, bright moonlight glinted off the windows of fighter jets. Bowcut stood alone on the starboard side, viewing the dark American coastline.

The country is dying right in front of my eyes.

Only the distant glow of fires had betrayed the locations of Los Angeles and Santa Barbara along the coastline. Several small towns still had power, though she wondered how many people remained alive in those cities. Even more pertinently, how many would survive once the creature attacks expanded out of the big cities.

The plan has to work before there's nothing left to save. Otherwise we're all screwed.

Bowcut zipped up her jacket to protect her from the cool night air before gazing out to sea. A cruiser led the way toward their date with destiny. Two destroyers flanked the *Nimitz*. In the distance, the dark shapes of more than a hundred vessels ominously plowed their way toward San Francisco.

One after another, seven carrier strike groups had joined the procession from different parts of the seven seas. Safe in the water. The mightiest, most powerful armada to have ever been assembled on the face of the earth. But the deadliest weapon at their disposal was right below her very feet. The 4,500 supersoldiers in the hangar, primed for battle upon their arrival.

A shooting star burst across the star-studded sky.

Does the universe even care about our fate?

In a thousand years, would anyone even remember humanity's brief reign on this planet?

She thought about how everything had led to this point. Three years ago, standing outside the Jersey City subway tunnel with SWAT team captain Larry Dumont, assuming terrorists had attacked the Z Train. Going below the Hudson River and discovering the creatures' terrifying nest. Her boyfriend, David North, giving his life to aid the escape of the survivors. She pictured him relentlessly firing his laser as a mass of creatures and wall of water engulfed him. When he died, part of her died right there with him.

Then the fallout. Cafferty, Ellen, Diego, and her versus the Foundation.

London. Paris. Antarctica. Lima.

Nobody saw it all coming, apart from Albert Van Ness.

She slipped a tattered Polaroid out of her thigh pocket. Everyone in the photo, other than her, was now deceased. Her brother and father—both police officers who perished during 9/11 when the South Tower collapsed—had their arms wrapped around

her smiling mother, who had died shortly there-
after.

*Everyone I get close to, everyone I've ever cared about,
is dead.*

First she had fought to honor their memory.
Then she had fought to get revenge. Now, she
wasn't sure what was left to fight for.

Footsteps neared, regimented and heavy. She
turned to see the imposing figure of Franco Roux,
dressed in his black-and-gray uniform. He dropped
a cigar and crushed its glowing end under his boot
and stood next to her, looking out into the darkness
of the sea.

"What's that?" he asked, noticing the photo in
her hand.

"The past," she replied.

Roux nodded in understanding. He reached into
his jacket pocket and pulled out a worn photo of
a younger version of himself standing alongside
a woman and small child. He rubbed his thumb
slowly along the edge.

"What's that?" Bowcut asked him.

"The past," he replied, distance in his eyes.

She nodded at the man, and the two stared out
to sea in silence for a long minute. "May I ask you a
question?" she finally said.

"Of course."

"Why do you keep fighting?"

Roux locked eyes with her, considering the query.
"For the same reason you do," he replied. "Because
it's the only thing you and I know how to do."

He's right.

It's all I ever knew how to do.

"Anyways," he continued, "I think your presence is required on the other side of the ship."

Bowcut raised an eyebrow. "Sounds official. What's going on?"

"The captain broke out the beer. Your boy Munoz is cranking up the tunes."

"The last supper, eh?"

"Let's hope not."

In the distance, the sound of "Working My Way Back to You" by the Spinners erupted on the far side of the ship. She smiled. Diego always played that song before their missions, rather than his usual maddeningly repetitive Pitbull selection.

As they headed to the port side of the ship, Bowcut stopped and faced Roux one more time. He stopped as well and turned to face her silently.

She knew what she was about to say was blunt, but at this point, what was there to lose? Besides, she trusted him.

Bowcut finally broke the silence. "You know you're working for a madman, right?"

"Yes," Roux agreed, looking away, almost embarrassed by the admission.

"Then why don't you stop him?"

Roux turned back toward Bowcut. "When the time comes, I will."

"We both will," she added resolutely.

"We both will."

"All right, Mr. Roux, let's get this party started." Bowcut smiled, grabbed him by the arm, and pulled him toward the fun. "You better know how to dance."

Roughly two hundred of the crew stood around open cases of beer from R&H, a brewery on Staten

Island that had recently been gaining popularity. She had to admit, it was damn good beer.

Music pumped from a Bluetooth speaker at full blast.

Munoz looked over to her and immediately approached with a broad grin, belting the song lyrics aloud.

"I think the creatures sing better than you," Bowcut said.

The pair laughed. He handed her a can of R&H and she snapped it open.

Bowcut took a couple of mouthfuls of the cool, crisp beer. She scanned the deck at the faces of the crew. Most seemed at ease—or as relaxed as they could be when heading toward a possible extinction. It was probably the reason the captain had let them have a drink.

"You're in a very good mood," Bowcut said to Diego.

"You're damn right," he replied. "If I discovered what I think I did, you'll be in a good mood tomorrow, too."

She looked at him quizzically.

"And because I'm a stickler for making backups, keep this safe for me, will ya?" With that, Diego slipped a flash drive into Sarah's hand.

"What is it?"

Before she could ask for clarification, he danced away, singing the next line in the song.

Sarah glanced over at the Caffertys, who stood at the edge of the group smiling at the scene. Ellen grabbed Tom's arm and encouraged him away.

"Hey," Bowcut shouted. "Where are you two going?"

Neither turned back.

She got that not everyone wanted to party. For her, cutting loose for the first time in months came as a welcome relief. For the crew and the team, this was possibly their last chance.

ELLEN PULLED TOM AWAY FROM THE PARTY. AS MUCH AS SHE liked the music and would've loved a beer, those two things were not her priority tonight. If this was her last night with her husband—and his mortality was at greater risk because of his deal with the devil— she wanted them to spend it together. Alone.

She silently led him to the deck below toward their room on the ship. He clasped her hand tightly. Neither spoke. There was nothing really to say. She could see the weight of everything on his shoulders. She felt it, too.

Ellen and Tom walked along a brightly lit corridor and slipped through the open door to their quarters. The room was sparse, just a small bed and even smaller dresser. She sealed the door behind them and pushed her husband up against the wall. She leaned into him and pressed her body to his.

They both closed their eyes, connecting physically for the first time in seemingly forever.

Ellen put both her hands around Tom's face and locked eyes with her husband. After a long moment, she broke the silence.

"Now you listen here, Mr. Cafferty . . ."

He smiled at her.

"No matter what the day brings, I expect you right back here tomorrow night, understood?"

"Yes, ma'am," Tom replied obediently.

Ellen kissed her husband passionately and unbuttoned his shirt.

VAN NESS WHEELED ALONG THE CORRIDOR TOWARD THE captain's quarters. Collingwood had requested he visit, alone. He knew what was coming, and so far, his plan had gone perfectly.

Let them think they're making the decisions.

The captain kept a tight ship. It impressed Van Ness. It took a high level of skill to run what was effectively a floating city.

He stopped outside the captain's door, raised his swagger stick, and gave three sharp knocks.

"Come in," the captain called.

Van Ness navigated his chair inside a surprisingly large office. Uniforms were hung along one wall. The jackets seemed to have too many medals for his liking. A room at the side had a bed and a bathroom next to it, very much like a cheap hotel's version of a suite.

Captain Collingwood sat behind a solid wood desk. He wearily looked up. "Thank you for coming, Mr. Van Ness."

"How may I be of assistance, Captain?"

Collingwood sipped from a glass on his desk, full of what Van Ness thought smelled like whiskey. He leaned forward.

"I was impressed by your supersoldiers' performance on the bridge."

"They are in fact impressive."

"You said earlier the creatures would target my fleet."

"That is correct," Van Ness replied. "The creatures are clearly aware of our impending counteroffensive. I'm afraid we tipped our hand in Lima."

"Which brings me to the point of this conversation," Collingwood said. "It seems as if these supersoldiers are the only effective means we have to combat these monsters."

"As I mentioned, they are a tool at your disposal, Captain."

"With that in mind, I'd like to disperse a portion of these soldiers on the various ships in our fleet to protect our mission."

Van Ness looked away, pondering the request. "Surely my supersoldiers would be better suited on the ground in the invasion of San Francisco, Captain. And a portion left behind on the *Nimitz*, protecting your ship. Don't you think that—"

"True," Collingwood said, cutting him off, "but if just one of those creatures reaches any of my ships, it could kill hundreds of soldiers before being stopped. We could end up losing the entire fleet. That is simply unacceptable to me."

"I understand," Van Ness replied. "But still, dispersing my army is . . ."

"Is good strategic decision-making," Collingwood said. "I still don't trust you or your men, and frankly, I don't want more than a handful left on my ship. I've instructed my XO to coordinate the dispersal and to order the supersoldiers not involved in the land invasion to protect our ships. Is that clear?"

Van Ness studied the man and sighed. "Very well, Captain. You know the best strategy for war. It is your decision."

"Then I've made it."

"Is that all?" Van Ness asked.

"Yes, thank you."

Van Ness turned his wheelchair around and headed toward the door. As he exited the room, a thin smile spread across Van Ness' face.

CHAPTER TWENTY-EIGHT

Joey sprang away from Karen to the chopper's cabin window. Despite their early departure, he remained bright-eyed and excitedly peered out at dawn breaking on the horizon. Karen was wearing a Coast Guard orange-and-blue coverall—the only clothing the camp had available so she didn't arrive on the *Nimitz* stained with the blood of victims.

Their ride from the military base on Treasure Island—a gunmetal-gray Sea Hawk helicopter—smoothly thundered through the sky. Directly ahead, long rows of ships plowed through the water, roughly a mile off the coast.

"Look at all those boats, Mommy," Joey chirped as he pointed down.

The sight below took her breath away. The largest armada of ships ever seen.

We've still got a dog in this hunt.

She guessed they were only an hour south of San Francisco, judging by the quick flight. The idea of her playing an influential role in the counterattack hadn't quite sunk in.

"Mom, look at that giant boat!" Joey said.

"That's where we're heading, baby."

A smile spread across her son's face.

The chopper descended. As it closed in on their destination, the *Nimitz* grew to an almost unimaginable scale. Sure, she'd seen carriers from a distance and plenty of times on TV. But up close, the dimensions appeared gigantic. Four acres of floating land. Everything a shade of gray. Dozens of planes lined the edges of starboard and stern. It was an incredible feat of engineering.

"Good God," she murmured.

The Sea Hawk's wheels bumped against the deck of the mighty ship. One of the ground crew opened the side door.

Karen thanked him, grabbed Joey, and stepped outside onto the mammoth deck. Two people stood waiting for her arrival: a middle-aged woman with steely blue eyes, wearing cargo pants and a baggy olive T-shirt—she looked familiar, though not in an immediately recognizable way—and a younger man in a uniform, who extended his hand. "I'm Petty Officer Dave McMaster. Welcome aboard the USS *Nimitz*."

"Hi, I'm Karen Green and this is my son, Joey."

Her son's eyes darted in all directions, visibly in awe—as she was—at the sight. All the fighter jets. The dozens of destroyers following nearby. Hundreds of soldiers and crew members working diligently on the deck of the ship. It was all so overwhelming, and encouraging.

For the first time in a long time, Karen felt optimistic again. Like humanity actually had a shot.

"Hi, Karen, I'm Ellen Cafferty," the woman said, introducing herself.

That's why she looks familiar . . .

"And hello, Joey," Ellen said warmly.

"Hi, ma'am," he replied.

Ever my polite little man.

"Shall we?" Ellen asked. "Everyone is waiting for us in the meeting room."

"Who am I speaking with?" Karen asked anxiously.

Ellen gave a reassuring smile. "The captain; the executive officer; my husband, Tom; and Albert Van Ness. Apparently you've got some good information to share?"

"I hope so," Karen said shyly.

"Listen, you're going to do great in there, don't worry," Ellen said softly. "Any information you have would be hugely helpful, and we appreciate it more than you know. I'll be right there by your side, no matter what."

Karen smiled. It was nice having an ally.

"Is it okay to leave Joey with his own personal tour guide?" Ellen asked.

"Hey, little guy," McMaster said. "How would you like to see a fighter jet up close?"

"Yes please!" Joey responded enthusiastically.

Karen set Joey down and knelt in front of him. "Be a good boy. I'll be back soon."

This was the second babysitter she'd left him with since this whole ordeal started, not that she had a real choice. Only this time, being on board this mighty vessel, far away from the specter of the creatures, made the decision a lot easier to stomach.

Joey left with the sailor, and Karen blew him a kiss when he looked back.

"Shall we?" Ellen motioned. Karen walked alongside her in silence. Now, on this ship, away from the horrors of the past few days, the enormity of everything overwhelmed her.

"Mrs. Cafferty, may I ask you a question?"

Ellen smiled at her. "Please, call me Ellen. Of course, go ahead."

"Um . . . are we safe on this ship?"

Ellen stopped walking and turned to face her. Tears welled up in Karen's eyes almost immediately.

"I heard what you and your son have been through," Ellen quietly said.

"It's . . . almost too much to bear, to even think about," Karen replied softly, breaking down. "And after everything my son witnessed . . ."

"I understand," Ellen said, clutching Karen's hands tenderly. "But we're gonna get through this together, all right? And I want you to know that no matter what, I've got your back. No one messes with the Green family anymore, not on my watch."

Karen laughed and wiped away the tears. "Thank you."

A QUIET HUM AND THE SOUND OF CHATTERING KEYBOARDS filled the *Nimitz*'s intelligence center. Crew sat in front of workstations around the tennis-court-sized room. Cafferty rested his elbows on the large central table.

The intimacy of last night now seemed a distant memory.

At least I had that.

At least I have her.

Ellen had pulled him back from the brink so many times, he had stopped counting. By now, Tom had gotten used to his wife saving him from himself, from his worst tendencies. Without her, there was nothing worth fighting for. She made him better. She made everything better.

The sunrise had yanked him back to their current harsh reality, though. Back to the realization of what he'd agreed to.

Captain Collingwood had urgently summoned his team and Albert Van Ness for a dawn meeting. A civilian apparently had information that might be useful. That was all he knew. And Ellen had gone to meet her on the flight deck.

Munoz and Bowcut sat to Cafferty's left. The captain and his XO sat to his right, all patiently waiting for Albert Van Ness to finally reveal his plans before their guest arrived. On the videoconference screen, a weary President Brogan listened in.

Across the table, Van Ness peered down at a huge map of San Francisco. He wafted a bony finger over the city several times, analyzing every inch.

Cafferty studied his nemesis from a distance. Van Ness was like one of those fractal portraits that you need to stare at for minutes before the real image reveals itself. The only difference being, with Van Ness, the true vision never became clear until a time of *his* choosing.

"So . . ." Diego said, breaking the awkward silence. *"How's everyone doing?"*

Cafferty smiled at him. Munoz was always a smart-ass.

"When do you plan on enlightening us on your attack strategy, Mr. Van Ness?" President Brogan asked on the video screen.

Van Ness lifted his head from the map.

"First, let us hear the good girl out who's on her way," Van Ness replied. "And then I believe the plan will make itself known."

Munoz leaned over to Cafferty and whispered, "That means he doesn't have a plan yet."

Cafferty smirked. But knowing Van Ness, he had every potentiality planned out. The questions consuming Cafferty, though, were this:

Regardless of whether I live or die, what's Van Ness' plan after the battle for San Francisco is won or lost?

And more important, how can I fuck those plans up?

The intelligence center's door opened.

Ellen led a young lady to the table and they took seats opposite the officers. Maybe thirty, Cafferty thought. She had dark rings around her eyes and nervously glanced around.

"Everyone, this is Karen Green," Ellen said. "She's a brave paramedic who escaped San Francisco with her four-year-old son, Joey, and has been helping victims as they arrive on the island."

"Good to have you here, Karen, and thank you for all your help," Collingwood said. "I am Captain Collingwood, this is my executive officer, Captain Vasquez. This is Tom Cafferty and his team, and Albert Van Ness."

Karen nodded hello at everyone in the room.

"And of course . . ."

"Hello, Karen," President Brogan chimed in, momentarily startling the woman. "Thank you for your help today."

"Oh, wow, um, hello, President Brogan."

"Captain Kohler filled us in briefly about what you witnessed, but we'd like to hear it from you directly."

"If I can help in any way, I'll do it," she responded.

"Tell us what you saw," Brogan said. "No detail is too small."

"Um . . . okay . . . well . . ." Karen stammered. "Well, my son and I were hiding on the top floor of an office building after my husband had . . . um . . . had been . . ."

Cafferty saw the woman's eyes fill with tears. "Karen," he said gently, "what did you see from the top of the building?"

She fought back the tears and continued. "All the smaller creatures gathered around the center of George Sterling Park, and the ground began to shake, like an earthquake . . ."

Van Ness straightened in his chair and leaned forward, listening intently.

"Then . . . the big one rose out from the ground."

"Exactly how big was this creature?" Cafferty asked.

Karen turned to him. "Almost three times the size of the rest. It was the size of a truck."

"Did it look any different from the rest?" Van Ness asked.

"Yes. Its . . . its eyes glowed red," Karen said. "And it had what looked like a crown of thorns on its head."

"Hey, Karen, my name's Diego," Munoz said. "I'm just an intern here."

Karen smiled at his joke.

"What did you hear when this creature rose from the breach?" he asked.

She closed her eyes, trying to recall what she'd experienced. Eventually she said, "It was like nothing I've ever heard before. Its screech shattered every window on the park. And . . ."

"And what?"

"It seemed like every other creature bowed in deference to it. Obeyed it. Like it was commanding them all. Like they were communicating with each other."

Van Ness leaned in closer to the map of San Francisco, studying it carefully.

"Sterling Park, you say?" Van Ness asked. "You're positive, my dear, of the location?"

"One hundred percent," Karen replied. "And then the smaller creatures surrounded it in thick lines. Like they were protecting it as it walked the streets, checking on their destruction."

"Fascinating," Van Ness commented.

"Did you see it return into the same breach in the park?" Cafferty asked.

"We didn't have the chance. Joey and I got the hell out of there."

"How can we be sure it returned to the same hole it dug up?" Cafferty asked Van Ness.

"We cannot with any certainty," Van Ness replied. "Although, all things in nature tend to take the path of least resistance."

"You're very brave, Karen," Captain Collingwood said. "Anything else to add?"

"Just one thing," Karen said confidently. "If there *is* a queen, *that* was it."

"Well said, my dear," Van Ness said to Karen. "President Brogan, as I thought, our attack plan has revealed itself."

He jabbed his finger against the map.

"The main assault teams will land at Hunters Point. Send every supersoldier there. But before we do, I'd humbly request the U.S. Navy turn the dock and surrounding neighborhood into a parking lot, Madam President. The more noise the better."

Cafferty studied the map, confused. "Hunters Point?" he asked. "That's *miles* away from Sterling Park. I thought our mission was to hunt down and kill the queen."

"And we will, Mr. Mayor," Van Ness responded. "Trust me, Madam President. No one knows war strategy better than an old German."

"Except maybe the Russians," Diego whispered under his breath.

"You need to launch everything you've got at Hunters Point, Captain," Van Ness said authoritatively. "All your weapons, all your men, all my supersoldiers, except for the ones protecting your fleet of course."

Cafferty shot a look at Ellen, suspicious.

Except for the supersoldiers protecting the fleet?

"In the meantime," Van Ness continued, "I will require a Chinook helicopter to transport myself and a small squad of twenty supersoldiers to Sterling Park on the other side of the city."

"Why would I agree to this?" Collingwood asked. "We need more details."

"My intention is to win this war, Captain. I'll let you do your job. Let me do mine. Your military will be safe and sound while my soldiers are the ones on the front line, bearing the brunt of all this. But if you don't agree, perhaps we can reverse that order."

Collingwood looked away, backing down.

"Oh, and one more thing . . ." Van Ness eyed Cafferty. "Thomas and his team will accompany me on my mission. Assuming that is amenable to you, Mr. Mayor?"

Cafferty nodded at Ellen, Diego, and Sarah, and then turned back to Van Ness defiantly. "Bring it on."

CHAPTER TWENTY-NINE

T he vanguard of the fleet cruised underneath the deep red splendor of the Golden Gate Bridge, still proudly intact, and entered San Francisco Bay. Five choppers swarmed in the clear blue sky around the deserted docks at Hunters Point. They were checking for any survivors before the overwhelming military force incinerated the area.

On the *Nimitz*'s flight deck, a Chinook helicopter landed, blasting Diego Munoz with its strong downdraft. He hunched over an ultrahigh-frequency distress beacon, a plastic briefcase-sized box with assorted switches, knobs, and waveforms on it. Diego had calibrated the device carefully. A theory had formed in his mind. Unproven? Yes. Useful or effective? He had no clue . . . yet.

But it's better than just sitting on my ass.

Bowcut nudged him with her knee. "You seeing that, Diego?"

"What?"

She nodded toward the smoldering city on the mainland. "What a god-awful mess."

A cruise liner listed against the rugged Marin Headlands. Its hull groaned against the rocks and a torn banner fluttered on the pool deck. The blood-stains on the balconies told their own story.

"Someone had their vacation ruined," Munoz said.

He gazed at the stage above the pool deck. Dried blood almost covered the entire area. Body parts littered the floorboards. Whatever went down, it must have happened fast. "And we thought we had it bad."

The aircraft carrier powered toward the city.

Munoz switched his focus to the military base on Treasure Island: a bastion of human survival, untouched by the carnage. It appeared oddly tranquil. People walked around the perimeter in civilian clothing. Vehicles moved backward and forward. They, unlike him, probably didn't possess the knowledge that the creatures were capable of tunneling under seabeds. He guessed a breach could happen at any second on the basis of never underestimating the creatures' abilities.

"You ready for action?" Bowcut asked.

"Nothin' prepares you for this."

"Damn straight."

Diego looked across the deck at Albert Van Ness and the Caffertys boarding the helicopter, along with twenty supersoldiers.

"This doesn't feel right," Munoz said.

"What do you mean?"

"Van Ness' plan. Sending thousands of super-soldiers and the U.S. military to the wrong location and only a handful of us to hunt the queen. Why?"

Bowcut shrugged. "Classic diversion. The queen will send hordes of creatures the wrong way, leaving herself vulnerable to attack when she least expects it."

"I suppose. But what if she keeps a few *thousand* creatures around to protect herself? Then we're royally screwed."

"I don't trust his intentions, either, but he's coming with us. To me, that means he's confident the plan will work."

"I guess we'll find out. I'm surprised the military put up with his demands."

"Like they had a choice. He's got the supersoldiers. And if his plan fails, it's his clones that get slaughtered. Better than our soldiers."

"I suppose," Diego replied. "Doesn't it also strike you as odd that he wants all of us off this ship to join him?"

Bowcut looked intently at Diego, considering what he said. She turned and walked across the deck to speak to Tom Cafferty as he climbed on board the chopper. Then she joined Roux and boarded an amphibious assault craft headed toward San Francisco.

Diego glanced across the bay at the carnage. Most of the skyscrapers in the city had transformed into charred skeletons. But the weirdest thing was the absolute stillness that had overcome the city. No movement at all. Like the place had transformed into a corpse.

But all that was about to change.

Forty amphibious assault crafts sliced through the water ahead of the fleet, creating white trails in the deep blue water. Black and angular, they bounced over the waves toward their drop-off point, each packed with hundreds of supersoldiers. U.S. forces followed them in countless more crafts. It looked like D-Day on steroids.

The missile bays opened on the *Nimitz*, and dozens of powerful projectiles shot from below deck and arced into the sky, flames burning behind them.

Munoz gazed up, shielding his eyes from the glare of the sun.

Simultaneously, missiles shot from every aircraft carrier in the fleet and rocketed toward the landing point.

"Holy hell," he uttered.

The missiles raced over the landing craft and struck the empty dock and surrounding buildings with tremendous force. Thunderous booms split the air, and the earth shook upon impact. Massive balls of fire shot upward. Debris rained onto the empty berths and destroyed warehouses. Everything within hundreds of yards was almost instantly flattened at the destructive power, including any creatures in the vicinity. They would probably have made things harder for the landing force, if it were human . . .

That should get the queen's attention, though.

Munoz gasped with awe at what he was witnessing. He couldn't see any creatures on land, but they were coming, no doubt. His experience told him that much.

The roar of fighter jets came next.

On every carrier, dozens of F18s took to the sky. They quickly gained altitude and swept toward San Francisco in formation. The jets homed in on known clusters of creatures near Hunters Point and simultaneously fired dozens of laser-guided AIM-9X Sidewinder missiles at various targets.

Munoz instinctively held his breath and closed his eyes a split second before the missiles hit, anticipating the shock wave.

In a flash, San Francisco had become a full-blown war zone.

Diego could only imagine the queen below-ground somewhere, clear across the city, just now learning about the massive human counterattack under way.

That bitch is gonna be pissed.

But this awesome display of power wasn't going to win the war. The main assault powered over the waves toward the raging fires in Hunters Point. The amphibious assault craft with thousands of supersoldiers on them were seconds from hitting land and launching a full-scale invasion . . . on the opposite side of the city from where Van Ness and Cafferty's team were about to head.

Let's hope the queen takes the bait.

"Diego, over here!" Cafferty bellowed.

Munoz turned toward the deck.

The Chinook helicopter's rotor blades had spun to a blur. Inside, Van Ness, twenty supersoldiers, and the Caffertys waited, the old man likely pissed that Bowcut hadn't joined them. Munoz doubted it put a serious dent in the crazy old fool's real plan.

He took one last look at the battered city, hoping they were bringing it salvation. Then he scooped up his tactical beacon and jogged toward the tailgate of the chopper. He leaped inside and the Chi-nook prepared to take to the sky.

A moment before it did, Ellen Cafferty kissed Tom on the lips and unbuckled her harness.

"You're not joining, Mrs. Cafferty?" Van Ness shouted over the sounds of the chopper.

"I think it's best for at least one of us to remain behind, to coordinate intelligence and communica-tion," she shouted back. "You know, just in case."

With that, Ellen leaped out onto the deck of the *Nimitz* and mouthed the words *I love you* to her husband one last time.

"Suit yourself," Van Ness said sternly. "It will make no difference."

Munoz studied his face and could tell Van Ness was definitely pissed at this sudden change of plan. It likely added to Bowcut's nonappearance for the smaller mission.

Perhaps Van Ness wants us all where he can kill us.
Tough shit for him.

As the propellers sped up, Diego noticed Van Ness lowering a syringe containing green liquid into his swagger stick. The same syringe Tom had pointed out in the Antarctic base two days ago.

With that, the Chinook took to the sky.

CHAPTER THIRTY

Sarah Bowcut and Franco Roux stood at the bow of the leading assault craft, lasers raised toward the shattered remains of the docks. They had a minute before reaching land. The putrid stench of death increased with every second. She had no doubt horrific scenes awaited on the battlefield.

An untold number of young and old, cut down without mercy. Maybe birds pecking at their corpses. Rats over them. Flies. She'd mentally prepared for the sights of the bodies that hadn't burned. The way Sarah saw it, this simply provided the backdrop for the fight. A real-time snapshot of the horrifying human cost.

She scanned between the flaming buildings for any signs of movement. There'd been sporadic creature sightings throughout San Francisco, but so far, the bulk of the enemy army remained hidden from open view.

Behind her on the boat, fifty supersoldiers packed every available foot. None moved an inch as a wave of sea spray lashed against them. They glared forward with determined stares. All the image of Roux. None probably understood the hope they carried for humanity, or cared.

In the distance, a Chinook helicopter lifted off the *Nimitz*'s flight deck and thwacked toward a different part of the city. Tom, Diego, and Van Ness' ride. She knew Ellen had decided to stay back. One of them had to. She hoped it wasn't the last time she saw her team alive, though. Didn't give a shit about the megalomaniac's fate.

Bowcut wiped a sheen of sweat from her brow.

Whatever happens, humanity isn't going down with a whimper.

Jets screamed through the smoke-filled sky, ready to lend their support. Drones circled over the surrounding neighborhoods of Dogpatch, Visitacion Valley, and Portola. So far, no warnings of an advancing horde had come through her Foundation earpiece.

"You think they're hiding until we arrive?" she yelled over the craft's powerful outboard motors. "Or hiding from the missiles?"

"Maybe both," Roux replied. "It won't stay like that for long."

"They'll be watching."

"Waiting. Deciding on how to deal with us. They only have one real decision, but they don't know it just yet."

His responses made sense. This battle was fairly straightforward. Supersoldiers versus creatures. A vicious struggle at close quarters. That's how the creatures liked to fight, and that's how they needed to be taken down. One at a time, until Van Ness and Cafferty could kill the queen.

Bowcut took a calming breath and nodded to herself.

You got this, Sarah.

The craft slowed toward the side of Hunters Point's mostly empty dock. Debris from the earlier explosions littered the concrete: torn steel from the warehouses, rubble from the craters, smashed pieces of wooden pallets. The port side reached within two feet of dry land. The supersoldiers immediately leaped to the concrete and arranged themselves into a tight defensive semicircle. Roux and Bowcut disembarked and stood behind them, facing a gentle grassy hill that led up to a group of seven low-rise apartment buildings.

Another three crafts reached the dock and disembarked quickly. Their squads moved alongside Roux's, forming a line between the landing point and the road. It created enough safe space for the entire invading force, if the creatures didn't breach their defensive line. Bowcut had been impressed with the Foundation coordination in the hangar and in Lima. This was equally impressive, though it seemed inconceivable that the creatures would simply allow them to arrive without attacking.

She nudged Roux. "This seems too good to be—"

A deafening screech rose over the roar of the fighter jets. Chilling. Possibly the loudest she'd heard. And this was aboveground, from behind the hill, without the confines of caverns to amplify the noise.

The supersoldiers collectively tensed.

A second screech erupted. Sharper.

Closer.

But where are they? Surely not right below our feet, about to explode out of the shell craters. That'd create total carnage.

Then nothing immediately followed.

Roux glanced back at the crafts. Several more had successfully landed. He planted his hand against his earpiece. "Get your asses moving, guys. We've got enough to hold the bridgehead, but we can't wait here forever."

"You sure about that?" Bowcut asked.

"We don't have a choice."

She aimed her laser at the top of the hill.

To her front, hundreds of windows in the apartment buildings exploded outward. In the blink of an eye, creatures rocketed out of every level. Thousands of them. Jumping from the higher floors to the road. Clambering down the external walls. Racing out of the entrances.

Did they somehow guess what was unfolding and lay in wait?

Whatever.

This is it.

Sun glinted off the creatures' black armored skin. Tails whipped from side to side as thousands of the monstrosities stormed down the hill toward the dock. They had the high ground and huge numbers on their side. The creatures moved at breakneck speed, using gravity to their advantage, guaranteeing that they'd reach their target within seconds with nearly unstoppable momentum.

The U.S. forces and Foundation team members who had managed to disembark raced behind the line of supersoldiers and aimed lasers over their sturdy shoulders. Bowcut did the same. She blocked everything out of her mind apart from bringing down as many creatures as possible until her laser lost its charge. She fired, and her weapon's searing hot beam joined at least thirty others, zipping into the massed front ranks near the bottom of the hill. Hundreds fell, sliced through their legs, chests, and heads.

The laser beams fizzed as they crisscrossed the battlefield, effectively butchering hundreds of creatures. But even as more weapons quickly joined the initial broadside, it was clear to her that this was nowhere near enough to stop the relentless charge. Other creatures instantly replaced the fallen, bounding over their dismembered bodies. They streamed over the road and funneled between the burning warehouses, tearing through the smoky atmosphere.

"Fall back!" Roux screamed.

Others yelled his order.

The supersoldiers stayed in position. More from the landing crafts bolstered their line to roughly a few thousand. They had formed into three ranks. U.S. forces and Foundation team leaders scrambled back thirty yards and aimed over the supersoldiers' heads for any creature that managed to leap high enough.

Bowcut took a moment to peer through the smoke toward the apartment blocks. During every one of her pounding heartbeats, a steady black flow poured out of the windows and doors with no signs of stopping.

We could be facing millions. Wherever the queen is, she's sending everything she's got to the front lines of the battle.

At least, we can hope.

The creatures rapidly closed to twenty feet, baring their rows of teeth, wildly screeching. The first thick cluster leaped into the air.

The front line of supersoldiers thrust upward to meet them.

The all-out war for San Francisco had begun.

Before the creatures had a chance to whip down their tails, most had the ends thrust into their chests. The Foundation's amazing creations didn't wait for a second to see if the wounds proved fatal. Every one of them moved on to the next creature, then the next, without yielding an inch of ground.

When a supersoldier fell and got dragged into the attacking throng for a brutal hacking, another sprinted forward to take his place in the front line. In front of them, black corpses piled to a height of six feet high. The soldiers didn't wait for the next creatures to scale the bodies to have a higher point to leap from. They slowly advanced together, stamping on the injured, fighting as they went with eye-watering, untiring speed.

Missiles rocketed over the bridgehead, targeted precisely at every hellhole the creatures poured out of. They slammed into each of the apartment buildings in quick succession, leveling everything in sight. The ground rumbled. Thick columns of fire shot into the sky.

Moments later, a dozen Sea Hawk helicopters thundered over from the direction of the fleet.

Side doors opened. Snipers in each cabin aimed their weapons downward, and a barrage of laser fire rained down on the creatures from above, carving whole swaths of destruction below.

The supersoldiers advanced another few paces, wading between the corpses on the battlefield.

If there is a hell, this is what it looks like.

Creatures began to switch their attack strategy, like they were evolving in real time. Instead of the first wave's method of leaping with thrashing tails first, which left them vulnerable, they now stayed low and rapidly lunged forward. This had a short-lived effect, increasing their success at tearing limbs off supersoldiers, before the soldiers themselves evolved and countered back effectively.

By now, all crafts had managed to dock and the advance continued.

Boots pounded the ground as landing forces either joined the ranks of the supersoldiers or knelt with their fellow humans, slicing down creature after creature with laser beams.

Three creatures appeared on the top of a burning warehouse, howling at the flames licking their bodies. They threw themselves off the side, over the lines of supersoldiers, using their suicides as an attempt to break through.

Roux and Bowcut rounded on them, aimed, and squeezed. Red-hot lasers sliced through the creatures' chests instantly. Roux calmly walked to each and fired between their eyes, making sure the job was done.

Bowcut edged across to him while keeping an eye on the warehouse roofs for any other creature stupid enough to try the same thing. "They can't keep coming forever," she shouted over the raging war. "How many more do you reckon are heading here?"

"This is only the start," Roux shouted back.

CHAPTER THIRTY-ONE

The Chinook powered over Treasure Island toward Fisherman's Wharf. Tom Cafferty crouched by the open side door with a perfect panorama of the glistening bay.

The view was terrible.

Boats, dead humans, and creatures drifted in the water between the fleet and the land. The city didn't look much better. No power or movement to reveal a single sign of life. In the distance at Hunters Point, Cafferty could see the battle raging. Two armies—creatures and supersoldiers—engaged in a fight to the death on the dock. Lasers spearing through the smoke from helicopters above. Countless buildings on fire. The warm wind carried the sound of thousands of piercing shrieks with it.

When this is done, there may not be a city left to save . . .

Cafferty couldn't tell from this vantage point which way the fight was going. He comforted himself with the fact that Ellen was keeping a close eye on the proceedings safely on board the *Nimitz*. Van

Ness clearly wanted Cafferty's entire team on this mission. So if Ellen staying back screwed up part of his plan, all the better. The same applied to Bowcut.

Munoz knelt next to Cafferty, gripping his tactical beacon case. He stared down wide-eyed at the torn-apart city, silent. The tech expert usually took everything in his stride, no matter how bad. This time his look reflected the events on the ground.

"This shit's crazier than a soup sandwich," Munoz said.

Diego always seemed to have the right expression no matter the situation, Cafferty thought.

"It appears as if the creatures have fallen for our diversionary attack," Van Ness said.

Cafferty spun to face him. "Let's hope. How do we know the queen will still be near Sterling Park?"

"We don't, now do we?" Van Ness replied disconcertingly. "But I'm sure one way or another, we'll root her out."

Van Ness' arrogance and presumption grated on Cafferty.

"How do you propose we root her out with only twenty supersoldiers on our side?"

"Oh, I'm sure the rest of my forces will join us soon," Van Ness replied coolly. "And let's not forget we have access to the most powerful, most advanced fleet ever assembled in history. I'm sure your mighty U.S. military will serve my purposes well."

"What do you mean by that?"

The men stared at each other for a lingering moment, Van Ness at ease in his chair—not even the horrors below appeared to rattle him—and Cafferty tense about what the next few hours would bring.

How can he be so certain his plan will work? Even with his soldiers, he's never actually encountered the queen. And yet he's sitting there, seemingly without a care in the world.

What the hell am I missing?

The chopper swept over Fisherman's Wharf and lowered toward the tennis courts in George Sterling Park. Trees lined the perimeter. No creatures were visible around the gaping hole in the grassed area.

They wouldn't leave her unprotected.

They won't just let us stroll in for the kill.

The Chinook touched down on the hard court, crushing two tennis nets. The surrounding chain-link fence, sagging and torn, rattled hard.

Eighteen supersoldiers quickly filed out and created a protective circle around the chopper. Two remained at either side of Van Ness' chair, along with two Foundation team members. Neither of the latter men had spoken a word. They clearly had their instructions, whatever those might be. Cafferty wondered if they were his death squad.

He followed Munoz, jumping to the ground with their pistols raised. Both aimed at the buildings surrounding the park, half expecting to be attacked at any moment. Butterflies danced in his stomach. It seemed odd, after all the devastation and slaughter, to stand in a seemingly deserted part of the city. Once bustling, now a ghost town. Sure, signs of the carnage remained, like the bloodstains on the road.

For Van Ness' ground zero—the site of the queen's first emergence—it didn't really fit what he'd expected to encounter.

The supersoldiers lifted Van Ness' wheelchair out of the chopper. He pointed over the chunks of earth toward the hole. It was exactly as Karen Green described. It appeared as if something massive had risen and broken through the earth right in the center of the park.

"My friends, it is time to lure our prey," Van Ness said. "Mr. Cafferty and Mr. Munoz, please accompany my supersoldiers as they inspect the breach." Van Ness tapped on the armrest of his wheelchair. "I, for obvious reasons, cannot come with you."

"That's convenient," Munoz said, shaking his head.

Van Ness slammed his swagger stick hard against the ground, losing his cool momentarily. "I have hunted and killed more of these creatures than you ever will, Mr. Munoz. Do *not* presume that I am a coward. I am in this wheelchair because a creature crushed my spine before you were born, and I will be fighting these monsters long after *you* are dead, sir."

Munoz swallowed hard and looked away.

"All right, let's do this," Cafferty said, finally breaking the tension.

They walked toward the open-air breach, with the eighteen supersoldiers matching their strides in a protective circle. Cafferty closed on the edge and slowed.

The ten-foot-wide hole corkscrewed into darkness. The incline was shallow enough to walk down, maybe thirty degrees. It brought back memories of entering the cavern under the Hudson River with David North and Lucien Flament. That time, he was searching for Ellen, not realizing that the Frenchman was trying to lead them to their deaths.

Munoz flung his arm against Cafferty's chest to stop him. "You hear that?"

"What?"

"Listen."

A tapping sound came from below, gradually building up to a clatter.

Heavy footsteps.

Lots of them.

Creatures racing up to meet their challenge.

Cafferty glanced around at the ring of super-soldiers. Only eighteen of them. And two to protect Van Ness.

This is suicide . . .

"Remain calm," Van Ness shouted. "She'll have sent her main force to extinguish the threat at Hunters Point."

"Are you sure about that?" Munoz shouted back, just as dozens of creatures burst out of the hole.

Cafferty staggered back a few paces and activated his mic, calling to the helicopter pilots. "Take off now!"

The Chinook's blades slowly began to rotate.

Munoz leaped to the side of a tree and aimed his laser at the horde. These creatures were smaller than the rest, wilder and faster. The queen's inner circle. Their screeches echoed through the park. They immediately attacked the ring of supersoldiers.

The sight made Cafferty freeze. He and Munoz were only a few steps from the creatures in every direction as they swarmed the group.

The supersoldiers immediately responded with lethal force, puncturing the tails of creatures through their chests and crashing fists through their skulls. Head stomps crushed the injured. Dozens of creatures lay dead in less than a minute.

Munoz steadily fired his laser across the mouth of the hole, keeping his beam going back and forth, slicing through any creature that followed the first wave. Cafferty followed suit, trying to make sure none made it to open ground. Aiming between their defenders proved difficult, but that was their only option.

It wasn't quite enough.

A few creatures managed to break out. They circled the group and entered the tennis courts. Cafferty twisted around and fired on them. He cut down several but eased his finger off the trigger when his laser beam neared the helicopter.

He turned to Van Ness. "Send a soldier to save the damned chopper."

"That is not our priority," Van Ness shot back.

"Goddammit, Van Ness!"

Cafferty fired again, clearing three creatures from the side door.

Four more creatures leaped on the front of the Chinook as it took to the sky, lifting to a height of around one hundred feet. They battered through the windshield and ripped out the two pilots. Both fell with creatures clutched to them, biting their faces and sinking claws into their bodies as they free-fell downward. Their bodies slammed into the tennis court with tremendous force, denting the concrete.

The Chinook lurched to the side and plummeted. The hulking body crashed to the ground, right on top of the creatures and pilots. Its rotors slammed into the pavement.

Cafferty instinctively ducked.

The helicopter ignited in a fiery wreck, and shards of metal spat through the air and tore through trees.

He quickly turned his attention back to the battle. Only two creatures remained standing; the rest had been effectively butchered by Van Ness' army. Outnumbered and outmatched, the creatures backed away still screeching, baring their teeth.

Without hesitation, the supersoldiers broke from their formation and charged. The two creatures retreated, bounding back down the dark hole into the now silent abyss below. The supersoldiers didn't follow.

Clearly under orders more comprehensive than we've been told.

The park grew still once again. The Hunters Point diversion had worked so far; most of the creatures remained on the other side of the city.

The crippled Chinook's engine wound to silence.

Cafferty shook his head in disgust at the sight of the downed chopper and the tangle of dead U.S. Navy men underneath. He turned to Van Ness.

"You son of a—"

"Now, now," Van Ness interjected, "there is no time to debate the events of the past. Those men are dead, Thomas. Now is the time to cast our bait for the queen."

"You're a goddamn madman."

Van Ness ignored the comment, turned toward the supersoldiers, and tapped something into the pad on his armrest.

Whatever the order, and however it was transmitted, Cafferty had never seen the soldiers look so intense. It was almost as if they sensed that they were close to their ultimate objective, their whole reason for being. He and Munoz exchanged a knowing glance, then walked away a few paces.

Diego leaned over and whispered to Cafferty. "So . . . what's the bait?"

CHAPTER THIRTY-TWO

The smoke around the old naval dock had become too thick to operate in without a gas mask. Strong morning sunshine beat down through the haze. Bowcut kept her breathing steady. She knew one lapse in concentration, one mistake, could end up being a terminal mistake. She searched for any creature that tried to flank the invasion force. Hundreds of other lasers did the same, providing covering fire for the supersoldiers and taking down anything else that moved.

The sea of monstrosities had been driven back over the road, step by step. She guessed at their peak there were a few hundred thousand creatures involved in the attack. That number had swiftly been quartered by the supersoldiers. But that didn't stop them from attacking with equal vigor.

The battle continued on a grassy hill in front of the burning apartment buildings. An extended line of four thousand supersoldiers, two ranks deep, continued to slaughter the creatures and stop them from ever reaching the U.S. forces. Van Ness' creations trampled forward over the corpses, which lay thick in all directions.

Then something changed.

All at once, the creatures stopped charging at their regimented opponents. They retreated to the top of the hill, snarling, falling back. It was as if they were receiving new orders and were revising their attack strategy.

"What do you think?" she asked Roux.

"Looks like they are trying to come up with a new plan."

"Looks like they're receiving new orders from on top, if you ask me."

Roux nodded. "That, too."

She hoped they weren't being recalled to defend the queen on the other side of the city. If so, the ruse was up and Cafferty was in mortal danger.

She held her breath to see what the creatures would do next.

After momentarily regrouping, the monsters charged down the hill once more, moving as one overwhelming force. It appeared their plan was to smash through the defensive line, like a spear penetrating its target, rather than spreading the fight out on all fronts.

It was a bold but risky offensive strategy. And potentially very effective.

But it meant they were still here, fighting Bowcut and Roux's forces instead of running back to Mama.

Thank God.

"Stand by!" Roux ordered. "Don't give an inch."

The supersoldiers took up their standard position, waiting for the attack, arms raised, on their heels. Ready to spring up or forward.

The two rival forces clashed again. The sheer weight of the onrushing mass pushed the super-soldiers back several yards, nearly breaking through the defensive line.

From a purely strategic point of view, Bowcut admired the speed at which the creatures were able to switch offensive approaches nearly instan-taneously in a baying mob. No doubt about it, Bowcut thought, the queen must be commanding and communicating with her troops in real time, testing different attack patterns methodically. Any war general would be jealous. Though it begged the question: How was the queen reacting so fast, and why hadn't she joined the attack?

After losing ground on the hill and taking a few dozen losses, the line of supersoldiers was able to hold firm, slicing down creatures from the tip of the spear again in quick time. Deafening screeches rang in Bowcut's ears from the dying masses on the ground.

To her, this barbaric duel was reminiscent of the images she'd conjured during history classes. A shield wall battle between the methodical Saxons and their wild Viking opponents. Unlike the TV depictions she'd seen, she knew the organization of the former won the day, just like how Van Ness' modern counterparts were winning.

"This is exactly what we want." Roux leaned toward his shoulder mic. "Mr. Van Ness, they continue to deplete themselves here. No sign of retreat to your position." After a brief pause he said, "How's it going over there?"

Nothing came through Bowcut's earpiece as Van Ness replied. That fact came as no surprise. The Foundation hierarchy clearly had its own command channel. Yes, it was a joint operation, but the U.S. side of the task force wasn't about to give the Foundation access to all of its secure communication systems, either.

Van Ness trusts no one . . .

Roux nodded intently, gazing toward the ranks of supersoldiers. "Copy, we'll get there as fast as we can. Out."

"We're going . . . now?" Bowcut asked.

Roux looked over at the steady line of supersoldiers, perfectly executing his orders. "They've got this under control and know the mission."

"Just you and me? Will the supersoldiers keep fighting without you here?"

"That's the order. Our soldiers execute all commands to completion given by the senior-most Foundation members, namely Van Ness and myself. Naturally, we'll run everything by your military. So yes, they'll keep fighting while I'm gone. For now, we're needed there."

"So there's no way we could command the soldiers?"

"It'd take months to teach anyone to effectively coordinate our squads. We simply don't have time. You have my assurances that that day will come."

"Understood." Though it wasn't exactly how Bowcut had understood the "joint" attack. Still, she trusted his word on the matter. And for now, everything was going well.

Roux ordered one of his team to send for a chopper. As it approached the dock, the creatures' roars intensified in anger at their inability to stop the ongoing aerial assault.

The chopper touched down.

Sarah grabbed Roux by the arm. "Remember our conversation last night?"

"I remember."

"Good. Never forget this—your boss *cannot* be trusted."

Bowcut jumped into the chopper's cabin, followed by Roux. They immediately took to the sky, giving her an overhead view of Hunters Point. Two long lines of supersoldiers held back a mass over twenty times its size, fighting over the countless bodies of creatures littering the hill and the road. Smoke and fire billowed out of the shattered apartment buildings. Everything focused on this point, with the streets around it completely deserted.

"It's some sight," Roux said, sounding proud of the battle below.

For the first time, a sense of optimism grew in Bowcut, though it was tempered. She trusted Roux with her life, but they were now going to join up with a man she couldn't trust as far as she could spit.

"Give it a couple of hours and we'll have taken the city back," Roux added.

"What's the point if the queen escapes, though, right?"

"Precisely. That's why we're headed there now. If she's not destroyed, these battles will wage forever, and time is not on humanity's side. And eventually, she'll find a weakness in our armor."

"Is there one?"

Roux looked away in thought, preferring not to answer.

Maybe it's too soon for optimism . . .

ELLEN STOOD ON THE STARBOARD SIDE OF THE *NIMITZ*'S bridge, watching drone footage from the city. So far, everything was going to plan. This fact pleased and saddened her simultaneously. She let out a deep sigh. Humanity might win the day, courtesy of Albert Van Ness.

But if he wins . . . Tom is dead.

By now, she knew the enemy. Van Ness, like her husband, was laser focused on his mission. Fanatical even. Winning was his obsession. Now, it was her husband's as well. She knew Van Ness would not stop until he defeated the queen, proving his own superiority, and then wiped her husband from existence.

But Tom will find a way. He always does.

"Stand by to load the boats," Captain Collingwood ordered.

His words rapidly snapped her out of her thoughts.

Boats?

Ellen moved over to the port side, behind two junior officers. Monitors in front of them showed supersoldiers lined up in one of the lower cargo bays. Six of the landing craft had drawn by the side of the *Nimitz* and bobbed in the water.

Seconds later, ten supersoldiers leaped off the side in turn and onto the first vessel. They organized themselves into two ranks and stood static, crowded near the stern. Another group leaped onto the second boat.

Ellen spun to face the captain. "What's going on?"

"I'm dispersing these soldiers throughout the fleet to protect all our ships," Collingwood replied.

"Why? The creatures can't reach us out here."

"But they could when we dock, or if they somehow managed to board a carrier. There're a hundred ways we could get attacked, like yesterday. That cannot happen. We *must* protect our fleet."

Ellen shook her head. "This sounds like Van Ness talking. Did he suggest this?"

"This was my idea, Mrs. Cafferty. I had to talk Van Ness into it."

"*You* talked *him* into it?"

Ellen looked away, thinking through the scene.
No one talks Van Ness into anything.

Dispersing these supersoldiers throughout the fleet seemed like a very bad idea to her. It was like a Foundation disease, infecting the infrastructure that would support the ongoing struggle. Van Ness with power and influence, no matter how small, on each major carrier and destroyer in the U.S. Navy.

The simple truth remained: nobody understood Van Ness like the team and she did. Every decision he made had a purpose, no matter how small, and was never flippant. It may be paranoid, but that's the way they had to operate if they wanted to counter any unexpected moves beyond the known plan.

"Captain, I know Albert Van Ness. He is a master manipulator. He *wants* his soldiers on your boats."

"That soldier saved my life yesterday and the lives of everyone on this ship. Not only that, but consider the strategic advantage we gain here. Spreading Van Ness' forces thin makes it *far* less likely they can mutiny. I don't trust them, either. But I'd rather have only a few on my boat than a few hundred. Rest assured, they will be under armed guard the entire time. Disperse them, dilute their power."

He had a valid point, but it still didn't feel right to her. She stepped toward him. "I'd rather face ten creatures than one of his men, Captain. At least with creatures, you know their intentions. With all due respect, what are these supersoldiers' intentions?"

Collingwood looked down at the remainder of Van Ness' men as they boarded the vessels. "I'm very sorry, Mrs. Cafferty. My decision is final."

"Fine, but ask yourself this, Captain: The creatures answer to the queen, right?"

"I suppose so."

"But *who* do these soldiers answer to?"

CHAPTER THIRTY-THREE

V an Ness straightened in his wheelchair and gazed up Lombard Street. He imagined Karen Green in one of the tall buildings, viewing the horrors below: the battered cars, the deaths, the queen . . . For a pawn in the grandest game of human existence, she'd proven far from sacrificial.

But I've *sacrificed more than anyone.*

And they'll soon learn my price.

Today, he felt invigorated, like in his previous fights before this debilitating injury. His spine crushed under the weight of a dying creature so many years ago.

The queen will pay for what she's done . . .

Being on the front line evoked memories of fighting side by side with his father, Otto—globe-spanning operations that had stopped countless human deaths. Jakarta, Warsaw, Strasbourg, Manila. Endless campaigns to protect humanity, until humanity stopped him in the form of Thomas Cafferty.

The world owes my family. It's nearly time for it to settle its debts.

Van Ness glanced at his watch. The grander plan was close to launch. Much of it depended on impeccable timing. And his assumptions about the queen.

I need her to rise to the surface. Only then can I claim supremacy.

Humans, he could control. The queen? He knew she wasn't as gullible. She was ruthless, calculating, strong. But he was hoping she was driven by the same instincts as him. He was depending on it.

A chopper thundered over the tops of the buildings and descended toward the park. As soon as its skids touched the ground, Roux and Bowcut disembarked. She headed for her team.

Van Ness waved Roux over. The head of his army sprinted across the grass.

"Hello, sir," he said.

Always compliant. Always efficient. An invaluable ally for the battle.

"As of now, the creatures remain occupied with our diversion," Roux continued.

"Excellent work, my friend. We do have one slight problem."

"Which is?"

"The queen hasn't come out to play yet. I believe we should provide her with some motivation."

"How do you suggest doing that? We could send down some soldiers—"

"No, no," Van Ness said, cutting him off. "I cannot descend downward, as you see. No, this fight needs to happen here, for all to witness."

"What do you suggest?"

"Something more personal," Van Ness replied. "Between her and me. One apex predator to another. Beating them in battle clearly isn't enough. I'm afraid we'll have to humiliate her out of her dirty nest."

Roux raised his eyebrows. "How? I mean, her army is taking a beating and she still hasn't appeared."

"Take your supersoldiers to find ten creatures. Then drag them over to the tennis courts and tie them firmly to the fence."

"Then what?"

"Then what, indeed. If the queen is anything like me, she'll react to my next move."

"Which is . . . ?"

Van Ness glanced over at Cafferty and smirked. "Do you know why people lose at chess, Mr. Roux?"

"Why?"

"They let their emotions get in the way. I'm betting she will, too."

EVERYTHING AROUND THE PARK FELT LIKE AN ODD REALITY. The distant sound of brutal conflict. The screeches of dying creatures. Choppers in the sky. Laser blasts. Closer, the menacing breach, intimidating and silent.

Yet despite all of this—and the stench of decomposition and the cloying smoke—the sunlit uplands of a free world started to appear tantalizingly close in Cafferty's mind. Roux's update told him that.

The apparent success of their mission likely meant that, for him, things were about to drastically change.

Van Ness could choose any moment to snuff Cafferty's life out, and they both knew it. He'd made his peace with that fact. Although he had no intention of going down as easily as Sonny Liston after Muhammad Ali's phantom punch in Lewiston, Maine.

However, they still had a few hurdles to clear before that moment would come.

Notably the queen.

Bowcut trudged across the parkland and joined Munoz and Cafferty by the side of a tree. She ripped her gas mask off, revealing her tired, sweaty face. "Good to see you guys in one piece," she gasped. "What's the latest here?"

"Dr. Evil is cooking something up," Munoz replied. He motioned his head toward the breach. "The queen is still in her lair, and Van Ness isn't happy about it."

"So what's the next move?"

"You tell me," Cafferty said, while gazing to the northeast side of the park.

Roux strode toward the tennis courts, looking troubled about his task. Behind him, ten supersoldiers followed, each dragging a writhing creature by its tail in one hand and holding a thick steel chain in the other.

"What the hell?" Cafferty muttered.

Munoz slowly nodded. "No shit."

Every creature had newly inflicted, visible wounds. Blood flowed from gouges in some of their chests. Others had missing limbs. None moved with their typically slick, violent intent. The supersoldiers pulled them to the side of the tennis courts, shoved them against the steel poles that supported the chain-link fence, and tightly wrapped the chains around the creatures' chests.

It looked to Cafferty that the creatures had been lined up to face a firing squad, a ritual butchering to match the cold barbarity humanity had faced. Then again, creatures didn't exactly stick to the Geneva Conventions.

Once the last creature had been secured, Van Ness wheeled across the grass at full speed toward Roux and his team.

"Let's find out what's going down," Cafferty said.

Munoz and Bowcut flanked him as they followed the wheelchair, half jogging to keep up with Van Ness.

Cafferty leaned toward his shoulder mic. "Ellen, you still there?"

"Got you loud and clear, Tom."

"Everything okay on the *Nimitz*?"

"I'm not sure."

"What do you mean?"

"Collingwood is spreading the supersoldiers around to all the other carriers, apparently to protect the fleet from any creatures and to dilute Van Ness' army."

"What?"

"He's spooked about what happened on the bridge yesterday and doesn't want to jeopardize the fleet. I can't say I blame him, but I don't like it."

"Neither do I," Cafferty said slowly.

"They're keeping the soldiers under armed guard."

"Not sure that makes a difference."

"Me neither."

This was a move he didn't see coming. He momentarily squeezed his eyes tight, forcing back the lump in his throat. "Make sure you closely watch those super-soldiers and let me know what's happening."

"*Will do.*"

"Stay safe, baby."

"*You, too, cuddle bug.*"

Cafferty winced.

Munoz stifled a laugh.

Ellen used this pet name as a joke because they both found it a bit corny. If anything, it was probably to ease his nerves, or, perhaps, to share a final moment of fun with him as the battle for San Francisco had finally turned in humanity's favor.

Van Ness headed straight for the chained creatures. His chair bumped over the grass and he brought it to a halt in front of the first one.

The injured creature bared its teeth and screeched at him. He stared back quizzically, appearing to question its pointless defiance.

Oddly, there was one spare pole at the end of the tennis court. Van Ness stared at it for a moment while drumming his fingers against the arm of his chair.

Cafferty's finger slowly curled around his laser's trigger. If the tennis court was his chosen execution site, he refused to die this way. Especially as he suspected that Van Ness would force Diego and Sarah to fire the shots.

The twisted asshole would like nothing better.

That isn't happening.

Maybe, he wondered, his saving grace was the nonappearance of the queen. Van Ness' victory wasn't assured until then, and he knew the madman would not stop until he killed her.

He's gonna make me watch him win . . . and then end my life . . .

ON THE CUSP OF WINNING AGAINST OVERWHELMING NUMBERS of creatures, Bowcut stood in front of the strangest sight in San Francisco. She watched as Van Ness bizarrely peered along the line of the ten injured creatures, probably contemplating his next moves.

Roux stood to the right of his wheelchair, awaiting further commands.

Munoz stepped across to her and whispered out of the side of his mouth, "It's like he's choosing from a Red Lobster menu."

"Shut up for a minute."

She concentrated on Van Ness. The cogs were turning in his brain. He was up to something. More than just lining up creatures for a cold-blooded kill. Something maybe more sinister than the chained-up creatures suggested.

Van Ness eventually waved Roux over. "Franco, you've done a most excellent job."

"Thank you, sir. If we continue at our current rate, the soldiers can move to their cleanup operation modes. We'll hunt the remnants of the creatures through the night."

"After we kill the queen."

Roux affirmed, "After we kill her."

"How many casualties did we receive?"

"Just over four hundred, sir. We're in great shape."

"Very good, very good. I could not have done it better myself."

"What is the plan now, sir?"

"Simple. We'll draw out the queen by executing her captured children, one by one, limb by limb. I'll slice through each of them and give them plenty of time to transmit their cries of distress. That should get her attention. But first, a quick matter to attend to."

Van Ness reached into his blazer pocket and pulled out a small Luger pistol. "This belonged to my father, Otto Van Ness. It was his sidearm in the Führerbunker on that last fateful day before Berlin fell. The first day he learned of these creatures. The first day of the Foundation and what would become my lifelong mission, my obsession. Quite a piece of history, isn't it?"

Roux shifted uncomfortably. "Yes, sir."

Van Ness inspected it, twisting the pistol from side to side. "You know, I gave it as a gift long ago to my former number two, Edwards. I'd like to give it as a gift to you now, Mr. Roux. You've earned it."

Roux eyed Bowcut for a second. A knowing look. She had seen that look before from her SWAT team when they knew they were in over their heads.

She tensed.

In the space of a heartbeat, Van Ness raised the pistol and fired. A bullet slammed squarely into Roux's chest, knocking him off his feet. His body crashed to the ground, and his head thumped hard against a rock. Blood pooled into the dirt surrounding him.

Van Ness tossed the weapon aside and wiped his hand with his handkerchief. He wheeled a couple of feet back. "Thank you, Mr. Roux."

"*No!*" Bowcut shouted.

She went to raise her gun.

To hell with Van Ness.

Before she could even level her weapon, a supersoldier surged across and ripped it free from her grip. Two more disarmed Cafferty and Munoz just as fast. All three stood there with a supersoldier breathing down each of their necks.

Bowcut grunted with anger. Her whole body shook at the injustice and needless act. She went to step forward, regardless of the consequences. At this moment, she was prepared to force her thumbs into Van Ness' eyes and do what the team should have done in Paris.

A strong hand clamped around her shoulder, stopping her dead. Unable to move, she peered down at Roux's motionless body and the blood-drenched rock his head was resting against.

Van Ness spun his chair toward Cafferty, Munoz, and her. "Don't be concerned, my friends. You are in no danger at present. Our immediate objective remains the same."

His words only increased her fury.

"Why?" Bowcut asked through gritted teeth.

"Because he was second-in-command, of course," Van Ness said matter-of-factly. He rubbed the stump on the end of his left arm. "You see, I simply won't be betrayed by my number two ever again."

CHAPTER THIRTY-FOUR

Clouds had rolled in from the sea, and light spits of rain dropped on the park. Van Ness stared at Bowcut, Cafferty, and Munoz in turn, studying their faces, watching their reactions to the events. Unadulterated hatred burned in their eyes. This was an irrelevance. They couldn't see the big picture, the tough decisions required to win the war of all wars.

Van Ness' mind drifted back to Edwards gruesomely slicing off his hand with a creature's claw over a year ago. A man whom he trusted, whom he was building humanity's future with.

Not again.

I will never be fooled again . . .

By now, at the dock, his creations would be trouncing their way through the last few thousand creatures that had brazenly colonized San Francisco. This fact alone should've told the queen everything she needed to know. That regardless of her vast armies, humanity—led by Albert Van Ness—would continue for the foreseeable future.

And no one, not Roux, not Cafferty, will stop me this time.

But only if I eliminate the queen . . .

Killing her wouldn't signal the end but the beginning of the end. Barring an unforeseeable disaster today, the human race hadn't tasted victory against the rise of the creatures until San Francisco. After taking this city and the queen's destruction, humanity wouldn't taste defeat again under his stewardship.

"I don't know who's worse," Cafferty said, glaring down at Roux's corpse. "You or the creatures."

"It's unwise to test my patience. I'll deal with you once we've gotten the next phase out of the way."

"Is there anything you won't do?"

"*No!*" Van Ness snapped. "No! There is nothing I won't do. I'm going to make *you* watch as I destroy the queen. And then I will destroy you, Mr. Mayor, once and for all. You alone caused this. I am the one who will undo your damage."

Van Ness rotated his chair away and faced the first creature. It struggled uselessly against the steel chains. The supersoldiers had once again done sterling work. He grabbed a laser pistol from one of the soldiers and fired his beam across the creature's knees.

The bottom half of the creature's legs dropped to the ground. Yellow blood hissed from the stumps. It roared in agony, spraying hot saliva over a few of the supersoldiers. They didn't move a muscle—a lot more obedient than Roux had ever realized and completely under Van Ness' ultimate control.

He waited and listened.

No sounds came from the breach.

Van Ness lifted his aim to the creature's face and fired, splitting its head in two from top to bottom.

The creature sagged against the chain, lifeless.

Still nothing from the breach. But he never expected only one would do the job. He had to show the queen this would happen again and again and again, all across the world, until none in her army was left. A callous slaughter to match her own planned destruction of humanity. Two could play at her game.

Van Ness moved to the second creature in line. He severed its arms with two blasts of the laser beam. The creature let out a piercing, painful screech. Loud. Long. Surely enough to register.

He waited.

Once again, nothing came from the depths.

Van Ness drew his laser beam across the creature's neck. Its head thudded against the grass. He wheeled to the third creature. This one already had an arm and leg ripped clean from their sockets. The creature seemingly whimpered at him.

Pathetic. Is it crying? An apex predator behaving like this?

He shook his head in disgust and killed this one in an instant, carving the beam across its soulless eyes.

"Nothing yet?" Van Ness shouted in the direction of the breach. "Afraid you've met your match?"

He wheeled to the fourth creature. This one had a gaping wound in its stomach. He fired the laser beam straight through the hole, carving it deeper. The creature howled, desperately struggling against the chains. He fired again, and the creature roared in agony.

A second later, a low vibration echoed from the breach below.

The ground began to rumble under his wheels.

"It's time for our final act, Mr. Cafferty," Van Ness exclaimed.

He tapped the digital interface on the arm of his chair. The supersoldiers behind Cafferty, Munoz, and Bowcut shoved them forward, pushing them all onto their knees, eye-level with his wheelchair.

Seeing the condescending Cafferty kneeling before him—as he should be—was immensely satisfying. The man who escaped the tunnels of New York, who stumbled his way through London and Paris and brought down everything Van Ness and his father had built, was now at his mercy.

Make him watch, and then break the man.

Now that the queen was moments from rising, there was no reason for Van Ness to delay the next phase. He locked eyes with Cafferty. "It gave me no pleasure to kill Mr. Roux. But you, Thomas . . . when I kill a Cafferty, *I'm going to enjoy it.*"

Cafferty attempted to lurch forward, but the supersoldier kept a firm grip on his shoulders. "Get it over with, goddamn it!" he yelled. "I'm tired of your games."

"That's precisely what I'm doing." Van Ness tapped the arm of his chair again. "All done."

"What?"

"When I said 'a Cafferty,' who said I was going to kill *you* first?" Van Ness smiled as his nemesis' face morphed from anger to sudden fear. "No, no,

Mr. Mayor, I've got other plans for you. But as we speak, my supersoldiers are about to take over your entire American fleet, the most powerful armada ever assembled, to quote your captain, and unfortunately, your wife is . . . expendable."

"You son of a bitch!" Cafferty shouted, struggling to break free from the supersoldier's grip. "Our deal was between you and me!"

"I will get to you, Thomas, I promise. First, though, I'm going to *hurt* you."

The failed mayor struggled again. But in all his wriggling, irritatingly, he managed to pull the mic out and pressed the transmitter button down.

"Ellen!" Cafferty shouted frantically. "Stop the soldiers! It's a tra—"

A supersoldier ripped the radio from Cafferty's body armor. Two others did the same to Munoz and Bowcut.

"How valiant, Mr. Mayor," Van Ness said, pressing the execute button on the arm of his wheelchair. "But alas, what's done is now done."

IN THE DARKNESS OF THE USS *NIMITZ*'S HOLD, AN ELECTRONIC pad beeped on the doors of an unmarked Foundation shipping container, the one carrying the vat of liquid that was meant to feed the supersoldiers. Two metal rods clanked down and to the side. Green slime spilled across the ground, and one of the doors creaked open a few inches.

Guttural breaths came from inside. The screech of claws grinding against steel. Heavy footsteps slapped against the metal floor, crunching on pieces of the vat's broken plastic body. Slow at first, then faster.

Both doors banged open and nearly flew off their hinges.

A massive creature exploded out of the darkness and raced for the exit.

ON THE CROWDED BRIDGE OF THE *NIMITZ*, ELLEN FRANTICALLY shouted into the microphone. "Tom, are you there? *Tom!* Can you hear me?"

The line went dead.

She exchanged worried glances with Captain Collingwood.

"Zoom in on the drone footage of their position!" Ellen commanded.

Collingwood nodded, and a navy tech complied.

She scrutinized the live footage of the park. The more it focused in, the blurrier it got. But it was obvious Van Ness was now in control and had Cafferty, Munoz, and Bowcut lined up in front of him.

Ellen looked at the expressionless supersoldier on the bridge, then glanced out the window at the various crafts carrying hundreds more fast approaching the rest of the fleet. It would be moments before the supersoldiers were on board every U.S. aircraft carrier and destroyer in the armada.

"Captain, it's a trap," Ellen shouted. "Van Ness has set you up. His men are about to take over the fleet. You have to stop this!"

Collingwood studied the drone footage from the field. He then lifted his binoculars to look at the distant transport boats.

Just then, a faint shriek came from somewhere far below, followed by crashing sounds and the faint crackle of gunfire.

"What the hell is going on?!" Collingwood shouted.

The XO jumped on to the comm. "Status report, all decks!"

The horrifying sound of sailors screaming and the unmistakable sound of a creature screeching came through the speakers, along with more gunfire.

"Help! There's a crea—"

Ellen's pulse quickened.

A creature loose on the Nimitz? *How?*

The sounds of sailors screaming and being torn to pieces grew louder and closer. Chaos erupted on the bridge as crew members shouted over each other.

The shrieks of the creature tearing through the ship grew closer still.

"Lock down the bridge!" the XO shouted. "And secure that door!"

A dozen navy crewmen took up defensive positions and drew their pistols, aiming them squarely at the heavy steel door at the front of the bridge. One junior officer went over to rotate the wheel to securely lock the heavy door, desperate to do so before the creature was upon them.

"Captain!" Ellen shouted over the cacophony. "Order the fleet to destroy those ships now before the supersoldiers reach them!"

Collingwood stood frozen with fear. Finally, he said, "I'm sorry I didn't listen earlier, Mrs. Cafferty."

Ellen grabbed the comm and thrust it into the captain's hands. "Send out the order before it's too late!"

Collingwood pressed down on the receiver. "Attention all U.S. ships, this is Captain Collingwood of the USS *Nimitz*. The boats approaching yours are carrying hostiles. Immediately target those vessels and destroy them. Do not let them board, no matter what. And may God hel—"

The bridge door that the crewman had been trying to seal blasted open and a massive jet-black creature bounded through. A barrage of bullets slammed into the monster, not slowing it down in the slightest. The creature's tail swept forward and sliced three crew members in half at the waist. Blood sprayed all over the windows, walls, and floor. It leaped through the air and tore through three more crewmen with its razor-sharp claws.

Ellen stumbled back in shock at the speed of the lightning-fast carnage. The creature had a box with a blinking red light drilled right into its brain. The same control box she saw a year ago on the rooftop of the De Jong Group building in London, attached to a hybrid.

This is no ordinary creature. This is Van Ness' genetic monstrosity.

And he's controlling it.

Ellen grabbed the motionless supersoldier by its uniform and screamed in its face. "Do something, goddammit!"

The supersoldier stood still, with no reaction whatsoever to her, the creature, or anything happening on the bridge.

The creature seemed to ignore it as well.

Collingwood grabbed Ellen and dragged her to the blast door on the other side of the bridge. "Come on! It's no use!"

The creature tore through sailor after sailor, crushing their skulls in its powerful hands, ripping them limb from limb. Within moments, everyone on the bridge was dead, save for Collingwood and Ellen. The captain frantically opened the back hatch as the creature turned its attention to its final prey.

"*Go!*" he shouted.

Collingwood pushed Ellen through the blast door and slammed it shut, turning the wheel quickly to lock himself inside with the creature.

Ellen turned back and futilely banged on the door, looking through a small glass window into the bridge. It was no use—the door was sealed and practically impenetrable.

Through the glass, the creature squared off against the captain. Collingwood desperately drew his gun and fired. Unaffected, the creature swung its tail just far enough to slice off his hands, as if it were teasing him. The useless gun and his severed appendages fell to the ground, soaking the captain in his own blood. He dropped to his knees in agony.

The creature loomed over Collingwood and slowly drove the pointed tip of its tail through his chest, inch by inch, impaling him in slow motion. Blood gurgled out of his mouth and his body went limp. The creature withdrew its tail rapidly, and the captain's limp carcass crashed to the ground.

Bile rose in Ellen's throat.

Then something caught her eye in the background. Through the bridge's blood-spattered windows, distant U.S. Navy ships deployed missiles squarely at the boats carrying Van Ness' supersoldiers. The report of missile fire and the shock wave of nearby explosions shook the *Nimitz*.

Thank God, the fleet got our message.

She prayed they destroyed every single one of Van Ness' supersoldiers in time.

Inside the bridge, the creature turned its attention to the door. Ellen instinctually backed away. The creature slammed its shoulder against the steel.

The door held.

The creature flailed wildly in the room, angry it could not reach its prey. It would be only a matter of time before it backed out the way it came and found her. And if the supersoldiers were of no help . . .

Ellen could barely think.

Where do I go? Where do I hide?

Her next thoughts went to Karen Green and her little son, Joey, who was only a year or two older than Ellen's own son, David. After the ordeal they had survived on the streets of San Francisco, they were now sitting ducks in their room two decks below.

I have to warn them. I have to protect them.

She cast her own safety aside, and any thoughts of her husband's predicament in the city.

CHAPTER THIRTY-FIVE

T he ground below Cafferty shook like the city was
experiencing a mini-earthquake. Dogs barked
in distant streets. In the buildings surrounding the park, shards of glass dropped from broken
windows and shattered against the sidewalks. The
shaking grew stronger by the second, and he thrust
a foot forward to maintain his balance.

A supersoldier ripped Cafferty back, keeping him
in a tight grip. He exchanged glances with Bowcut
and Munoz. Both gave him a wide-eyed stare. The
queen was most definitely rising, and the three of
them were weaponless and being held hostage.

Van Ness lowered his laser from a chained-up
creature that he'd just decapitated. He briefly swept
the barrel across the team, stopping at each one of
them in turn, and smiled.

Bowcut spat in his direction in defiance.

"A pity you've never been taught manners, Ms.
Bowcut," Van Ness said, visibly disgusted. "Without manners, without integrity, we are no different
from them, I fear."

Bowcut spat again, closer to hitting Van Ness this time.

"Enough!" Van Ness snapped. "I have waited a very long time to meet our guest, and I'd like to be ready for her."

He turned his attention back to the breach, his face deadly serious. The shaking of the ground grew stronger and stronger by the second.

"Any moment now, she will reveal herself," Van Ness said.

"No shit, Sherlock," Munoz barked back.

Cafferty had no firm idea about the monstrosity they were about to witness, but he should've seen Van Ness' move against the fleet coming. The megalomaniac had likely gone over his plan a thousand times, preparing for this moment.

His thoughts raced to Ellen, there aboard the *Nimitz*, not knowing what mortal danger she was in. He should've realized Van Ness would try to hurt him in every way possible, twisting the knife hard before eventually killing him. Breaking his spirit first, then breaking him. Ellen was the closest thing to his heart. Only now did he realize she was always Van Ness' first target.

And now his entire team stood at their most vulnerable.

The ground below Cafferty's knees jerked a few inches upward, snapping him out of the scramble of thoughts flying through his mind. He drew in a shuddering breath.

Just like in Paris, when the hybrid creature had held him by his neck, he was at the mercy of Van

Ness again. But back in the French capital, he saw a way out. Right now, his team could only play the role of useless witnesses to Van Ness' victory or defeat.

And both scenarios spell my death.

The supersoldiers rushed over to the breach and formed a circle around its perimeter, preparing for battle. Two remained by Van Ness' side, and three others held Cafferty's team firmly in their grips.

A mound of grass rose unnaturally in the center of the park. Fast. About the size of a town house. It crashed back down after a second, leaving a huge patch of disrupted earth. The supersoldiers turned from the breach.

A second later, the ground rose again, higher this time. Chunks of soil and rock rained down on the team. Cafferty wrapped his arms around his head and ducked. Munoz and Bowcut did likewise.

Van Ness sat motionless in his chair, unflinchingly observing the phenomenon. It appeared that nothing would distract him from the first view of his ultimate prey.

It turned out Tom needed to see it, too.

Cafferty's heart raced, watching the spectacle unfold. Van Ness' apparent calmness baffled him. This really was it. They were about to come face-to-face with a monster the likes of which the world had never seen. Sure, the supersoldiers had been ruthlessly effective against her minions. However, nothing could prepare them for what was about to come.

A muffled screech emanated from the abyss below.

Huge chunks of earth exploded upward with tremendous force. Through the tornado of dirt and debris, a massive creature thrust out of the ground.

The queen.

As Karen Green had noted, she was almost three times the size of any of the killers Cafferty had ever seen, at least twenty feet tall. Viscous fluid dripped from her jet-black skin. She had talons the size of machetes, a serrated tail the length of a vaulting pole.

And her eyes . . .

The queen's eyes glowed demonic red through the dirt and haze.

Her feet crashed against the ground with an earth-shaking thud less than a hundred yards away. She quickly scanned her surroundings and focused on the metal poles surrounding the tennis court, at her dead and wounded children.

The queen opened her mouth, revealing three rows of teeth that looked like long, sharp icicles, chiseled to razor-sharp points.

Then she roared.

The force blasted Cafferty, Munoz, and Bowcut off their knees, along with the supersoldiers holding them. Cafferty's head slammed against the ground hard. For a moment, he lay stunned.

If just her scream can do that . . .

Van Ness' wheelchair skidded back and slammed against the tennis court's chain-link fence. His body jolted in the chair, and he used his remaining hand to stop from falling. The two supersoldier guards, along with the others, leaped back to their feet and quickly took up position protecting Van Ness.

Seizing the freedom from the grip of Van Ness' men, Cafferty scrambled to the side of a tree and took cover behind its trunk. He peered around its edge, expecting a vicious attack to come at any moment.

Munoz scrambled behind a giant mound of dirt, still clutching his plastic briefcase tightly in his arms.

Bowcut ducked behind another tree a few yards from Cafferty.

The supersoldiers took position near Van Ness, no longer interested in his team. Cafferty knew Van Ness wouldn't expect them to run. Despite being his prisoners, just like him, they still had to see this through.

Simultaneously, the supersoldiers surrounding the breach sprinted toward the queen. The first one to reach her hurled himself at her chest with incredible speed. She swung a muscular arm and batted him away, as if he were a fly. The soldier hurtled fifty yards in the air, out of the park and across the road, and his body crashed into the side of a building.

Holy hell.

Maybe Van Ness underestimated the bitch.

Two supersoldiers wrapped themselves around the monster's ankles. They pulled hard and she dropped to her knees. More supersoldiers followed, latching on to the queen, driving their fists hard into every part of her body. Some drew their laser weapons and fired at point-blank range, but it had no effect.

Nothing punctured her scaly black armor.

Just then, Cafferty noticed the queen had stopped moving entirely. She was frozen in place during the attack, focusing.

Oh shit . . .

Suddenly, every attacking supersoldier burst away from her body at tremendous speed, including the ones attached to her legs and back. They rocketed through the air, out of control, across the park in all directions, slamming into trees, cars, and buildings.

"She's using her telekinetic powers!" Cafferty shouted.

The queen rose to her feet, towering over them, eyes glowing red with anger, and took three hulking strides directly toward her shackled children. Directly toward Van Ness.

As quickly as the supersoldiers had fallen, they climbed to their feet and sprinted straight back to fight. They lined themselves between the queen and Van Ness, trying to stop her advance. She hunched, letting out a deafening screech. The force of it shoved the soldiers back a couple of strides, but they closed back in.

The queen thrust out both of her clenched talons, punching the air.

A massive, invisible telekinetic shock wave burst out of her body, sending the soldiers flying backward once again. They crashed against the tennis court's chain-link fence.

Debris soared past the tree that Cafferty knelt behind.

The queen took three more heavy steps forward, getting close to striking distance of Van Ness, close to where he had been executing her children, close to the man who had spent his life attacking her nests across the world.

The battered supersoldiers sprang back up and returned to block her path.

The queen whipped her tail at the left edge of their line.

A soldier on the end caught her tail and grasped tight. His arms shook and sweat poured down his face as he desperately tried to hang on. The queen thrust a talon in his direction, sending a single, focused telekinetic shock wave directly at him. The invisible force ripped the supersoldier into pieces instantly, sending chunks of him flying in all directions.

Cafferty quickly looked at Van Ness. He recognized the expression on his face. The same expression Van Ness had had when the creatures lifted him against the glass and tried to squeeze the life out of him in Paris.

Fear.

Van Ness is afraid.

With her incredible telekinetic powers, the queen was unstoppable, and Van Ness was only now realizing it.

Another supersoldier leaped directly at the queen's head, but she let out another focused telekinetic blast wave, instantly ripping him apart.

The queen bounded directly at Van Ness, destroying soldier after soldier as she went.

Munoz and Bowcut crawled over to Cafferty, faces terrified.

The queen thrust her talon in the direction of

another soldier, blasting him with another direct shock wave. Pieces of him zipped across the tennis courts and clattered against an umpire's chair, turning it into a twisted wreck.

Van Ness' army was being picked off one by one. Thousands of supersoldiers may have stood a chance against this powerful enemy, but they were still occupied by the distant battle at Hunters Point. Rather than a clever diversion, today's strategy now appeared more like a death warrant.

"Her telekinetic powers are too strong!" Cafferty shouted at his team.

"How the hell do we stop that?" Bowcut replied.

Munoz fumbled to open his plastic briefcase containing the ultrahigh-frequency distress beacon. "I, uh, I've got something that might work."

"*Might?*" Bowcut asked.

His hands trembled as he frantically flipped open the locks on the case.

"I found the exact frequency the creatures use when deploying their telekinetic powers. So maybe we can interrupt that signal."

"Diego, whatever you've got, do it fast!" Bowcut shouted.

He flipped the power on, and the lights illuminated on the control board. In the center of the board was a button to activate the ultrahigh-frequency beacon.

The queen tore through soldier after soldier and was now only feet away from Van Ness, Cafferty, and his team. It roared again, nearly knocking them off their feet.

We're moments away from slaughter . . .
"*Diego!*" Cafferty shouted. "*Hit the damn thing!*"
"Here goes nothing . . ."
Munoz held his breath and slammed his fist down hard on the activate button.

CHAPTER THIRTY-SIX

Ellen watched as the creature darted out of the bridge of the *Nimitz* at lightning-fast speed. She had to move. Before she could, though, she thought:

Where are the few remaining supersoldiers aboard the Nimitz? *Are they a threat, too? Or only standing by while Van Ness slaughters everyone on board?*

She shook her head. Those questions could wait until she ensured her own safety.

The distant report of gunshots snapped her out of her reverie. Some of the crew likely had weapons on them, but she wasn't sure how many. It wouldn't matter. This monster was unstoppable.

Karen and Joey . . .

Ellen had to move, fast. She spun and clanked down several sets of metal steps, past the flight deck and into the depths of the superstructure.

She entered the main hangar deck and rushed past two prepped fighter jets, both waiting on the elevators, ready to be lifted up to the main deck for battle. She headed for the entrance to the sleeping quarters. That area was tight, with bunks packed into rooms like sardines, though Karen and Joey had been assigned their own compartment.

The long, brightly lit corridor had been sealed off at the halfway point as part of the lockdown procedure. A solid steel door had been slammed shut, compartmentalizing the *Nimitz*. This new retrofit had done its job, so far . . . It seemed as if the creature had not yet reached any of the crew quarters.

Ellen raced in the direction of Karen and Joey's compartment.

Marines burst out of two rooms at the far end, weapons raised, and aimed through each doorway as they made their way toward Ellen.

"Are you okay, ma'am?" one asked as they hurried past.

"I'm fine. Did you see a woman and kid back there?"

"Yep. Second-to-last door on your right."

Ellen already knew the location, but the answer eased her concern. She jogged along the highly polished floor toward their room.

As she reached to within twenty yards, a thunderous hollow boom rocked the corridor. She veered to the left and thrust her hands against the wall to maintain her balance.

What the hell was that? A missile strike?

Ellen steadied herself and launched herself forward again, determined.

Then she saw the damage and the sight made her skid to a stop.

The steel blast door at the end of the hallway had

a slight buckle in the top left corner. She remembered Tom telling her how the creatures managed to smash down the entrance to the command center in the Visitors' Pavilion. That door underneath the Hudson had been the strongest available, but it was still no match for the creatures. She had no clue about the strength of the door in front of her, but she had no intention of hanging around long enough to find out.

Another loud boom came from the other side. The top left portion of the door buckled farther. Small pieces of mechanical and electrical debris shot across the ground.

"Holy shit," Ellen uttered.

She sprinted for Karen and Joey's room. As she neared, Karen poked her head out of the entrance.

"Grab Joey," Ellen yelled as she ran toward them. "We need to leave! Now!"

The creature slammed the far side of the door again. The shudder-inducing noise of groaning metal echoed down the corridor.

Karen disappeared for a few seconds, then returned with her terrified son in her arms. The wide-eyed look of fear on both of their faces told its own story. They were back in a living nightmare. All Ellen could do was keep cool for their sakes—despite the sickly feeling of dread in her stomach—and try to use all of her experience battling these monsters to keep them alive.

Karen reached Ellen's side. "Where do we go?"

"Away from here. That's a good start."

The creature battered the door a few more inches, forcing it open enough to create a small gap.

Not big enough for the monstrosity to enter, but one more hit would likely do the job.

Ellen turned and raced back toward the hangar deck. Karen's footsteps followed closely behind. The marines reentered the corridor, and she pressed herself against the wall as they rapidly moved past, weapons raised.

Brave . . . but foolish.

"Your weapons won't stop it!" Ellen shouted at the soldiers as they ran by. "You need to fall back!"

The marines didn't listen and took up firing positions in the hallway.

One final thunderous boom from the far side of the hallway and the steel door came crashing down.

A creature stood behind it on bent, muscular legs, its powerful arms by its sides. Staring forward. It let out a bloodcurdling screech and bounded along the side wall toward the marines at an incredible speed.

Rifle shots reverberated around the corridor.

Joey covered his ears.

Karen looked to Ellen for guidance. They were still only forty yards clear of the marines. A creature could make that ground up in the blink of an eye if they failed to stop its attack.

That, she accepted, was the likely scenario.

"Keep moving!" Ellen shouted.

The rapid fire from the rifles quickly decreased as more and more screams filled the corridor. One by one, the marines were slaughtered. The last few active weapons discharged. Then two final cries of agony.

Everything fell silent in the corridor.

Ellen looked over her shoulder as they neared the opening to the hangar deck.

The creature stood above the butchered corpses of the soldiers. It slowly raised its head in her direction. A second later, it rocketed forward, heading directly for Ellen, Karen, and Joey.

Just then, Ellen finally realized.

I'm the target. It's after me . . .

And it will slaughter every living thing on this ship to get what it wants.

CHAPTER THIRTY-SEVEN

The queen had closed to near striking distance of Van Ness. Two more thumping strides and her tail would carve him to pieces. He frantically pressed the control pad on his armrest, but the wheels of his chair spun in the dirt without gaining any traction. His face had whitened. His lips trembled. Through all of Van Ness' detailed planning—and all of his graceless bravado—Cafferty knew his mortal enemy hadn't seen this coming.

But apparently the queen already had ideas about this meeting. It appeared she wanted to kill Van Ness up close, unlike the supersoldiers, which she continued to dispatch with her terrifying telekinetic power. Another Roux look-alike shot across the park in several pieces and splattered against the side of a wrecked ice-cream truck.

"Diego," Cafferty bellowed above the queen's roars. "What the hell?"

"Give it a second to work, Tom."

"We might not have one."

Bowcut sprang to her feet and sprinted for a laser in a crouching run. She reached within a few feet and dove for the weapon.

The queen, momentarily distracted from Van Ness, flicked a talon in her direction, sending Bowcut toppling across the grass. Her body slammed into one of the tennis court's steel poles. Blood from a creature's corpse dripped onto her now motionless body.

"Sarah!" Cafferty shouted.

Bowcut slowly rolled onto her side, eyes half closed.

Still alive.

For how much longer, though?

Cafferty shuddered.

Sarah wasn't getting up any time soon, though she was spared being ripped to pieces. He guessed his team would be the next target for the queen's personal treatment, considering they'd destroyed two nests.

The queen took another crashing step toward Van Ness. She screamed, and the force rammed his chair back against the chain-link fence. His gray hair and face were soaked with her sticky saliva. He snatched the laser from his lap and raised it in her direction. She flicked a talon toward him. The laser flew from his grip and cartwheeled hundreds of yards away through the smoky air.

"Goddamn it, Diego," Cafferty growled.

"It's fired up, Tom. I'm just not sure it'll work."

Just then, a high-pitched, nearly indiscernible whistle came from Munoz's device. Cafferty waited, desperate to see if it had any effect.

The queen jabbed out her talon in the direction of another advancing soldier, trying to use her telekinetic force to stop his attack.

But nothing happened.

She tried again, but the action failed to slow the soldier's charge. He slammed into the queen and crashed his fist against her teeth.

"Holy hell, you've done it, Diego!" Cafferty blurted out while staring at the remaining supersoldiers launching themselves forward. "You've taken away her power!"

"For now. Whew!" he replied, wiping sweat from his brow.

Cafferty grabbed Diego's face and kissed him on the cheek.

Munoz stayed focused on his device, gazing at the measurements streaming across the LED screen. He tweaked a few dials, oblivious to the desperate fight that was taking place only a stone's throw from the tree.

Two more supersoldiers hammered into the queen. They shoved her back several yards while punching her face and chest. She swung wildly at them, screeching. She managed to batter several away, though the force of her strikes had visibly waned. Van Ness' creations staggered back only a few feet now before immediately reengaging the enemy.

The battle is turning . . .

"I'm checking on Sarah," Cafferty said. "Keep that damned thing going."

Munoz looked across to him. "That's my plan, Stan. I'll keep her jammed. We've gotta take this boss-level bitch down."

Cafferty slapped him on the back. He rose to his feet and rushed across the grass to Sarah on unsteady legs. Adrenaline propelled him forward. His rapid pulse hammered in his ears. He took a wide berth of the area where the soldiers continued their fight with the queen and skidded down by Bowcut's side.

He gently placed his hand on her shoulder. "How you doin'?"

Her eyes flickered open. "I've seen better days."

"We all have," Cafferty added. "I think Diego just saved our asses."

Bowcut winced and let out a grunt. "The queen?"

"Going down."

"Thank fuck."

The soldiers had pushed the queen to the right of the tennis courts, away from Van Ness and toward the trees that lined the park. Closer to Diego, but the shuddering blows inflicted on the queen had visibly started to take their toll. Her confident roars had turned to frantic howls. Swings from her arms and legs missed their targets. She spun wildly, attempting to throw off two soldiers, but they maintained their grip.

Seven supersoldiers now attacked the queen, all throwing weighty punches. It seemed only a matter of time until the repeated blows ended her resistance.

The proverbial death by a thousand cuts.

Van Ness peered across to Cafferty. The fear in his eyes had gone, replaced by a look of curiosity. The wheels on his chair bit into the dirt, and he powered to the other side of Bowcut's prone body.

"I'd say our agreement is terminated," Cafferty shouted.

"Nonsense," Van Ness said. "While I owe a debt of gratitude to Mr. Munoz, you were never going to survive, Thomas, no matter what."

The supersoldiers pummeled the queen closer to the trees. One hung off each arm and leg. One on her back. Two attacking her torso. Munoz kept peering from behind the tree with an increasing look of panic etched across his face.

The queen staggered closer and closer to Diego's position by the second. Cafferty realized what was happening and shouted, "*Diego!* Move! Right now!"

Sudden fear in his eyes, Munoz obeyed immediately and sprang to his feet, clutching the military-grade tactical beacon under his arm. He needed to get out of the line of fire—fast.

A supersoldier took a running jump at the queen. He pounded both fists into her chest, sending her staggering back a few yards . . .

. . . right to within striking distance of Munoz.

He lurched away from the tree trunk and sprinted toward Cafferty.

The queen's head whipped in Diego's direction.

A split second later, her tail rose to strike.

"Diego, fucking *run*!" Cafferty screamed, searching desperately for a weapon, any weapon, on the ground.

Munoz glanced over his shoulder—the queen was upon him. There was no way to outrun her wrath. He turned and looked back in the direction of Cafferty and Bowcut, locking eyes with his friends one last time. He smiled that classic Diego smile they had come to know and love.

As he did, the queen's tail lashed forward, so fast that the movement was a blur.

The tail impaled Diego right through his chest, piercing his heart instantly. He clutched at the new appendage with one hand, knowing that when the tail withdrew from his torso, he was doomed. Blood spurted from his mouth.

He looked back up at Cafferty, and with his dying breaths, mouthed his last words:

"Finish this . . ."

The queen withdrew her tail, and Diego instantly crumpled to the ground.

"*No!!*" Cafferty cried out in anguish. Bowcut turned away in agony at the sight.

As Munoz's body went limp, the beacon he was holding crashed to the ground as well, smashing to pieces.

The piercing signal it emitted abruptly stopped.

Sensing the device's shackles now removed, the queen let out a deafening screech. Her posture stiffened, followed by the sound of a low boom.

Then a massive telekinetic shock wave left her body, stronger than any previous one. So powerful that the soldiers around her were instantly ripped to pieces, along with Diego's lifeless body.

The air distorted as the wave raced across the park in all directions, picking up anything loose and blasting it away like pieces of shrapnel.

Before Cafferty could move, the wave slammed into him, picking him up and hurling him back at a terrifying speed. Bowcut's injured body was also lifted and thrown, knocking her out.

Van Ness' wheelchair was thrust clear across the tennis court, and he sailed alongside Cafferty, screaming in agony.

With the beacon now destroyed, there was no stopping the queen.

They were all likely flying to their deaths.

And Diego . . . was gone.

CHAPTER THIRTY-EIGHT

Ellen sprinted into the massive hangar bay, looking back every few seconds to ensure Karen and Joey hadn't become separated from her. They had to stick together. The young paramedic remained hot on her heels, only a few steps behind while carrying her son. Heavy footsteps pounded after them, closing with every heartbeat, as did the snarls and the screeches of the monster giving chase.

The creature was in a frenzy like she had never seen, coming directly for her. She'd seen these things enough times before to recognize the intent and persistence, but never directed against a single individual like this.

Ellen frantically scanned the area for any sort of cover: crates, a maze of pumps and piping, the packed missile bay—all easily searchable by the creature. A brutal game of hide-and-seek would not work.

I need to stop this monster . . . somehow.

Ellen raced through the options in her mind. The first time she'd come down to this level, she was so focused on reaching the crew quarters that she hadn't noticed the corpses littering the floor. Engineers, pilots, and whoever else had had the misfortune of being here after the creature had made its first pass through. Blood slicks that looked like oil surrounded the dismembered bodies.

At the far end of the hangar, twenty supersoldiers stood in two ranks, unmoving, seemingly uncaring about what was about to unfold. It became clear to her on the bridge that the supersoldiers would not help. Thankfully, the majority of them had been destroyed on the boats. She knew these remaining few on the *Nimitz* would not provide her salvation.

A light gray Super Hornet fighter jet lay to their left, sitting on one of the elevators with a clear blue sky overhead. The windshield was raised. A ladder was attached to its side. The jet was armed, ready for a mission. Firing a missile inside an aircraft carrier seemed like a very bad idea to her, though, and besides, Ellen had no clue how to operate the plane or the lift. But she had to do something.

"This way," she shouted.

She led Karen and Joey to the rear of the fighter. The first task was to get out of direct sight of the creature, who was about to burst through the corridor.

They ducked beneath the Super Hornet's wing and headed for the tail.

A split second later, the creature bounded into the area.

Ellen craned her neck around the fighter.

Blood dripped from the creature's three rows of teeth. The red light on the box drilled into its brain kept blinking, confirming to Ellen it was still under Van Ness' direct control. It peered around the hangar, then leaped onto a fighter jet on the opposite side of the area. From there, it sprang from plane to plane, scanning the hangar bay for anything left alive.

It's only a matter of time before it gets to us . . .

The creature screeched and dipped out of sight like it had identified something of interest. A moment later, a distinctly human scream rang out, then abruptly stopped. The monster sprang back into view, landing next to a prone sailor, and rammed the point of its tail through the back of his head. The man's body briefly jerked.

Joey went to scream at the sight, but Ellen quickly covered his mouth. She was well aware of the creatures' heightened senses compared with those of a human. The slightest mistake and they'd be toast.

The creature vaulted into the air toward their side of the hangar. Its feet slammed against the body of another Super Hornet, roughly fifty yards away. The metallic clank chimed around the area. The creature slowly turned toward the supersoldiers, eyeing them for a brief moment.

Please God, have the supersoldiers stop this thing.

Nothing happened, though. They stood there, motionless, careless. A far cry from what Ellen had witnessed in Lima.

Shit.

We're on our own.

The creature ignored the supersoldiers and continued on its hunt, thrashing equipment and crates around.

Ellen leaned close to Karen and, keeping her voice low, asked, "Don't suppose you know anything about fighter jets?"

"Like what?"

"Like how to fire their weapons?"

She shook her head. "No, I'm sorry—"

"Hey," a weak male voice called out from a few feet away.

Ellen twisted to face a bank of batteries.

"Hey," the voice repeated.

Karen went to head over.

Fear instantly shot through Ellen. She grabbed the younger woman by the shoulder. "Don't trust any repeated phrase."

"Huh?"

"They can mimic any sound."

Karen grasped Joey tighter and crawled back a few yards. Ellen was unsure what to believe when it came to these creatures.

"Please help me," the male voice continued.

Definitely human.

Ellen crawled toward the bank of batteries on her hands and knees, cautious not to get too close. It didn't seem like a trap, but she couldn't afford a single misstep. A man lay behind the pile, dressed in a green coverall. He had slash wounds on his arms and legs.

"Can you move?" Ellen asked.

"I think I'm a goner." He winced, revealing his red-stained teeth.

Ellen scanned his body up and down. Blood poured from deep gashes all over his body. It looked to her like his femoral artery had been pierced. He'd be dead in a matter of minutes.

She noticed a name tag on his uniform. "Are you a pilot?"

"Best in the fleet," he replied, forcing a smile.

Loud crashing continued inside the hangar bay as the creature manically tore through everything.

"Can you tell me how to fire a missile from that jet?" Ellen asked.

The pilot turned his head in the direction of the creature, understanding what she was asking. "You do that in here, no one survives on this ship."

We're out of options.

The pilot's eyes widened. "Wait. The afterburner. We could fry that motherfucker."

"How do we do that?"

"Get me up to the cockpit, and I can ignite the afterburner. But . . ."

"But?"

"We need to lure the creature behind the plane."

Ellen realized what he was saying. "We need bait."

"Precisely."

Ellen drew in a shuddering breath. The last time she felt this way she was being tied to that pole in Van Ness' lair with a snarling creature only feet away. Even if she *could* lure it into the perfect spot, the odds of her surviving the blast were slim to none.

She looked over at Karen clutching her terrified son in her arms, tears running down his face once again. Ellen and Tom's son, David, was only a year younger. She couldn't bear the thought of their lives ending this way, in fear.

Ah, fuck it.

Ellen frantically beckoned Karen and Joey toward the injured man. They crawled to her position, keeping low to avoid being spotted by the increas-ingly furious creature. Karen immediately knelt and tied her belt tight around the pilot's thigh to slow the bleeding, swiftly and skillfully, without any cer-emony. He pursed his lips, trying desperately not to scream. He had lost too much blood already, but maybe that would buy them the few extra seconds they needed.

A plan had started to quickly formulate in Ellen's head. She remained convinced that she was the rea-son the creature had been let loose on the *Nimitz*. With that in mind, she had to take responsibility for the biggest risk.

Ellen leaned in close. "I'll give you the bait. You *fry that motherfucker.*"

"You got it, boss."

"Listen up, guys," she said. "Karen, you and Joey help the pilot to the cockpit and lock yourselves in the rear seat. I'll lure the creature into position."

"How?" Karen asked, her face full of fear. "I mean, are you sure?"

"I made you a promise," Ellen replied to her. "I intend on keeping it." She winked at Joey and tousled his hair.

At the far end of the hangar, the creature tore through more crates, methodically on the hunt. Then it paused and appeared to sniff the air in a primal way and slowly turned in their direction.

The creature stared at them.

"Christ," the pilot wheezed.

Before anyone else could utter another word, the creature bounded straight for them, direct and fast, locked on its next victims.

"Move! Get on the plane!" Ellen yelled to the pilot and Karen.

She didn't wait to see if they followed her order or even if the pilot would be able to climb the ladder.

Ellen darted in front of the plane and grabbed a rifle from the mutilated body of a crewman. She knew bullets wouldn't pierce the scaly black skin, but that wasn't the point. She needed to piss the thing off. She shouldered the weapon and fired— all the training she'd done with Sarah coming back in a flash—taking single aimed shots as the creature rapidly closed on them.

The creature took the bait and raced faster at Ellen. A tracer round smacked the monster in the chest, slowing it only momentarily. In her peripheral vision, Joey scampered up the ladder and jumped behind the seat. The pilot followed, with Karen below him, shoving him up with her shoulder, blood still running down his leg.

Ellen ran to the starboard side of the plane, still taking single aimed shots, continuing to keep the creature away from the far side. She had no idea how long it would take the pilot to get everything ready.

If it takes more than ten seconds, I'm dead.

We're all dead.

The creature was twenty bounds away, and she had no idea if the magazine was about to run dry. Adrenaline and fear pumped through her veins. The only thing that passed through her mind was the safety of Karen and Joey. And the fact that if this was her final action, she had owned it and made it count.

Whether or not the pilot was ready, there was no time left.

Ellen raced toward the back of the plane.

The Super Hornet's engines wound up.

Please be enough.

She spun and fired three rapid shots at the creature, who was mere seconds away. That emptied the magazine.

Ellen tossed the rifle to one side and moved directly behind the plane.

Directly behind the massive engines.

"Come on, you fucker!" she screamed.

The creature leaped onto the wing, then jumped down within striking distance.

She staggered backward. Her boots hit something hard and Ellen crashed to the floor.

The creature paced toward her, letting out guttural breaths. It was as if it knew it had her and was going to enjoy the moment. Its tail lazily wafted from side to side, then rose in preparation to impale her.

"*Punch it!*" Ellen screamed, and rolled to the side.

Two bright orange jets blasted from the throats of the Super Hornet's twin nozzles. The scorching 1,700-degree heat engulfed the creature, sending it flying back against the wall and pinning it with the ferocious discharged power.

The hybrid creature's black skin burst into flames and peeled off its body. It screamed in agony as it incinerated. Yellow blood cauterized around its shriveling tendons and muscles. Its entire body convulsed under the intense heat, and the red blinking box screwed into its head disintegrated.

Finally, the afterburner died out, leaving only the sound of the crackling fire in the hangar deck. The charred carcass of the once mighty creature lay only a few feet away, now just a smoldering heap.

Ellen scrambled to her feet and ran to the side of the fighter jet. Karen and Joey climbed out of the cockpit, safe. The three embraced.

"You saved our lives," Karen said, wiping her tears away.

"And you saved mine," Ellen replied. "The pilot?"

She looked up. His head leaned against the side of the cockpit. His eyes vacantly stared at nothing.

Ellen let out a deep sigh. The man was a hero who had fought until his dying breath to save others.

"You okay, little man?" Ellen asked Joey.

"Yes, ma'am."

Karen smiled at her always polite baby boy before turning to Ellen. "What now?" she asked.

"First, we get away from those supersoldiers. Who knows if Van Ness will turn them on us next?"

"And then?"

"Then we find out if my husband is still alive."

CHAPTER THIRTY-NINE

Cafferty's back slammed hard into the base of a tree. He crashed to the ground in a heap, surrounded by torn body parts of supersoldiers. For a brief moment, he lay still on the grass in a fetal position, groaning as searing pain throbbed through every joint. He attempted to draw air into his winded, aching body. His lungs felt like they wouldn't inflate.

A high-pitched tone whistled in his ears. He detected only a single muffled sound, like he was underwater. It was still instantly recognizable: a bellowing, dominant screech was coming toward him.

He blinked, attempting to focus. The world around him had transformed into a confusing kaleidoscope of colors. The frantic mix of thoughts in his head crystallized into three straight facts as he attempted to come to his senses:

The queen has prevailed.
Our best hope of killing her has been obliterated.
And Diego . . . Diego is dead.

Shock and guilt overtook his senses and tears welled in his eyes. He could not process what had just happened, could not process losing such a close friend. The brightest beacon in this three-year war.

And then he replayed Diego's final words in his mind, over and over again.

Finish this . . .

Finish this . . .

Get up, Tom. Get up and finish this. For Diego.

Cafferty grunted to all fours, using all the strength he had. He sagged against the tree, struggling to rise. In the distance, a dark shape moved in his direction—a twisted version of the grim reaper, preparing to carve him to pieces.

He sucked in a deep breath.

Come on, Tom.

Cafferty shook his head. His vision began to clear.

To his left, Van Ness' chair lay on its side, the left wheel still spinning. Cafferty couldn't see Bowcut, unless she was part of the mangled torsos around him.

"Thomas," a weak voice called out.

Van Ness dragged himself toward Cafferty and propped himself up against a tree. Bloodshot eyes. Panic-stricken, bruised face. Dirt covered his usually immaculate suit jacket. He appeared even more terrified than when the creatures had forced his body up against the glass in Paris, attempting to squeeze the life out of him.

This time, Cafferty couldn't save him. He couldn't even save himself. As a consequence, everyone he knew, including his son, would likely die.

"Thomas," Van Ness rasped. "The time has come for the final solution."

"What are you talking about?"

"We are here, in this position, because of you, your failures. There is only one chance left to stop the queen, to save the world."

"Which is?"

Van Ness reached for his swagger stick and unscrewed the top. He pulled out a syringe holding the same color solution as the one Cafferty had seen in Antarctica, the one he had seen Van Ness prep getting onto the chopper on the *Nimitz*.

"*Sacrifice yourself* . . ." Van Ness said.

The queen crossed the tennis courts in their direction, growing closer by the second. She swiped a section of the chain-link fence out of the way as if it were paper.

Cafferty studied the green liquid inside the syringe. "What does this do?"

"The serum will rapidly mutate your DNA. In a word, you'll become more creature than human."

"And what happens to me afterward?"

Van Ness leaned closer to Cafferty. "There is no afterward. You knew it would come down to this."

The queen closed within fifty yards and roared, blasting back the branches of the surrounding trees.

"This is the only way. Please, Tom . . ." Van Ness gasped. "Inject yourself, now!"

The desperation in Van Ness' eyes was obvious as he held out the syringe in his quivering hand. This time Cafferty believed every word. He and his nemesis were both facing certain death. There was no longer an agenda.

The queen kicked the bloodied torso of a super-soldier to one side and was nearing striking distance.

Van Ness' hand trembled as he pushed the syringe toward Cafferty. He looked at him with bloodshot eyes. "One must live . . . and one must die."

A million thoughts raced through Cafferty's mind in an instant. If the serum worked and he could stop the queen somehow, his son would live. Ellen would live, assuming she wasn't dead already. Humanity would live.

He thought back to last night on board the *Nimitz*. Kissing his wife's neck. The curve of her lower back. The passion and desperation. Holding each other for what could be the last time.

He thought of Diego, giving his life for the team. For him.

It has to be done.

All my failures, all my hopes . . .

. . . forgiven and realized in one final moment.

Cafferty grabbed the syringe resolutely. He ripped up his sleeve and went to plunge the needle into his weakened arm.

Before he could inject himself, though, a massive telekinetic shock wave hit him. The syringe dropped from his hand and his body flew backward a dozen feet, hammering to the ground yards away. Van Ness' frail body had been forced against the tree, likely crushing a few ribs in the process.

And the syringe lay at Van Ness' feet, too far for Cafferty to reach.

The queen was nearly upon them, intent on tearing them to pieces.

Van Ness looked down at the syringe with resignation. After a moment, he eyed Cafferty and spoke. "Mr. Mayor, do you know the only thing I hate more than you?"

"What?" Cafferty replied.

"*Losing.*"

Van Ness lifted the syringe and rammed it into his chest.

His body immediately went into convulsions and writhed on the ground. Cafferty watched in shock as Van Ness' body twisted on the grass. His arms trembled. His legs flipped. Finally, he went completely still.

The queen took two more bounding steps toward them. Seeing Van Ness' body on the ground, she stopped and aimed her talons in his direction, preparing to unleash a directed telekinetic force that would instantly tear him to pieces.

Instead, Van Ness sat up, stiffly but unnaturally fast. His eyes bulged from his head; his veins had turned green and protruded from his face, neck, and hand. He lifted one leg, then the other, and for the first time in decades, he stood on his own two feet. The creature serum had undone his shattered spine, undone the frailty and age of his bones.

He rose.

He stood there, in defiance of the queen. He stared down his true nemesis, eyes burning with anger. It appeared as if unparalleled strength coursed through his muscles. His pounding heart made his chest protrude a few inches.

He made a fist and slammed it into his own body.

"*Come on!*" Van Ness screamed at the queen, his voice growling and suddenly powerful. "*COME ON!*"

As if answering his challenge, the queen fired a focused telekinetic blast right at Albert Van Ness. He leaned into the shock wave as it slammed into his body, but incredibly, he held his ground. The shock wave tore apart the tree behind Van Ness and shredded the clothing on his body, but his footing held.

Cafferty shuffled around the tree on his backside. He dropped to his chest and peered around the trunk to watch the spectacle unfolding.

Impossibly, Van Ness took a step *closer* to the creature, leaning into the shock wave like a battleship cresting a wave head-on.

Furious at the defiance, the queen blasted another telekinetic wave at him.

He took another step forward, forging a path through the tornado.

The queen swung her mighty tail directly at the man.

Van Ness raised his arm, deflected it, and took another step forward.

Tons of dirt and debris pummeled his body, now coursing with creature DNA.

But he still advanced.

Van Ness' body transformed rapidly. His veins looked like they would burst any second as his human DNA unsuccessfully fought the genetic abomination happening internally. It was clear to Cafferty that he'd soon be dead.

But hopefully not before he does something to stop her.

Van Ness took another powerful step toward the queen. He reached down to a torn-apart torso of a supersoldier and grabbed a grenade from his belt. Van Ness pulled the pin with his teeth and took another step forward.

The queen let out a deafening screech at her enemy, trying everything to stop his approach. Van Ness deflected all her attempts.

Finally, he was upon her.

The queen's eyes glowed devil red. She roared, revealing her razor-sharp teeth. It seemed her plan—as her powerful force was no longer stopping him—was to bite him in half.

As if helping her with the task, Van Ness thrust his fist into her mouth and released his thumb off the detonation trigger. The queen snapped her jaws shut around his arm.

They glared into each other's eyes.

"This is for my father, you son of a—"

A massive explosion ripped through the queen, tearing her to pieces, along with the body of Albert Van Ness, in one horrific final moment.

Cafferty ducked to avoid the shrapnel and viscera. Yellow blood spattered the trees all around him.

After a moment, the entire park fell silent.

The queen was destroyed.

Albert Van Ness was gone.

No visible signs of them remained. Only a charred wheelchair betrayed their final location. Smoke drifted off the blackened wheels. The brass knob of Van Ness' swagger stick had melted.

The man Cafferty had hated for the best part of three years had given his life to save humanity.

Faced with a choice between his ego and humanity's survival, Van Ness had made the ultimate sacrifice.

Cafferty's head was in too much of a spin to comprehend the events. He grabbed the trunk and forced himself to a standing position. Where he went from here, he had no idea.

But he needed to know if he was the only one left alive.

CHAPTER FORTY

T he explosive boom rocked Bowcut awake. It was somewhere close, sounding like a bomb had just gone off. She had no idea how long she'd been unconscious, but at least she wasn't dead. Yet. And at least somebody was still fighting.

Her last memory was hurtling across the sun-lit park, then coming to a violent halt against the park's wrought-iron fence. It was all a complete blur in her mind. Intense pain from the collisions burned in her right shoulder and hip, adding to the agony of being hit by the queen's shock wave.

The sound of the distant battle at Hunters Point had grown quieter than before.

Perhaps it's coming to a close.

But are they too late to stop the queen?

The final thought made her force open her heavy eyelids. She dreaded what she might see. She mentally prepared herself for the sight of her team dead, or the huge creature towering over her injured body.

Bowcut focused on the surrounding area.

All was still.

No sign of any ongoing battle.

Nothing moved in the park. Massacred pieces of supersoldiers were spread around the lumps of dirt and grass. Roux's body lay in the same place, unmoving. Van Ness' wheelchair was a mangled mess. Sarah scanned the area for any life.

"Dammit," she hissed, grunting to her feet and limping toward the tree line, sensing the worst.

As she neared the trees, she spotted movement to her right.

Bowcut froze. The action of stopping made her wince as pain shot through her body. Then she sighed with relief.

Cafferty gingerly emerged from behind a maple tree. He looked like he'd been thrown through a ceiling fan. Caked blood and a dozen cuts peppered his face. His arms and legs were covered in filth. But he was alive.

When he met Bowcut's gaze, he gave her a weak smile.

"Tom, thank God," she said, and embraced him. "Where's Van Ness?"

"He took out the queen. Blew her to pieces, and himself along with her."

"So . . . it's over?"

"Yes, but . . . Sarah . . ."

Fear and nausea instantly rose up inside Bowcut. She scanned the area left and right, frantically searching, remembering what had happened right before she was knocked out . . .

"Diego . . ."

"*No!!*" she cried out, tears streaming down her face in an instant. Cafferty clutched her and pulled her close, tears streaming down his face as well.

There were no words to be said.

He was gone.

After a few moments, Sarah weakly asked, "Ellen?"

Cafferty leaned toward the mic he'd collected from the side of a butchered supersoldier. He silently prayed as he hit the transmit button. "Ellen, please tell me you're there." He held his breath in anticipation.

After a few seconds, his wife replied, "*Tom, thank God you're alive.*"

The emotion on his face was obvious. He glanced at Bowcut, beaming like the morning of the Z Train's inaugural launch. She knew everything in his life had gone to shit after that, and all of their lives had been catapulted to this point through determination, resolution, and violence.

"I can't tell you how good it is to hear your voice, baby," Cafferty said, fighting back tears.

"*And I can't tell you how good it is to see you again,*" she replied.

See?

Bowcut looked up and noticed a chopper approaching the park. It set down fifty yards away, and Ellen practically leaped out of it. She ran toward Cafferty, and the two embraced, kissing each other.

"I promised you I'd be back tonight," Cafferty said, holding her tightly.

She smiled at her husband and kissed him again. "Good man, Mr. Cafferty."

Ellen hugged Bowcut, but then noticed . . .

"Tom, where's Diego?"

Their silence told her the answer.

"No, no, no, no, no . . ." Her head dropped, and tears streamed down her cheeks. Cafferty embraced his wife, sharing in their collective grief.

He gave his life . . . for us . . .

After a few moments of silence, Cafferty asked, "The fleet?"

"Is safe," Ellen replied, wiping away her tears. "The queen?"

"Is dead. Along with Van Ness. In the end, he sacrificed himself to stop her."

"I guess he completed his lifelong mission."

"He did," Cafferty replied solemnly.

"We still have to deal with the supersoldiers," Ellen said. "With Van Ness gone, how do we control them? We need their help to stop the creatures worldwide."

Bowcut turned toward Van Ness' number two's motionless body a dozen yards away. "Roux said only he and Van Ness could give them orders. I saw him using a tablet to input commands, like Van Ness was using. Maybe he still has it on him."

The team headed across the tennis courts and approached Roux's body.

When she was within several feet, Bowcut spotted his left hand twitch.

Surely not?

Bowcut quickened her pace, puffing her cheeks with every painful step, and reached the side of his body.

Roux smiled up at her. "What did I miss?"

"Franco, thank God!" Sarah said, clutching his face. "How?"

"You told me not to trust him," Roux said. "So I didn't." He pulled open his shirt, revealing two protective layers of Kevlar underneath his uniform with Van Ness' bullet firmly embedded in it. "Didn't see that rock coming, though. Concussion for sure, but I'll live to see another day."

Bowcut rested her forehead against his, overwhelmed and surprised by the strength of her emotions that he was alive.

She helped him up, and they embraced.

"Roux, the supersoldiers?" she asked.

He took out his tablet and surveyed the data. "They've eliminated the creatures from Hunters Point. Any remaining ones in San Francisco have fled underground. There are over two thousand supersoldiers still active and on their way to secure our location."

"Still active?"

"Ready if any creatures come back. We're safe."

"The supersoldiers on the *Nimitz* didn't attack us," Ellen said. "If Van Ness was in control of them, why not?"

"You're welcome," Roux replied. "A very smart person reminded me that I was working for a madman, so I took it upon myself to circumvent his orders and have them stand down."

"How?"

"Dr. Liander gave me an override."

"Appearances can be deceptive."

"You're telling me—"

"I knew I liked you," Bowcut interjected. "Thank you."

"Don't thank me yet. We've got to liberate the world now. And I could use all your help and expertise."

"After all this, you still work for the Foundation?"

"The Foundation is dead. Let's call this the World Alliance."

CHAPTER FORTY-ONE

SIX MONTHS LATER

A roaring fire crackled in the hearth of the Caffertys' log cabin. Tom and Ellen sat relaxed on two armchairs, facing the orange glow and warmth of the fireplace. To his left, little David slept on the couch, thumb in his mouth, covered by his favorite blue blankie.

A Frank Sinatra record softly played in the background. The old-school crackle gave the songs a comforting, familiar feel.

Ellen took a drink of her favorite Pinot Grigio and set her glass down.

Cafferty reached over to the table to grab his glass of Jameson.

Snow fell outside and had already deposited a thick layer on the trees surrounding Oneida Lake. Everything about this upstate New York property was perfect. Tranquil. A welcome escape from the rebuilding efforts around the country and around the planet. Exactly how he'd envisioned the future for his family before circumstances had dictated a different path.

Right now, nests were being systematically destroyed all over the world, under the capable eyes of Roux and Bowcut. Humanity was firmly on the front foot with those two at the forefront of operations. Without a queen to lead the creatures, the surviving monstrosities had stayed underground, rudderless. And with the flash drive Diego had slipped Bowcut on the *Nimitz*, containing a backup of all his research, the World Alliance was able to build many more devices to stop the creatures' telekinetic power. They would all soon perish. The day when they were finally eradicated couldn't come soon enough, but more important, people had started to feel safe again.

Humanity was back in business.

Cafferty sipped his whiskey.

The couple sat there in companionable silence, both staring at the flames. He guessed Ellen thought about what they'd come through every single day. He did as well, but expected those memories to fade with time—never to completely disappear, just ease in terms of their immediacy.

The cell phone in Tom's pocket pinged three times—Sarah Bowcut's assigned alert.

Ellen rolled her eyes. "I suppose you'd better get that."

"Suppose I should."

She was playing with him. Cafferty had shed his obsession with the mission and had devoted himself to the two most important people in his life.

He was an entirely different man from the one who had stood in front of the press three years ago with President Reynolds, not knowing what was about to come at him.

Cafferty read the message on his device's screen.

Tom, hope you're happy with the shipment. If you accidentally kill yourself with the goods, please don't haunt me from the afterlife.

He smiled at the last part and climbed to his feet.

"Going somewhere?" Ellen asked.

"Just getting a new bottle. Need anything from the basement?"

"I'm good, thanks. Don't stay down there too long . . ." Ellen unbuttoned the top two buttons of her blouse and walked into the bedroom seductively.

"Yes, ma'am . . ."

Cafferty made his way through the living room and down a creaky set of wooden stairs. He hit the basement light.

A jumble of boxes filled the forty-foot space. They still hadn't properly unpacked. A few days of relaxation had been the first priority.

He snaked between the boxes to a gloomy corner. A wooden crate sat there. It'd arrived yesterday from Philadelphia. Cafferty grabbed a crowbar and wedged it underneath the lid. One quick heave popped it open.

He swept the packing straw to one side, revealing a dozen laser pistols, chargers, and a bandolier of grenades.

Nice work, Sarah.

The rest of the world thought Cafferty had officially retired. And for now, he had. But he'd also vowed to never take civilization's safety for granted.

He fished out a laser and held it in front of his face.

If war ever commenced again on a grand scale, nothing would stop him from joining the fray. He'd be ready. He'd been through too much to simply sit on the sidelines. He owed it to humanity, owed it to the likes of Diego Munoz, David North, President Reynolds, Captain Collingwood, and so many others.

He even owed it to Albert Van Ness.

He owed it to all of them, especially Diego, to finish this. And no matter what, he would.

Cafferty took another sip of whiskey and exhaled. With his family secure, they could look forward to a bright future. Together. Uncompromised.

And if he lived to a ripe old age, and his grand-children asked him what he and Ellen did during the war against the creatures . . . Thomas Cafferty's answer would always be the same.

We survived.

ACKNOWLEDGMENTS

When I wrote *Awakened* back in 2005, I never imagined it would one day become a trilogy, and that I'd get to work with one of the best publishing houses in the world and one of the best, most charming co-writers out there. I hope you enjoy our epic culmination to this story and our characters, whom I've come to love.

Thanks to David Pomerico from Harper Voyager, Lisa Sharkey and the excellent team from Harper-Collins, and Karen Davies and the team from Harper360. Thanks to my colleagues and friends, Joseph, Carsen, Nicole, Susan, Chá, and Ethan, for their tireless and inventive work. Thanks to Jack Rovner and Dexter Scott from Vector Management, Nick Nuciforo and Brandi Bowles from UTA, Danny Passman from GTRB, Phil Sarna and Mitch Pearlstein from PSBM, and Elena Stokes and team from Wunderkind PR. And special thanks to Brad Meltzer, R.L. Stine, and James Rollins for all your incredible guidance, support, and friendship.

Mom and Dad (and my entire family)—love you all. Spear—sorry, Liander lives at the end. And special thanks to my love and fiancée, Melyssa, who singlehandedly has the power to change lives.

And finally, thanks to all our amazing *Impractical Jokers* fans for always supporting what four guys from Staten Island do.

—James S. Murray

My life has changed quite a lot while writing this book. I'm a husband to a great wife, Jennifer, and father to a lovely daughter, Maple. Jen's parents, Faye and Joe, have also been incredibly warm and welcoming to me during my time in Canada. I'm proud of how this trilogy turned out after James and I committed to writing the series. He's a great guy and friend and I deeply value our partnership. Every time I visit America, James and Melyssa are always kind and generous hosts. I'd also like to thank three other people. First, Paul Lucas from Janklow & Nesbit. Paul is my agent and works tirelessly on my behalf. Second, David Pomerico from Harper Voyager. I've already said in the *Awakened* acknowledgments what David brings to the party, but his patience and understanding are also two admirable traits he possesses. Third, my family and friends for being there. Lastly, and most importantly, a huge thanks to you for reading *Obliteration*.

—Darren Wearmouth